ROMANCING THE CROWN

Long live the prince! All of Montebello holds its breath for the news of their beloved prince's wedding. Join the kingdom for the final stormy and sensual confrontation as the lovers reunite and passion reigns supreme!

**Meet the major players
in this royal romance:**

Prince Lucas Sebastiani: In losing his memory, he found his heart—but can love survive where duty is sovereign?

Jessica Chambers: She survived hell only to discover that the man she loved has become a handsome, royal stranger. It will take more than luxury and riches to turn this feisty rancher into Cinderella.

Baby Luke: His existence is a miracle, but can this precious prince bring his prideful parents together?

King Marcus and Queen Gwendolyn Sebastiani: Montebello's beloved rulers are ready to guide their son through the most delicate—and important— negotiation of his life.

Princess Julia Sebastiani Kamal: The wise princess knows well ~~~~~~
learn before he can ~~~~~~
taught her own belov~~~~~~

D1413601

Dear Reader,

As the year winds to a close, I hope you'll let Silhouette Intimate Moments bring some excitement to your holiday season. You certainly won't want to miss the latest of THE OKLAHOMA ALL-GIRL BRANDS, Maggie Shayne's *Secrets and Lies.* Think it would be fun to be queen for a day? Not for Melusine Brand, who has to impersonate a missing "princess" and evade a pack of trained killers, all the while pretending to be passionately married to the one man she can't stand—and can't help loving.

Join Justine Davis for the finale of our ROMANCING THE CROWN continuity, *The Prince's Wedding,* as the heir to the Montebellan throne takes a cowgirl—and their baby— home to meet the royal family. You'll also want to read the latest entries in two ongoing miniseries: Marie Ferrarella's *Undercover M.D.*, part of THE BACHELORS OF BLAIR MEMORIAL, and Sara Orwig's *One Tough Cowboy,* which brings STALLION PASS over from Silhouette Desire. We've also got two dynamite stand-alones: Lyn Stone's *In Harm's Way* and Jill Shalvis's *Serving Up Trouble.* In other words, you'll want all six of this month's offerings— and you'll also want to come back next month, when Silhouette Intimate Moments continues the tradition of providing you with six of the best and most exciting contemporary romances money can buy.

Happy holidays!

Leslie J. Wainger
Executive Senior Editor

Please address questions and book requests to:
Silhouette Reader Service
U.S.: 3010 Walden Ave., P.O. Box 1325, Buffalo, NY 14269
Canadian: P.O. Box 609, Fort Erie, Ont. L2A 5X3

The Prince's Wedding
JUSTINE DAVIS

INTIMATE MOMENTS™

Published by Silhouette Books

America's Publisher of Contemporary Romance

Special thanks and acknowledgment are given to Justine Davis for her contribution to the ROMANCING THE CROWN series

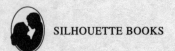 SILHOUETTE BOOKS

ISBN 0-373-27260-X

THE PRINCE'S WEDDING

This edition published by arrangement with Harlequin Books S.A.

® and TM are trademarks of Harlequin Books S.A., used under license. Trademarks indicated with ® are registered in the United States Patent and Trademark Office, the Canadian Trade Marks Office and in other countries.

Visit Silhouette at www.eHarlequin.com

Printed in U.S.A.

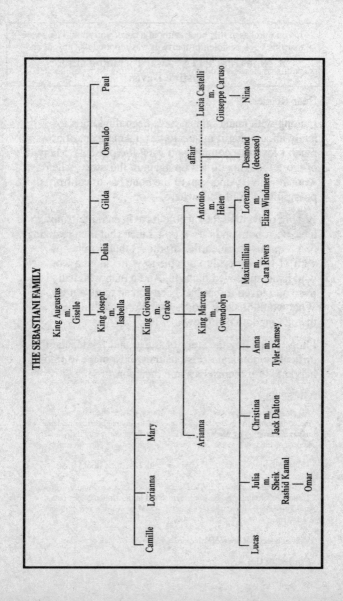

THE SEBASTIANI FAMILY

King Augustus
m.
Giselle

King Joseph — Delia — Gilda — Oswaldo — Paul
m.
Isabella

Camille — Lorianna — Mary

King Giovanni
m.
Grace

Arianna

King Marcus
m.
Gwendolyn

Lucas — Christina — Anna
         m.   m.
      Jack Dalton   Tyler Ramsey

Julia
m.
Sheik
Rashid Kamal

Omar

Antonio
m.
Helen

Maximillian — Lorenzo
m.   m.
Cara Rivers   Eliza Windmere

affair .... Lucia Castelli
                  m.
                  Giuseppe Caruso

Desmond   Nina
(deceased)

A Note from RITA® Award-winning author Justine Davis:

Dear Reader,

I, along with many others, have been thinking a lot lately about what it means to be an American, of how much I love this country and what it represents. Many of those thoughts turned up again in this story, when a woman who is American to the bone has to confront the possibility of a life elsewhere.

Having often thought I would have been quite happy to have been born and raised on a ranch (but then realizing that requires much earlier mornings than I'm happy with), I was pleased to be able to write about a woman who lived and loved that life. And a man who had also lived and loved it, but had been forced to give it up. What would make it worth giving up? Nothing less than a kingdom of his own.

I hope you enjoy the story of Lucas and Jessie, and the difficult, emotional decisions they must make to find happiness for themselves and their son.

All the best,

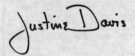

Chapter 1

At least it didn't show.

If nothing else, Lucas Sebastiani was certain of that. All those years of training, virtually from the cradle, on how to put on a public face were paying off now in a way he'd never expected. No one would be able to guess at his agitated state of mind.

But never before had it been such an effort to maintain that practiced facade—a fact he was very aware of and not particularly happy about.

"We'll be landing in Colorado in approximately one hour, Your Highness."

Lucas nodded without looking at the attendant in the Montebellan uniform. Not because he was fascinated by the view out the small jet's window, but because he didn't want to see the speculation he was sure would be in the woman's eyes. She would never say anything—anyone who worked for the Sebastianis was too well-trained for that—but Lucas suspected they were all wondering how he was feeling as they headed toward the scene of his own personal disaster, the place where his last flight had ended so abruptly and painfully.

How did they think he felt? That crash had done more than rattle his brain, temporarily wiping out his memory. It had changed his life—and he himself—forever.

"May I get you anything, Your Highness?"

"No, thank you, Mareta. Why don't you relax for the rest of the flight."

The woman nodded, then turned and walked toward the front of the plane. Restlessly, Lucas stood up. Normally when he felt like this he would head for the cockpit and take over the controls for a while. Flying his beloved new Redstone Hawk V was usually just the thing to settle his nerves. Something about flying the responsive craft made all his problems fade in significance, although it set Roark, the Sebastianis' chief pilot, on edge not to be at the controls himself.

If he'd been flying the Hawk that night, Lucas knew he likely would have beaten that storm. He even had the passing thought that flying it here and now, nearing the place where he'd come to grief all those months ago, would be a good thing, sort of like getting back on a horse after you'd been thrown.

But instead of heading for the cockpit, he found himself moving the other way, toward the stateroom at the back of the plane's cabin. Once he'd been pleased with the richly appointed fixtures and lush furnishings of the powerful little jet. Now he barely noticed any of the many amenities. The sleek plane was merely the quickest and easiest way to carry out this all-important mission.

Once, he thought wryly, *you were the walking personification of a stereotype, the guy the term "playboy prince" was coined for. And now?*

He wasn't sure who he was now.

He stepped through the door of the stateroom, and immediately some of his tension eased. That carefree, sometimes heedless man had died in that plane crash in the mountains ahead of them. The man who stood here now had been reborn, given a fresh start, and he was determined to make the most of it.

The reason for his determination lay sleeping peacefully in a small portable crib. As Lucas approached, the older woman who sat vigilantly beside his baby son's bed rose to her feet and inclined her head respectfully.

"Your Highness."

"How is he?"

"He is sleeping quietly, Your Highness."

"Thank you, Eliya. I'll watch him for a while."

The nurse nodded, reached into the small crib to adjust the blanket, gave the baby a last gentle pat, then gathered up the length of silk she'd been embroidering and quietly exited the stateroom.

Lucas sat in the chair she'd vacated and stared down at the tiny being, this miracle who was part of him, and part of history. The next prince of the kingdom of Montebello, heir to the more-than-a-century-old island throne that had been held by his family since its inception in 1880.

Luke Marcus Augustus Sebastiani. Such a big name for such a little boy.

Of course, when he'd come to them he'd been only Luke. But once his identity had been confirmed beyond doubt, he'd been renamed after his father, grandfather and illustrious ancestor in an official royal ceremony designating him as Lucas's—and Montebello's—heir.

Now, at three months old, he was blissfully ignorant of the fact that he was aboard a royal Montebellan jet, winging his way toward a reunion with the mother he'd never known. The mother he'd been stolen away from on the very day he'd come into the world.

Lucas shrugged his shoulders rather fiercely, as if the sudden action could somehow shed the memories of the confused emotions he'd felt when he'd first gotten word of Jessica's death. And his state of confusion had only gotten worse when he'd pressed for details and his cousin Drew had reluctantly told him that she'd died giving birth to a stillborn child. It was only later that he'd learned she'd been kidnapped by Gerald Hanson, who posed as the caretaker of the ranch, and who'd been in league with Jessie's sister in the plot to murder her and steal the baby.

The thought that Jessie had been pregnant when he'd left her had been a hammer blow. First had come wonder, that they had created new life out of their love. Then had come more confusion—why hadn't she told him? Judging by the timing, she had to have known.

Of course, he had to admit with much reluctance, he hadn't exactly stayed around long enough to give her time to work up to it.

When his memory had suddenly returned, he'd left her for her own good, he'd thought, knowing what chaos would descend on her beloved ranch if he stayed and was discovered there. He'd spent many a long night since torturing himself with guilt, especially after the report of her death—if he'd stayed, would she still be alive?

And the knowledge that his child, a baby whose existence he hadn't even been aware of, had also died had made the hollow ache inside him almost unbearable. He'd told himself he couldn't possibly feel so bad over a baby he hadn't even known about, who hadn't even lived to draw a breath.

But he had. And there it was.

He'd thrown himself into a passion of work, until even his father had suggested he slow down. He'd ridden on his favorite horse over the island of Montebello from one end to the other, until rumors about the mental state of their returned prince began to circulate among the people.

And then the miracle had happened. Out of the morass of evil hatched by Jessica's sister had come a tiny, precious bit of goodness. Gerald had lied, and his son was alive.

There had been the formality of paternity testing, but Lucas hadn't needed any DNA report to prove what he'd known the moment he'd looked at the child. His mother had gasped aloud when she'd first seen the boy, and then tears had come to her lovely blue eyes as she'd looked upon the very image of her own firstborn child.

Lucas stared at his sleeping son. He saw a chin and cheekbones familiar from photographs of his own babyhood, the dark hair, knew that when the baby's eyes were open they were the same dark blue as his own. But the beautiful, trusting smile that made Lucas's chest tighten painfully, was a gift from his mother.

From Jessica.

Jessie.

A shiver rippled through him. She'd been his touchstone, his center in a world spun out of control, the only anchor in the storm that had swamped his life. She'd quite literally saved his life and his sanity. She'd given him peace, a reason to go on, and hot, sweet love in the darkness.

And he'd walked out on her, in the middle of a Colorado winter night.

"I didn't know about you," he whispered to his sleeping son. "I didn't know."

And what would you have done if you had?

He didn't answer the self-directed question. He didn't have an answer. Because the man who had walked out that night was not the man who sat here with this child

now. Just as the man who had fallen in love with Jessie
wasn't that man. The man who had fallen in love had
been Joe, a simple ranch hand who led a simple life,
knowing nothing of his own past yet finding beauty and
a sort of peace in the present, in the arms of the loving
woman who had captivated him with her courage, her
strength, her gentle caring, her beauty.

The woman he'd been mourning since word had come
that she'd been murdered in the plot to cash in on the
existence of the child sleeping here so peacefully. The
woman who had haunted his days and filled his nights.

The woman he'd thought dead and buried until just a
few days ago.

His pilot's instincts told him when the plane's slow
descent began. In his mind he could picture the rough
terrain at the foot of the Rocky Mountains, that backbone
of America. They must have passed over Denver while
he'd been lost in thought. With the big city behind them,
he could picture the little town of Shady Rock, nestled in
the shadow of the towering peaks.

And somewhere, tucked away in a beautiful but isolated
corner, was Jessie's ranch, those beloved acres of land she
ran herself ragged to maintain. The ranch he'd come to
love himself, along with the quiet, peaceful life he'd
found there. Even when he'd been haunted by what he
couldn't remember, he'd loved it.

It was nice, he thought vaguely, not to have to worry
about the details. The limo was waiting for them, with a
driver who knew exactly where they were going. The
aide, Lloyd Gallini—who was also the bodyguard his father refused to let him travel without—was busy scanning
the area, although there was no one in sight who seemed
at all interested in them.

He couldn't blame his father, not after what had happened to him. Being captured, even intentionally, by ter-

rorists hadn't been much fun. That his efforts had been instrumental in the FBI's bringing down the Brothers of Darkness cell in the U.S., a danger not only to America but to the safety of his family and perhaps even his entire country, was the only thing good to come out of it.

But he still felt cramped. He'd had security around him all his life—it was the price of being the crown prince of Montebello—but it was somehow worse here, in this place. This was America, where such things as royal titles meant little to everyday people, and here he'd always been able to move more freely.

"We will be at the hotel within fifteen minutes, Your Highness."

Lucas suddenly tuned in to the aide's words, realizing he should have been paying more attention.

"Your suite is prepared, and—"

"No."

Gallini blinked. "Your Highness?"

"We'll go to the hospital first."

"But the security hasn't been finalized—"

Lucas shook his head. "The hospital. This has waited too long already."

It was odd, he thought as Gallini passed along the new instructions to the driver, that back here in the still-wild country of the Rockies the quiet obsequiousness of the people who served him seemed out of place. As if the land itself had created the mind-set of its people, that everyone was equal, and should be treated so.

I'm thinking like Joe, he realized.

Joe had been just another guy, an average citizen, his only uniqueness being his condition, that wall he'd come up against every time he tried to remember anything beyond the time when he'd awakened in the wreckage of the small rented plane, after losing the battle with a Colorado blizzard. It had been a wall so blank he'd only known he'd been the pilot because there was no sign anyone else had been aboard.

Joe had been able to go anywhere, do anything, talk to anyone, without worrying about protocol, image or threats to his life. Joe had been able to work happily until he was exhausted without being cautioned about overdoing it. Joe had been able to rant against fate without fear of his complaint being overheard and hitting the tabloids within twelve hours.

Joe had been able to fall in love simply because the right woman was there, not because his parents had arranged a suitable and advantageous match.

An image of Jessie as he'd last seen her, asleep in her huge old brass bed, coalesced with all-too-perfect clarity in his mind. A shaft of winter moonlight turning her long, blond hair to silver as it lay, still tousled from his eager fingers, across both her pillow and his. Her soft lips, slightly parted, curved into a slight smile even in sleep, and if the sheet had slipped one more inch down the soft swell of her breast, one of the lovely pink nipples he'd caressed and sucked and rubbed until she cried out in pleasure would have drawn him irresistibly back to her.

She'd had the look of a woman who'd been well loved, and leaving her had been the hardest thing he'd ever done in his life. Only the fact that he'd known it was the best thing he could do for her had gotten him through it.

Now he was about to see her again, for the first time since that night. And he didn't know what to expect from her.

Or from himself.

Lucas was aware of the charged atmosphere the moment they went through the hospital doors. He'd once accepted it as a matter of course, the odd reaction people had to royalty. As Joe, ordinary ranch hand, he'd lost the knack, and now that he was Prince Lucas again—or trying to be—he wasn't sure he'd ever get it back. The nanny lagged slightly behind on the order of the bodyguard, whom Lucas had instructed to protect his son at all costs.

Clearly they'd known he was coming. The usual phalanx of security and staff clustered around him before he got halfway through the lobby. He supposed the hospital had planned it out in the hours since they'd entered American air space. He wanted more than anything to tell them all to shut up and simply take him to Jessie, but he no longer had that option. Joe Benson could say anything he wanted to anyone, if he was willing to take the consequences. Lucas Peterson Sebastiani had had the consequences of incautious speech drilled into him since he'd been old enough to talk.

Joe, he thought wearily as he smiled and nodded endlessly, *had had it easy.*

It seemed forever, although he knew it was only a few minutes, before someone finally gestured him down a hallway to a large, private hospital room.

"Everything is as you wished," a woman with rather false-looking black hair gushed. He thought she had identified herself as some sort of public relations person for the hospital, which was typical. He would much rather deal with the frontline people, but knew this was simply another cost of being who he was.

Joe had definitely had it easy, he thought, realizing even as he thought it the irony of thinking a man who'd lost his entire past had had it easy.

"Thank you," he said as they paused outside the door to the room. He looked at Gallini. "Now, if you will give me a moment, please?"

His father's man was nothing if not well-trained, and he immediately ushered the entourage away. Lucas hesitated, bracing himself, then reached for the door handle. He inched the door open and stepped inside.

She was asleep.

Jessie had always had a fragile look, a look belied by an incredible inner strength. She had constantly amazed him—or rather, Joe—by the amount of work she did on the ranch, the things she was capable of that he never would have believed. If her physical strength wasn't enough, she put that clever mind to work and found another way.

But now she didn't just look fragile. She looked nothing short of frail, and it frightened him. He'd wondered if he would see her differently, now that she was the mother of his son, but all he could see right now was that frailness. The knowledge of how close he'd come to losing her hit with gut-sinking power, that the report of her death had very nearly been true. The dark circles under her eyes and the paleness of her skin as well as the bruises that marked her slender body told him this was a woman who had been through hell. A woman who still had a fight ahead of her to fully recover, physically and emotionally.

He could only hope he'd brought the right medicine.

Jessie woke up slowly. The now-familiar sounds registered first, voices in the hallway, the distant bell of an alarm as some other patient rang for assistance. She held off opening her eyes—as long as she kept them closed she could pretend it wasn't real. She'd never been one to avoid reality, but lately she'd found herself doing it more and more often.

Why not, she muttered inwardly, closing her eyes more tightly, *when my reality is just plain rotten? My baby is gone before I even had the chance to hold him, my own sister betrayed me in the worst possible way, I was held captive in a cellar by a mentally ill man for months....*

She smothered a sigh, knowing she was feeling sorry for herself. And even telling herself she had reason didn't make her feel any less guilty about it.

"Jessie?"

For a moment she thought she had gone back to sleep and was once more hearing Joe's low, husky voice whispering her name. God, she'd been such a fool. Falling in love with an itinerant ranch hand was bad enough, but falling in love with a prince? That was idiotic.

"I know you're awake."

It *was* Joe's voice.

Her body became rigid as knowledge came back to her in a rush. She'd known he was coming, she'd heard the hospital staff buzzing about the impending visit of Montebellan royalty. There was protocol to learn and follow, security arrangements to be made, she'd heard it all. Including the whispers about the tabloid stories of an amnesiac prince who had dallied with a rustic American woman, only to regain his memory and realize she was utterly unsuitable. She'd tried to dismiss it as tabloid sensationalism, but the common-sense logic of it had dug deep into her heart.

The nurses had even come to her for help, full of their excited questions, and she'd laughed so hard even she couldn't miss the hysterical edge that had tinged the sound. And she couldn't explain the absurdity of them asking her how to address a crown prince when she'd known the man only as Joe Benson, a good man with a horse, but one without a past.

And a good man in bed. Oh, yes, she knew that, too.

Great. What a thing to think of just before you have to open your eyes and face him.

With an effort that taxed her minimal stamina just now, she forced the vivid, erotic memories out of her mind. And opened her eyes.

She had thought she was prepared. She'd spent every hour since the call from the Montebellan royal family's advance man getting ready for this moment, telling herself what to expect. But now that she was face-to-face with it—with him—it did no good at all, and her heart broke all over again.

This man standing beside the bed was a stranger. Oh, he had Joe's face, his dark hair, his lean, rangy body, his beautiful deep blue eyes, so much darker than her own. But he was a stranger. Joe had been haunted by what he couldn't remember, but this man's eyes were even more grim, as if the memories he'd regained haunted him even more. This man stood just as straight, yet seemed weighed down, as if with an even greater burden. This man had an air about him that Joe had never had, something she couldn't quite put a name to. And it wasn't just the fact that he was dressed in an elegant, obviously expensive suit and tie, clothing she could never have pictured her ranch lover wearing.

She opened her mouth to say his name. She shut it again when she realized the name she'd been about to say was Joe. She remembered the discussion she'd heard between a couple of the nurses, about what you called a crown prince. Certainly not Joe....

"I suppose I should say 'Hello, Your Highness,'" she finally said.

He winced visibly. "Jessie, don't."

"I'm sorry. Was that not the proper form of address? Or should I simply be flattered that the 'playboy prince' has come to visit?"

She thought he winced again, but he controlled it so quickly she couldn't be sure. She knew she sounded bitchy but she couldn't seem to help it. She was tired, aching in more ways than one, and emotionally spent. She had to gather what defenses she had, and right now they were rather meager.

"I'm still the same man I was on the ranch," he said. "It's just that my name is Lucas, not Joe."

"Are you the same man?" she asked. "Are you really?"

She saw the brief flicker in his expression, and knew she'd struck a nerve.

"Inside I am. Somewhere."

His voice was tinged with such pain that she dropped the sarcasm in her own. And bit back, as she had been doing since the moment he'd walked in, the urgent questions about her baby. If crazy, twisted Gerald had lied, if the Sebastianis had kept the truth from her and her baby wasn't alive and well, she didn't want to know. Not yet.

"Will you answer a question?" she asked him instead.

"Of course."

"When did you know? When exactly did you remember who you were?"

"That's two questions."

She let out a compressed breath as he dodged answering directly.

"I mean, each has a different answer," he said quickly, as if he sensed her reaction.

"Oh?"

"I knew who I had to be when I saw my photograph on the news. But I still didn't remember anything more than what I'd told you."

She frowned. Then why had he left her like that, skulking out in the middle of the night, leaving nothing but a note? She understood now what he'd written, about not being the man she thought he was, but why had he run, if he still had no memories of his past?

She reached for the small control panel on the hospital bed and pushed the button to raise her head. She was quickly reminded of her every bruise and aching muscle, but she hated lying there helpless, looking up at him.

He leaned over, as if alarmed, and she supposed she must have winced at the various pains. She eyed him warily, not wanting him any closer, not now, not while she was battling to sort out her confused emotions. Again as if he'd read her reaction, he backed off.

Joe had been like that, she thought. He'd been seemingly able to read her every mood. So maybe there *was* some of Joe left in Prince Lucas Sebastiani.

She tried to hide the shiver that went through her as she thought the name, a name she had heard long before the battered, lost man called Joe had come into her life. The name she'd connected with the other glitterati of the world, kings, queens, princes and princesses.

The name she still found so difficult to connect to the man she'd known and fallen in love with during those glorious months on the ranch that was her life.

She'd allowed herself the fantasy, allowed herself to picture herself and Joe making their life on the land her family had lived on for generations, to picture a happy life with another generation of Chambers's to work this ranch she so loved.

But her Joe was the man often called the most eligible royal bachelor in the world. She had known when she first realized who he was that there was no future for them. Prince Lucas Sebastiani was far out of the league of a modest Colorado rancher who loved her quiet, peaceful life. She understood that. But her heart broke a little more on the knowledge that Joe, just plain Joe, had loved that life, too.

When she'd discovered she was pregnant with his child, she'd been both thrilled and terrified.

Terrified, she thought now as she stared up at this

stranger with Joe's face, had been the more appropriate reaction of the two.

"Why?" she asked. "Even if you did realize you were...who you are, why did you go like that?"

He lowered his gaze. "The more I saw of the news story, all the media fuss, the more I realized that if I was found at the ranch it would destroy your life there. I can't explain it, but in my gut I knew it would be chaos." He grimaced. "It was like some part of me still remembered what it was like to be constantly hounded by the media, even if I couldn't remember anything else yet."

"But later...you did remember?"

"Jessie," he said quietly, and there was an undertone in his voice that made her hold her breath. "I'll tell you everything, answer every question you have, I promise. But...."

She held her breath once more, waiting in tense silence as he walked back to the door of her hospital room. He opened it partially, and she heard him speak quietly to someone outside, although she couldn't make out the words.

When he turned around, he held a small bundle in his arms. Jessie smothered a gasp. She hadn't thought he would...she just hadn't dared to think about it at all.

She sat up quickly, despite the protest of various body parts. Her heart raced. She forgot to breathe at all. And every last ache and pain was forgotten as Joe—Lucas— laid that bundle gently in her arms.

And at long last, after countless weeks of agony and heartache, she did what she had feared she would never do again.

She looked down into the eyes of her son.

Chapter 2

Lucas felt his heart pound solidly in his chest as he watched the tender reunion. From what he'd been told, Jessie had barely been able to hold baby Luke before he'd been snatched away by the near-bumbling madman to play his pivotal role in the insane scheme hatched by her vicious sister.

He couldn't even begin to imagine what it had been like for her. His own mother, the serene, unruffled Queen Gwendolyn, had been moved to tears at the picture painted by the American investigator's report on how Jessie was found.

"She will be fragile," his mother had warned him before he left, "and you must treat her gently."

His mother, as usual, had been right. Jessie was making no effort to halt the tears that flowed freely down her cheeks. Perhaps she wasn't even aware of them. It wouldn't surprise him, given the absolutely rapt look on her face as she stared down at little Luke. His throat was tight and he was having a hard time holding his own tears back. He knew that feeling so well, that sense of disbelief and wonder. It was a long, silent moment before he could speak.

"I'd been trying to contact you, calling the ranch at different times of day, but you never answered. I was afraid you had…that it was because I'd left you that way, that you were avoiding even talking to me. I couldn't blame you for that, told myself you had every right."

She flicked a glance at him, and he read in her expression that there was at least a little truth to his guess—that if she had been there at the ranch when he'd called, she would have done just that.

When she looked back at the baby, wonder again filled her face, and she lowered her head to nuzzle Luke's dark hair, and reached out to gently touch his cheek. With an effort, knowing it had to be said no matter how much he didn't want to say it, Lucas went on.

"When they told me you'd been killed, that Gerald Hanson had murdered you, I felt like the sun had gone out. When they told me you'd been pregnant, but the child had been stillborn, I no longer cared about anything."

Her gaze came up to him again, and this time she didn't look away.

"I went through the motions, but without purpose. Nothing mattered to me, not my life, my country, my crown. Nothing. And then—" He had to swallow to get the rest out past the lump in his throat. "Then they brought me Luke. And I had a reason to go on."

He reached out and laid a hand on their son's dark head. "He was the only thing that got me through," he said softly. "I had to keep going, for him."

Something warm and beautiful came into her eyes then as she looked up at him. Something he imagined he might have seen had things been normal, if he had been there when his son had been born. He wasn't sure he'd earned that look from her, but he couldn't deny how it made him feel. And how much he wished he *had* earned it.

She cuddled the baby closer, cooing nonsensically to him. Luke gurgled back, which seemed to delight her. When she looked up at Lucas again, her expression was eager as she asked, "What's he like?"

That took him a little aback. *He's like a baby,* didn't seem like what she'd want to hear, yet he wasn't sure what else to say. So he thought for a moment, searching for something to tell her.

"He has your smile," he finally said. "And he likes my father's beard."

Jessie smiled at his first words, but at the rest, the smile slowly faded. Lucas saw her changing expression and wondered what he'd said wrong.

"All those weeks I missed," she said, sounding so forlorn his chest tightened. "You know him, even your parents know him, but I don't."

"No more," he said. "He's with you now, you can make up for lost time."

She started to say something, then stopped. She let out a weary sigh, but hugged her baby even closer, leaning over to lay her cheek against his forehead.

"Jessie? What is it?"

"I want to go home," she whispered. "More than anything, I want to go home and be with my baby."

"Then that's what will happen."

She shook her head. "They won't let me out of here," she said. "The doctor said that I needed to stay another day, at least."

"We'll see about that," Lucas said.

He walked to the door and signaled Lloyd. The man hastened over, and before he could open his mouth and say that annoying "Your Highness," Lucas spoke.

"Get her doctor. Find out if there's anything that she needs that can't be handled at her home by a competent nurse. If not, find one, and pay her whatever it will take to get her to stay at the ranch full-time until Jessie doesn't need her anymore. Then arrange whatever equipment we'll need. I want her out of here today."

"Yes, Your Highness."

It had been a long time since he'd used the power of his position, but for Jessie and his son he would get back in the habit, and quick. What was the point of being a prince, of having wealth and power at your command, if you didn't use it to help those you loved?

And he would do everything in his power to make up to Jessie everything she'd gone through because of him. He knew she didn't have much reason to love him anymore, not after he'd walked out on her with only a cryptic note of explanation. And he especially knew it after he'd found out he'd left her pregnant. He should have thought of the possibility, of course, but somehow, amid the chaos of his memory returning and the mission that had lured the Brothers of Darkness to its end, he hadn't.

You're the best catch in the world, his sister Julia had said loyally before he'd left the palace. *You're handsome, rich and a prince. What's not to love?*

A lot, he thought now, rather grimly. Especially if you were an independent American female like Jessie.

He watched her drink in the simple presence of baby Luke, exploring, counting tiny fingers and toes, just as he once had. He tried not to think of the rest, of what she'd gone through to bring this child of theirs into the world, but he couldn't manage it.

"I'm sorry," he finally whispered. When she looked up quizzically, he added, "I should have been there."

Something flickered in her eyes then, and although she

said nothing, he felt sure "Yes, you should have," was her silent answer.

She deserved more from him, he knew that, but he didn't know what to say. Finally he just talked.

"I can't imagine what you went through, Jessie. In the hands of that crazy man, knowing he might kill you at any moment, and then even worse, finding out your own sister was behind it all...."

Every time he thought of Ursula, and what kind of woman it would take to murder her own sister and steal her newborn baby for profit, he felt a churning sickness inside. His family had been involved in a feud with neighboring Tamir for ages, but that had been mostly political, although it had begun with an arranged marriage and a murder. But even that paled beside the personal nature of this treachery. He couldn't even begin to imagine how Jessie must have felt when the entirety of Ursula's reprehensible plot had been revealed.

"A bit different than recovering from amnesia and remembering you're a prince," she said, her tone so neutral he couldn't tell if she was being sarcastic or not. Then she added, "And letting yourself be captured by terrorists so the FBI can shut down their U.S. operations."

He drew back slightly, surprised. "You know about that?"

"You're big news, even in America. The media adored the story of the Playboy Prince turned undercover agent."

He winced. He supposed she was quoting a story she'd heard, but that didn't make it sit with him any better. "I hate that nickname. Even when it fit, I hated it."

"And it doesn't fit now?"

He took in a breath, telling himself she had every right to ask. "I'm doing everything I can to make sure it never does again."

She studied him for a moment. "What you went through…it changed you, didn't it?"

"You changed me," he said bluntly.

She blinked, drew back slightly, and he knew he'd spoken too soon. She wasn't ready to hear that, wasn't ready to believe it, not yet.

He knew that he had to give her time. She deserved as much as he could give her. He'd been through his own trauma, true, but he'd also had more time to recover. And her ordeal wasn't just more recent, it had been as bad if not worse psychologically than his. His, after all, had been an accident, not trauma at the hands of someone he trusted.

He was almost glad when Lloyd inched open the door behind him.

"Your Highness?"

Lucas saw the odd expression that crossed Jessie's face, and wished the man had simply called him Lucas, or Mr. Sebastiani. But he couldn't deal with that now. He turned and walked to the door.

"The doctor says that if there will be a nurse on duty twenty-four hours for at least three days, he will release her into your care. I found a local agency that can arrange a nurse by this afternoon."

"Good. Have someone transport the baby's gear to the ranch. I don't want Jessie to have to worry about setting things up. And make sure Mrs. Winstead is there to cook," he said, referring to the Chambers's former housekeeper who had retired years ago but still helped Jessie prepare meals from time to time. "And get someone to clean, Jessie needs to rest. And—"

He stopped abruptly, realizing he was stating the obvious, that after years with the Sebastiani family Lloyd knew perfectly well what he was to do.

"You know what's necessary," he said.

"Yes, Your Highne—"

"And while we're here, Mr. Sebastiani or 'yes, sir,' will do," he interrupted.

An expression of surprise flitted across Lloyd's face, but he merely nodded. "I'll get right on it."

"Thank you," Lucas said.

"My pleasure. Sir," the man added before he turned to do his prince's bidding.

Sometimes, Lucas thought, being royal had its uses.

By the time they finally reached the outer hospital doors, Jessie had nearly lost her joy in going home. It was impossible not to notice the stir they caused, impossible not to see the way people whispered as they approached and then hushed as they passed. And most impossible not to notice everyone—females especially—gaping at Joe. At Lucas. At the prince. Whoever he was.

It still rattled her just to think about it, but now, seeing the dynamic for the first time, she knew she'd been right. There was no future for a simple rancher and the heir to the throne of Montebello.

All right, she told herself. *There's no future. So enjoy the present. You have your baby. And for the moment, you have Joe. Don't think about tomorrow.*

And she meant it. She had the child she had feared lost forever in her arms, and nothing else mattered much beside that. She would happily put off the inevitable.

The sight of the long limousine with its darkly tinted windows startled her, but she realized she should have known. Royalty was used to traveling in style. She got out of the wheelchair they'd insisted on and into the limo without comment. She even managed not to jump when Joe—no, Lucas, she had to remember that—took her arm to help her into the spacious passenger compartment.

Spacious and luxurious, she amended as she shifted the

baby in her arms. She'd refused to relinquish baby Luke to the nanny. She'd expected the woman to protest, but the nanny had only nodded and given her such an understanding and warm smile that Jessie had felt oddly comforted.

She'd been in a limo once, the night of her senior prom. But it hadn't been anything like this. Nothing like the rich, deep pile of the seats, the gleaming fixtures, a small TV screen, a telephone that looked like it could teleconference around the world and a built-in bar with a rack of glasses she would swear were real leaded crystal. She supposed a royal family took such things for granted, but to a girl from the rugged hills of Colorado, it was a different world.

A world she could visit but never live in.

As the countryside began to look familiar, with its memorable landmarks—Big Turtle Rock there, the Aspen Creek bridge over there—the troublesome thoughts faded away. A sense of welcome, of coming home, welled up inside her, burgeoning, growing until there was room for nothing but the joy of returning to the ranch she loved.

"You'll love it on the ranch, baby," she crooned to the bundle in her arms. "It's the most beautiful place in the world. The sky is so clear it feels like you can see forever, and the air is so clean the only thing you smell is the scent of pine trees. And just wait, baby, and you'll have the sweetest little pony—"

She stopped, suddenly aware of the steady gaze of the man sitting across from her. The nurse and the man who had introduced himself as "The prince's—I mean, Mr. Sebastiani's—aide," were looking rather pointedly out the tinted windows, giving them at least the illusion of privacy.

"His name is Luke," Lucas said softly. Then, after a

moment's hesitation, he added, "Your sister said you named him, but I suspect that was just another lie."

Jessie fought the tears that threatened whenever she thought of her sister's mad scheming. Once past childhood they'd never been the kind of close, loving siblings she'd always wanted them to be, but she would never have suspected that her glamorous big sister was capable of such treachery.

"No," she said. "I didn't name him. I never had the chance to."

"He's been officially named, now. But if you want to change it—"

"No. Luke is fine. He is your son, after all." She didn't think her voice had an edge, but his expression seemed to tighten. "Officially?" she asked.

"In a ceremony investing him as my heir."

"Oh."

"The full name chosen is Luke Marcus Augustus Sebastiani." She blinked and drew back a little, and he hastened to explain. "After my father and King Augustus, my great-times-about-seven grandfather, the first monarch of Montebello."

"I see."

Her voice had gone cool, she knew, but she couldn't help it. Had she been allowed to name her child, she might well have chosen Luke, but she certainly wouldn't have saddled him with all the rest. Perhaps a middle name of Alexander, after her father, or even Chambers, as a reminder of the other side of his heritage. But now it was done, and it was as if anything outside of his royal lineage was meaningless. And then Lucas spoke again, softly.

"I made a change in that, though."

She lifted her gaze to his face.

"The declaration reads Luke Marcus Augustus Chambers Sebastiani."

The tightness in her chest eased. She wanted to thank him for that much, but the words wouldn't come. She felt almost as if she owed him an apology for what she'd thought, but those words wouldn't come either. Not now.

With a great effort of will, she focused on her baby and the wonderful days just ahead, when she would have him to herself on the ranch, where she could finally, really heal. The peace she found there worked like no other medicine to soothe away her troubles, and she had no doubt it would work again, even after the kind of ordeal she'd been through.

She had so much to learn, she thought. So much to learn about her child, and about being a mother. She felt a twinge of fear, hoping she would be up to the task.

She lifted her head, looked out at the passing landscape, her pulse picking up as she realized they were getting close to home. She could walk it from here, she thought. She had before, when the old ranch truck had finally given out. Even though it was five tough miles, she'd done it. Somehow that made her feel safe, just being within reach of home.

For now she would just try to enjoy it. And try to quash the feeling that she was merely postponing the inevitable.

Lucas began to have a strange, unsettled feeling as the landscape became more and more familiar. In the months he'd spent on the Chambers ranch, he'd ridden virtually every inch of it, because on horseback and in Jessie's arms were the only places he'd felt sane. The only places where the befuddlement that hung over him didn't seem like the most important thing in the world, and the most insurmountable.

He hadn't had a clue who he was, but he'd known he was at home around horses, that the movement of a powerful mount beneath him was loved and familiar. That he

knew the way of thinking that took place behind those
liquid-brown eyes, that he knew what would spook them,
what would move them, what would charm them. Even
Jessie, who had grown up with the animals, had trusted
him completely with her valuable string of quarter horses
after watching him with them for a single day.

"They know you know them," she had told him. "It's
clear they trust you already. Their judgment is good
enough for me."

He'd been merely a new hand to her then, and he'd
never dreamed he would become anything more, no matter how her quiet strength and courage attracted him. He
knew he had no right to even consider it—what woman
in her right mind would want to get involved with a man
not simply without a past, but with no idea what that past
might contain?

Yet over time the pull between them had become irresistible. He'd had the brief thought that it was her loneliness, isolated out here on this ranch, and his own confusion and disorientation that had been part of it, but in
the end the unexpected passion they'd found was so fierce
no other reasons mattered.

He suppressed a shiver at the memories of night after
night spent in a sort of erotic, sensual haze, days spent
feeling weary from lack of sleep yet oddly energized, as
well, and eagerly awaiting the coming night's replay.

He doubted Jessie was feeling anything of the sort. She
was returning to the home she loved, and if it was haunted
with memories of their time together, he was sure that
was overshadowed by the joy of her return after her ordeal. He would do well to remember that, he thought.
Every corner of the place was, to him, a reminder of what
they'd found together here. To her, there were many more
memories he was no part of, thoughts he would never
intrude on.

As they rounded the last turn, Lucas leaned forward to be sure the driver didn't miss the boulder that marked the nearly hidden entrance to the ranch. But all the while he was wondering if he would ever again have memories she didn't creep into.

Not likely, he told himself.

Chapter 3

The moment Jessie walked into the kitchen, Lucas gave up on what he'd been dwelling on all morning, which was how to convince Jessie that the Playboy Prince didn't exist anymore. With everything that had happened to her, he wasn't sure she'd had enough time to even absorb the fact of who he really was, let alone accept that he was no longer what the gossip rags said he was. He'd only walked back into her life hours ago, after all.

The fact that he himself wasn't certain anymore who and what he was was something he tried not to dwell on. That solid certainty would come back, he was sure, once he had all the facets of his life in place. He was simply suffering from aftereffects. The doctors had warned him he might feel unsettled for a while.

He hadn't expected the feeling to be so strong, but he decided now that it was because he didn't have this in order yet. Once Jessie and Luke were where they should be, everything else would fall into place. And he was sure that would happen as soon as Jessie was sure he wasn't some spoiled, profligate wastrel, good for nothing except making tabloid headlines. But he would have to move slowly.

Jessie needed time. Time to feel safe again, time to put the nightmare of her abduction and awful captivity, her near death and the kidnapping of her baby behind her.

As much as she could, anyway, he amended, remembering his mother's warning that Jessie might be haunted by those events for a very long time.

Yet looking at her now, she seemed almost unchanged by her ordeal. The woman who walked into the homey, country kitchen looked just like the woman he'd fallen in love with all those months ago. Her long, slender legs were encased in faded blue jeans, and she was wearing one of the long-sleeved T-shirts she favored, soft from many washings. Her long hair was braided into a single, thick, golden plait down her back, the tip nearly brushing the worn leather belt at her waist.

But when he looked closer, he saw the darker circles beneath her eyes, saw that the jeans were a bit loose on her. Whatever weight she'd put on during her pregnancy, she certainly hadn't hung on to any of it. And when she gave him an uncertain smile, he knew she was still very fragile.

Careful, he warned himself yet again.

"Did the nurse check you?" he asked.

"Yes, she did," Jessie said, her mouth quirking. "I seem to have survived my hair-raising excursion in a vehicle that's obviously designed not to allow a single bump in the road to be felt."

"Good," Lucas said, ignoring her wry humor. She might as well get used to being treated properly, because from now on that's the way it was going to be.

Jessie walked quickly to the table, where Eliya sat giv-

ing Luke his bottle. She looked at the child hungrily, and
Lucas suspected it had been all she could do to be away
from the baby long enough to be examined by the nurse
he'd hired.

"Do you wish to finish?" Eliya asked her politely.

Jessie hesitated, her gaze flicking to the window that
gave them a view out to the barn.

"Take him," Lucas said to Jessie. "Eliya, will you
leave us for a moment, please?"

With a quick nod the woman carefully handed over the
baby, his blanket and the bottle, and departed. Jessie
looked a little startled at the speed with which it had happened, but she sank down into the chair the woman had
been using and cuddled her son close as she held the
bottle for him.

"You need time with him," Lucas told her when they
were alone.

"Yes," she agreed. "I need that." She gave him a
hesitant look.

"What is it, Jessie?"

"I'm a little afraid," she admitted. "Of really being a
mother to him. I feel like I've got so much to learn, so
fast."

"You were always a fast learner," he said. "And you'll
have plenty of time."

"But the ranch, I've been gone so long, it needs—"

"I'll take care of the ranch."

Her gaze snapped up to his face. "You?"

"You don't think I can?"

If he'd still been Joe, she wouldn't have doubted it,
Lucas thought. She knew he could work hard, that he
understood the running of a ranch, and that what he didn't
know he'd learn fast.

"I guess I didn't think about it," she said. "But it can't
be typical prince's work."

Lucas drew in a compressed breath. "Jessie, I'm the same man I was. Remembering my identity didn't change that."

"Remembering he was the crown prince of Montebellan royalty didn't affect just plain Joe?" she said, disbelief in her voice.

"I didn't say that. I just meant I can still be the man who helped you run this place. So you can not worry, and spend time with Luke."

"Oh." She lowered her gaze to the baby's face, to his tiny hands clutching at the bottle. "You'd do that?"

Lucas swore to himself. He'd known he must have hurt her badly, but he hadn't realized—despite a rather stern warning from his sister Julia—just how badly. But he didn't want to get into it now, not when she was still weak, still fragile. So instead, he gave her a part of the truth he knew she would understand.

"I like this life. There's something about the American West that's always appealed to me."

Jessie frowned. "You mean even before you…landed here by accident?"

He nodded. "I used to read about it, see it in films. Even as a child, I was fascinated by the freedom of it, the incredible openness and space, the sparse population. Montebello is an island, after all, with a finite amount of space. Your West seems…infinite."

"Wide-open spaces," she said.

"Yes. And the people are so different here. No one cares where you were born, or who or what you were, but only what you are now. And if your word and your work are good."

"Joe's work was good," she said wistfully, as if the man she'd known as Joe was still gone, not standing right in front of her.

"When I was here, I used to live in daily dread of being

asked questions I couldn't answer,'' he said quietly. ''It took me a very long time to realize that people out here give you the right to keep your secrets, as long as you're not hurting anyone else.''

For a long moment she stared at him, and he regretted using those words about hurting anyone when he'd hurt her so much. But finally all she asked was, ''Is keeping your secrets so important to you?''

He grimaced. ''It's something that was taken away from me the day I was born. The heir to the Montebellan throne is public property, and expected to live for the people first, his country second, the monarchy third, and himself somewhere much further down the line. Trying to keep secrets isn't very wise in that environment.''

''You sound like you resent it.''

He frowned. ''I didn't mean to sound as if I do. And I don't, really. It's who I am, and resenting something you have no choice about is pointless.''

But still, her observation made him uncomfortable enough that he excused himself, telling her he would do an assessment of conditions on the ranch and report back to her in a few hours. He didn't want to leave her, not so soon after finding her again, not so soon after he'd thought she was lost to him forever, but he knew she would worry until she was certain the ranch affairs were under control. Her wicked sister had tried to sell off all the animals. Luckily the ranch hands Ursula dismissed had worked together to keep Jessie's prized horses at one of their own small places, and to place the cattle with a nearby rancher who had graciously sold them back when Jessie's story became known.

Lucas was thankful that the hands had suspected something wasn't right and had saved the herd Jessie had worked so hard to breed. He wanted her calm and at peace before he broached the touchy subjects they had yet to deal with. And that was going to take time.

He only hoped he had enough.

Jessie didn't miss the tension that radiated from Lucas. She knew there were things hovering, things to be discussed, things to be decided. But she was more than happy to put them off. Right now all she wanted to do was hold her baby, learn everything about him, from those perfect little toes to his silken dark hair, and revel in having him back.

She knew the ranch would work its healing magic on her. It had already begun. And thankfully, there weren't many memories of Ursula here. Her sister had hated the place, and had forsaken it long ago, when Jessie was twelve, for the bright lights of city life and dreams of stardom.

Ursula had been bitter beyond Jessie's ability to tolerate when she'd come back from New York after breaking up—Jessie suspected she'd been dumped—with the man she'd claimed was her manager. She'd not found the success she'd dreamed of, and the world—and for some reason her little sister—were to blame. It was as if Ursula had hated her for being content to stay here on the ranch, for not having big dreams like Ursula's own.

I wonder if she would have loved me more if I'd failed at something big, too? Jessica thought.

If Ursula was capable of love at all. Somehow, somewhere, Ursula had changed completely. The sister Jessie had once loved had turned vicious. It was still hard for Jessie to comprehend that Ursula had actually plotted her death so she could feather her own nest by stealing Jessie's baby and using him to curry favor with the Montebellan royal family. Or if that failed, to blackmail them.

"Are you all right, sweetie?"

Mrs. Winstead, who had been the cook and house-keeper at the Chambers's ranch during Jessie's childhood, was a welcome familiar presence after the overwhelming proximity of Lucas and his small entourage.

"I will be," she said, "given time. I'm going to need your help, Mrs. Winstead. I'm terrified of making mistakes with him."

"Well, don't you worry your head, you'll have that," the older woman said brusquely, "and plenty more help if the crew that man has brought in is any indication. I mean, really, I kept this house for twenty-three years, and took care of you, as well. I think I could manage it again until you fully recover."

"He means well," Jessie said, a little surprised at how quickly she jumped to his defense.

"Joe would never have taken over like that, ordering people around," Mrs. Winstead pointed out.

Jessie sighed. "No. No, he wouldn't."

Mrs. Winstead sniffed. "I guess finding out he was a prince did that."

"He's changed," Jessie agreed, almost sadly. She couldn't argue Mrs. Winstead's assessment. Joe had changed when he'd become Lucas. He'd changed tremendously. "But it isn't just that…snowplow way he's got now, pushing everything out of his way. It's more than that."

"More?"

Jessie nodded slowly, thinking it through for the first time since the father of her child had strode into her hospital room in all his royal glory.

"He's weighed down, just as he was carrying that awful weight as Joe. But now he's carrying it in a different way. I'm not sure what it is, but it's there."

"Maybe," Mrs. Winstead said grudgingly. "I suppose being a prince isn't all it's cracked up to be sometimes."

Jessie turned that over and over in her mind as she retreated to her mother's old rocking chair with her son and Mrs. Winstead went about the business of preparing a meal, grumbling under her breath about the number of people there were to feed. Jessie smiled, knowing the woman was justifiably proud of her cooking, and that a few extra people were hardly a challenge to her skills.

Jessie rocked in her mother's chair, coming down from that fever pitch of panic and nerves that had enveloped her from the moment her baby had been taken from her. When Luke went to sleep contentedly in her arms, her heart ached with a fullness she'd never experienced, and she knew she would lay down her life for this little being in an instant, no questions asked.

But living for him was more difficult. She suppressed the nagging fear she'd been fighting ever since his father had put Luke back into her arms. What did she know about raising a child? For that matter, what did she know about taking care of a baby? She'd never even been around one, not a human one, anyway. She'd hand-raised many animal babies—foals, puppies, calves, rabbits, even a fawn once when she'd been a child—but she didn't know a blessed thing about human babies. And instinct could only do so much in today's complicated world. There was a very big difference between the instinct that told a mare how to take care of her baby and the instincts necessary to keep a human baby safe amid all the dangers of life.

She wondered if Luke could sense how frightened she was.

Poor little guy, she thought. *You don't even have a mother who knows what she's doing.*

But she'd learn, she promised him silently. She would learn, and pray she didn't do any irreparable damage in the process.

In what seemed like mere minutes, hours passed, and there was the sound of strong, male footsteps coming from the front of the ranch house. There were three male hands on the ranch, but still she knew who it was. She wasn't sure how, but she knew.

She supposed the idea that she could hear a certain arrogance in the stride was fanciful. And she had no real reason to assume it was there—he'd done nothing any rich, powerful man wouldn't do. It was just that the change from the quiet, unassuming, almost shy man she'd known as Joe was so startling, and even more so now that they were back here in the place where she'd first met him.

He hadn't been shy, she told herself, *he'd just been lost, uncertain. It made him seem shy.*

She was right, of course, the footsteps were his. He stopped in the kitchen doorway. She looked at Luke a moment longer, wondering if she would ever be able to face his father with the ease she once had.

Finally she lifted her gaze.

The look of pure longing she caught on Lucas Sebastiani's face startled her. It vanished quickly, hidden behind a steady, neutral expression she'd never seen on Joe's face. She was left wondering what—or who—it had been directed at.

"I've talked to the hands," he said, in a tone as neutral as his expression. "They checked up on the place and kept it in good shape, despite Ursula's treatment of them. Gant left a couple of weeks ago, but everyone else stuck it out. They all suspected something wasn't right."

She was glad to hear it. Not every man was willing to work for a woman even in this day and age, and she'd honed her crew down to those to whom it didn't matter.

"They respect you," he said, as if he'd read her thoughts. "And they all know you work as hard if not harder than any of them. You love this place and this life just like they do, and that's enough for them.''

"Thank you," she said, pleased.

"There are a few things," he said, going on as if what he'd said had been simply fact, not a compliment. "As usual, there's fence to repair. The liver chestnut mare got a wire cut, but Barney says it's not serious. And the reservoir up on the flats is clogged again."

Again Jessie's gaze shot to his face. As Joe, he'd suggested a way to fix the problematical reservoir permanently, with a supply and drainage system that was, for the moment, beyond her means. When she'd asked him how he'd known about such things, he'd gotten the strangest look on his face. And at last, rather forlornly, he'd answered simply, "I don't know."

"I presume you remembered how you knew those things?" she asked.

"Yes. There's an area of Montebello that has no water of its own. As my engineering project in college, I designed a system to deliver and store water from elsewhere on the island."

"Did you ever build it?"

"Yes. That's how I knew it would work, apparently. I knew that much, even if I couldn't remember the rest."

She glanced down at her son, noticed as never before his resemblance to his father. "It must be a relief to you, to have your past back in place."

"It is," he agreed, then added, "and it isn't."

Cryptic, she thought. Like Joe had sometimes been. Only with Joe she'd always thought it was unintentional. Now she wasn't so sure.

"I will build it now, if you like."

She shook her head. "I still can't afford it."

"Jessie," he began.

She went still, knowing he was about to offer to pay

for it himself. To his credit, he must have realized that was the wrong tack, because he stopped.

This was something else she hadn't really had time to think about, that her Joe was now a man with resources beyond anything she'd ever dreamed of. But right now, all she could think was that the offer he'd almost made smacked of an effort to ease whatever guilt he felt from walking out on her.

"You think that makes everything okay? You come back and throw money around? You think I can be bought?"

A muscle along his stubborn jaw jumped. "I never said that."

If he had, she thought, he would no doubt be offering all he could give. Joe might have been content to stay, to become part of the fabric of her life here as she'd always hoped he would. But Joe was as gone as if he'd died the night he had walked out on her. Prince Lucas Sebastiani— she didn't even know what his full royal name was, she realized—was a horse of another color altogether. A horse in designer slacks and silk shirts. She found herself longing for Joe's faded jeans and second-hand-store shirts, which had been all he'd been able to afford when she'd first hired him.

"I was just trying to help," Lucas said, his voice tight. "I know you want and need that done, so why shouldn't I do it?"

"What I want," she said slowly, "you can't give me."

"Try me," he said, sounding almost desperate now.

"The crown prince of Montebello can't give me what I want," she amended.

Something weary flickered in his eyes once more. "It's who I am. My first loyalty must always be to Montebello."

She saw both that he meant it and that it had cost him.

He had a loyalty to his country that he would not forsake. This, she thought, was what had changed most. Joe had been fairly carefree, despite the burden of his amnesia. Lucas carried a responsibility that was almost a visible thing.

And while that made her admire him, it also answered the question she hadn't dared ask. He would go back, back to that life, that glittering, glamorous life that to her was no more than a fantasy, a fairy tale that happened to be real enough to make the gossip columns and on occasion the nightly news.

Even what had happened to him was the stuff of fantasy; the rich, royal, jet-setting playboy crashing his private plane, stricken with amnesia, recovering just in time to go undercover for an FBI anti-terrorist operation, then home to a glorious welcome for the prodigal prince.

She much preferred Joe, itinerant ranch hand with no past and a future of his choosing.

For a long, strained moment, Lucas stared at her. He started to speak, then stopped himself. "Let's not talk about it now," Lucas said at last. "There's time yet. Just heal and get well, Jessie."

She appreciated his concern, but long after he'd left her there with their son still in her arms, she was still wondering what he'd been about to tell her. And why he'd changed his mind about it.

Something made her shiver, and she wasn't sure why. She shrugged off the feeling, telling herself nothing bad could possibly happen now that she had her baby back.

Chapter 4

It's one of the strangest sensations of my life, Lucas thought. *Like being a stranger in a familiar land.*

He'd saddled up the big bay gelding he'd ridden when he'd been here before. He fancied the horse remembered him by the way he'd nudged Lucas's shoulder familiarly.

It felt strange to be back in a Western saddle, since at home he rode with English-style tack. He had to confess, he'd missed the easy, long-legged way of Western riding. The big, solid quarter horse also seemed strange after the fiery, dish-faced Arabians that were his father's pride and joy.

I'd like to bring home one or two of these horses, he thought as he leaned back to pat the powerful hindquarters that could accelerate the animal faster than any other horse over short distances. The combination of Arab endurance and quarter horse speed off the mark could be an interesting combination.

He'd ridden a lot since returning to Montebello, on his

own black Arabian. In the beginning it had been the only peace he'd found as he'd struggled to assimilate everything that had happened. When he'd thought Jessie and the child she'd never told him about were dead, it had been the only way he could feel close to her.

When Luke had been brought to him, miraculously healthy and alive, he'd gone riding both when panic had filled him about being responsible for this tiny life and when he wanted to give thanks that some small part of Jessie still lived on this earth.

So now here he was, riding a familiar horse over familiar ground, yet knowing and feeling that he was a completely different man than he had been then. He remembered the days on the ranch with perfect, wistful clarity. They were like some long ago, treasured childhood dream—except that there was nothing childlike about what he'd felt for Jessie Chambers.

He rode on, memories coming back to him at a faster and faster rate, this hill, this stand of trees, this bend in the river. He remembered the long, hard days, the strenuous work that had left him exhausted at the end of the day. But it had been a pleasant sort of exhaustion, the kind that meant the satisfaction of a job well done, and a peaceful night of sound sleep.

He didn't know that kind of simple satisfaction anymore. Even the memory of it had faded amid the glitter of his other life. It was only now that he'd returned here that an echo of the feeling filled him. And a longing to experience it again, made more poignant by the realization he likely never would.

He hadn't appreciated the simplicity of that life when he'd had it. And he probably would never have realized the lack he felt now had he not spent those quiet months here. But now that lack was an aching, empty place inside that he didn't think he could ever fill again.

Unless he had Jessie. It was all tied up with her, and now that he thought about it, he wasn't sure how much of that peace had come from this place and how much had come from Jessie herself. Jessie and her love, a treasure he had had for all too short a time. A treasure that made all his wealth, his position, his much-envied title pale by comparison.

He pulled the bay to a stop on a rise. He looked back, knowing that from here he could see the ranch house. He'd ridden up here before, in that time when the only past he'd had dated from the day he'd come to in the wreckage of a small plane, with no idea of who he was or why he was there. The smell of aviation gas had spurred him to quick movement, and he'd dragged himself away from the crash site just in time—the fire had begun barely moments after he'd got clear. He'd saved only the clothes he'd been wearing, including the distinctive ski cap he'd had on in anticipation of the weekend in Aspen, the cap that had led his sister Anna to believe he was still alive.

But now all he thought about was the peace he'd felt then, looking back at the ranch from this spot. He remembered thinking he could make a good life here, even if he never remembered. But he had remembered, and while it had given him back what he'd lost, it had taken away what he'd gained in the interim.

A small column of smoke rose from the chimney, and another from the flue of the woodstove that warmed the kitchen. It gave the place a welcoming feel. Hearth and home, Jessie had called it. And he realized that Jessie and this place were so intertwined that it mattered little which was the source of that peace.

He thought of what life would have been like for Joe, coming home to this every night. Nothing more complicated to worry about than the range and the animals and beating a storm home. Knowing a warm, loving woman would be working right alongside you. And with the thought of warm, loving nights to get you through the days.

But instead, here he was, a man out of place. Prince Lucas Sebastiani, with a kingdom as his birthright, the media and paparazzi as his constant companions, and the fate of his people someday in his hands.

He wondered wearily if perhaps he hadn't been luckier as Joe.

Despite her worry about the ranch, it was two days before Jessie could tear herself away from baby Luke long enough to even step outside.

She stood on the front porch, taking in the fresh morning air, looking out over the ranch land she loved. The Chambers ranch was and always had been a small but quality operation, raising mostly blooded cattle and horses for sale to other ranchers for improvement of their own stock. They'd done well with that approach, although there had been lean times, as any ranch had.

She made herself, just for these moments, let go of the tension that filled her. Luke was napping, the air was clear and inviting, and she needed this. After that nightmare time in that awful cellar, expecting Gerald to kill her at any time, and after mourning the baby she'd barely held, and the man she hadn't been able to hold at all, she needed this badly.

She walked to the main barn, taking a deep breath as she went in, savoring the familiar earthy smells of hay and grain and horses. She'd never realized how much she loved those smells. How much they meant home to her. So much seemed new, and more precious than ever because she'd come so close to never seeing, hearing or smelling it again.

As she walked the length of the barn, she stopped at each stall to greet the horse inside. Lucy, the little sorrel, tried to nip as usual. Buddy, the big pinto who had three times tossed Joe on his backside, nuzzled her so enthusiastically he nearly knocked her over.

And then she heard the familiar, demanding whinny that made her smile. Brat, her baby, the mare she'd raised since she'd been foaled seven years ago, was making her irritation widely known. How dare she, the horse's indignant vocalization seemed to say, come into the barn and greet those other horses first?

With a laughing apology to Buddy, she hurried to the end stall.

"I'm sorry, honey," Jessie crooned lovingly as she rubbed under the buckskin mare's jaw. The horse had a long, dramatic registered name derived from the names of her sire and dam, but it had quickly given way to the frequently used appellation she now answered to.

Brat snorted energetically, but wasn't quite ready to forgive her just yet. The horse eyed Jessie somewhat balefully until she tugged two sugar cubes out of her pocket and gave them to her. Forgiving her at last, Brat nudged her with a velvety nose.

"Have you been good?" Jessie asked as she patted the sleek neck. "Or have you been giving Barney a bad time?" She cringed just thinking what might have happened had not Barney kept the horses at his own small farm when Ursula had tried to sell them.

The mare blew gustily at her, nudging her again.

"You need a good grooming," Jessie said frankly, examining the mare's dusty and disheveled coat and mane. "I suppose you made it too difficult, Brat."

She would have wondered if the head wrangler had been slacking off if she didn't know his dedication to his job, and didn't know perfectly well that Brat made grooming a misery for anyone except her. If it wasn't for the animal's amazing intelligence and incredible cow sense—she'd taken the county championship her first year of cutting competition—she wouldn't be worth the trouble to many. But Jessie loved her sassy personality and her honey-and-black good looks, and the bond that had grown between them was something she treasured.

Jessie slid back the latch on the lower half of the stall door. Brat stamped a hoof as if to say "About time!" She danced eagerly as Jessie led her out of the stall.

Moments later she had the horse secured in the cross ties, and went to get her bucket of grooming tools. She'd have to begin with the curry comb, she thought, the mare had obviously found some mud to roll in somewhere.

She had one flank nearly free of dried mud when she heard the barn door slide open, followed by quickened footsteps. She looked up over Brat's back to see Lucas approaching. Glowering. Apparently at her.

"What do you think you're doing?"

His imperious tone irritated her. She looked from him to the horse to the tool in her hand with an exaggerated expression of puzzlement. "I think it's called grooming a horse."

He grimaced. "I can see that. Why?"

"Because it needs doing," she pointed out in exasperation, for the moment forgetting she was addressing royalty. "What is your problem?"

"My problem is that you're just out of the hospital and have no business riding a horse all over creation!"

She drew back slightly. He'd sounded almost irate at the thought. It was rather touching, really. "Riding. Grooming. Two different things."

"You weren't going riding?"

She shook her head. "I wasn't. I know I'm not ready. But she doesn't like anybody but me to groom her."

"I know."

She blinked. And suddenly remembered he did know—he'd seen her deal with the horse before, and had seen the frustration of the others who'd tried. How odd, she thought. She'd almost forgotten he was Joe, so completely had he changed.

Had he still been Joe, she would have assumed it was concern for her that had set him off. But this was Prince Lucas of Montebello, and she wasn't sure what his motivation was. She supposed he still felt something for her, although she wasn't sure what. He had come for her, after all, and had arranged all this.

And he'd brought her baby to her. That above all. For that alone, he deserved her thanks, and a bit more patience, she thought. No matter who he was now. But she was grateful when he left her alone with her horse. Brat, at least, didn't confuse her.

With this new resolution in her mind, Jessie spent the next few days concentrating on getting well. She didn't think she was as fragile as Lucas thought, and she soon realized her nurse was an ally. The woman departed after her assigned three days, telling Jessie to do as much—but only as much—as she felt like doing.

First she would walk, she decided, staying close to the house and barns. And on the second day of those walks, she got a wicked shock. She went to the small family graveyard, where her parents and grandparents had been laid to rest on the land they loved. She felt the need to be close to them, to pour out her fears and her confusion, as she had in the days after discovering she was pregnant with the child of a man who had already walked out on her.

As she stepped through the gate in the low, picket fence that surrounded the small plot, she was vaguely aware of something different, something wrong. But it wasn't until she walked to her parents' graves that she realized what it was.

There was a new grave next to theirs. A very new one, one the grass hadn't yet covered. Set at the head was a plain metal marker.

And on the marker was her name.

It gave her such a start she nearly screamed. This was a detail no one had told her, that they had carried the farce this far, to dig a grave for a body that didn't exist.

"Damn it, why didn't they get rid of that?"

Lucas's voice came from close behind her, but she was so rattled by what she'd found she didn't even jump. His arms came around her and he turned her away from the eerily gruesome sight of her own grave. And for just that moment she let herself believe he meant it, that he was comforting her just as Joe would have. But it lasted only that moment as he held her then reality returned in a rush and she pulled away. He let her go and perversely, she didn't like that either.

In the days that followed, Jessie continued to take her walks, but she avoided going that way again. And as her strength grew, along with her restlessness, she decided to take that first ride. She couldn't resist the urge any longer. She needed to see for herself that everything was all right, that the ranch hadn't changed somehow during her absence.

There was nothing really physically wrong with her, she thought. It was exhaustion from her ordeal, coupled with being rundown after a birth with no medical care. But remembering Lucas's reaction last time, she announced her intention first.

"You're sure you're up to it?"

"I'm sure. I'm only going for a short while, the first time."

"I'll come with you."

"That's not necessary."

"It is for me." There was that imperious tone again, she thought. She didn't care for it.

"You don't need to."

"It's me or Lloyd, take your pick."

She frowned. "Look, I don't need an escort. All that's over now."

He started what she thought would have been a sharp retort, then stopped himself. And again she wondered what he'd been about to say.

"Then let me come because I want to," he said instead. "I've missed this place."

That, she thought, she could understand completely. "All right."

He seemed surprised by her easy capitulation. She knew she was a sucker for anyone who could understand her love for the ranch. A real sucker.

So as she saddled Brat and headed out, Lucas rode beside her on the big bay gelding he'd ridden as Joe. And for an afternoon she tried to pretend that nothing had changed, that the man beside her was still the man she'd fallen in love with all those months ago.

The man she still ached for, every night she spent alone. An ache that had come back full-force now that they were under the same roof.

But any time she looked at him straight-on, any time she saw his eyes, the illusion was shattered. This wasn't Joe, the man with no past, no ties, the man with the puzzled, haunted look in his eyes. This man knew exactly who he was, knew his place in his world.

Or his realm, she thought with silent irony. In the literal sense of the word, relating to kings. She still found it hard to believe. But she knew it was true. Unlike the quiet Joe, Lucas had a place in a bigger world—in fact, a place on the world stage. A stage where there was no role for a simple Colorado rancher.

It was Brat who warned her, her ears swiveling back, her tail swishing. Jessie turned, and as she'd half expected, saw the big bay approaching. Whenever she went out to ride, it seemed he came after her. She wondered if he was watching her, or if he just had everybody on the ranch reporting to him whenever she left the house.

Irritation flickered through her, but she was determined nothing would spoil today. She'd been waiting to make this particular ride since she'd arrived back at the ranch, and she wouldn't let her self-appointed keeper interfere. She wheeled Brat back around and continued on, and was honest enough to admit she'd just decided to take the much trickier shorter route, up the sheer side of the mesa on a trail narrow enough to have her scraping a stirrup on one side while her other foot hung out over space.

He kept up with her, of course. She hadn't really expected him not to; that hadn't even really been her intent.

Sometimes it seemed like her life had narrowed down to two things—her baby and his father. Every minute that wasn't taken up with Luke—which admittedly wasn't many—was taken up with battling her feelings for the man sleeping just across the hall.

She went very still as something struck her for the first time. Brat's head came up. The horse was incredibly sensitive to the slightest new tension in her body. She whispered a soothing word to the animal, but kept on thinking about what she had just realized. That unlike Joe, who had stayed in the bunkhouse even after they'd become lovers, Lucas—and his entire entourage—had moved into the house without any hesitation, or even asking her.

It wasn't really arrogance, or royal prerogative. It only made sense—he'd want to be close to Luke. And she couldn't deny she was glad to have all that help handy, she was still very new at this mothering business. But it just pounded home to her how things had changed, how Joe was just as gone as if he'd never really existed.

So why did she lie awake at night, listening for the slightest sound, not just from Luke's crib, but from the room across the hall? Why was she unable to sleep even after he'd gone to bed and silence descended on the house?

Why did she so often wake up from dreams that were a tangled mass of emotions, with the only constant being the hot, erotic images drawn up out of the depths of memory?

She shuddered, and Brat's head came up again. And again she spoke to the horse, and forced herself to turn her attention back to the rather precarious trail. She felt the buckskin's powerful muscles bunch as Brat prepared for the push up and over the rim of the mesa, and for a few seconds at least, she had room in her mind for nothing else.

Once she reached the flat of the plateau, she sent Brat to the east at a slow trot, glad to now have the task of searching the landscape to distract her. She knew from the sound of rolling pebbles and the swiveling of Brat's ears that the bay had just come over the rim. She didn't look back. Five minutes passed, then ten. Suddenly the buckskin's ears shot forward, and her head came up.

They're here, Jessie thought, that old excitement that never left her rising anew.

She reined the buckskin down to a walk, reached back and pulled a small pair of binoculars from her saddlebag, and intensified her visual searching. Still, it was a few minutes more before her human eyes picked up what the mare's sensitive ears and nose had already located.

She spotted the black colt first. The darkness of his coat

stood out on the mesa long dried out by the summer sun and ready for the blanket of snow to come. Coming two now, he was bigger, stronger, and looked fat enough to make it through the winter, as long as he stayed healthy.

The black colt's mother looked good, as well, perhaps because this year there was no foal at her side. And there was the pinto, and the jug-headed bay, over there was the liver-chestnut filly—wait, did she have a foal? Jessie leaned forward, trying to see, and after a moment was sure; the three-year-old was now a mother. And over there—

She stopped her own thoughts as she spotted the stallion. He was a wiry, compact sorrel with a flaxen mane and tail, who made up for what he lacked in stature in sheer muscle and power and spirit. He was off to the north, atop a rise, watching over his small band. And in the moment she saw him, he became aware of her. His head came up sharply and he wheeled to face her, even from the distance of at least two hundred yards.

She lifted the binoculars to her eyes, unable to resist the lure of simply looking at this wildest of wild things. The magnification showed her the flared nostrils, the intense gaze, the sharp ears as the horse analyzed this new possible threat. His body showed the scars of many fights to maintain his leadership, but he was still young and strong, and likely to remain in charge for a while yet, unless he got hurt.

Usually she would have been up here several times already this year, and he'd be used to her by now. Still, he should know he didn't need to fear this familiar and harmless intruder in his domain.

She frowned as the horse stomped one forefoot, then wheeled and raced down the rise, trumpeting his warning to his band, sending them racing away. And then she realized what she had forgotten in the joy of seeing the wild ones again—she wasn't alone.

When Lucas rode up beside her, she was just irritated enough that his presence had sent the wild ones running to take it out on him. But the moment she looked at him, saw the wonder on his face, she bit back the words.

"Wild horses?" he asked, his tone full of an awe that went a long way toward making her forgive him for his intrusion on what was normally a special, private time for her. "Is that what they were, real mustangs?"

"Yes," she said, realizing she'd never shown Joe this. They'd been too busy with…other things. "They've been up here on the mesa for a long time now," she finished hastily.

"I've seen film, but to see them in the flesh…."

His voice trailed off as he looked wistfully after the vanishing herd. And she forgave him completely, because she could see he felt just as she did.

"I come up every year to see how they're doing, if they need supplemental feeding before winter. They look good this year. And they only lost a couple."

"Lost?"

She nodded. "The old white mare, and a three-year-old colt. She may have died naturally, and the colt may have been driven away by the stallion."

"May have?"

"Or they may have been shot, or poisoned."

He blinked. "What?"

"A lot of ranchers hate them. Think they take up range and graze that should go to cattle. A lot of them aren't above doing a little thinning of their own. Some of them would like to just kill them all."

"I can't believe that," Lucas said, shaking his head.

"It's their livelihood that's being affected. They've got families to feed, and since ranching isn't exactly the most profitable venture these days, they can't afford to cut any slack for anything but their moneymakers, which are the cattle. I understand. I don't agree, I think the horses are too precious to destroy, but I understand where they're coming from.''

"And you can afford it because you're specialized?'' he asked.

She nodded. "My money comes from quality, not quantity, so I can afford the range space.''

For a long moment they just sat there, in the old, companionable silence she'd once known with Joe. She sighed inwardly, knowing that longing for the past was useless, but still unable to help herself. She'd loved Joe with all the passion and emotion she had in her. And she thought that maybe, just maybe, she could come to love this man beside her in the same way.

But even if she could love a prince, she didn't think she could ever live with one.

Chapter 5

The full moon washed the vista in an eerie silver light. Lucas shifted in the saddle, staring out across the vastness of the Colorado landscape from his vantage point on the ridge. Behind him were the Rockies, the towering peaks that still inspired awe in him. He remembered how, as Joe, he'd often stood outside at night and just stared up at them. He'd known that these "serious mountains," as Jessie called them, were something his home—even though he couldn't remember it—didn't have, yet somehow they seemed familiar.

Now, of course, he knew that the Sebastiani family owned a large cabin in Aspen, a cabin that was one of his favorite places to retreat, and was, in fact, where he'd been heading when the plane he'd rented for the spur-of-the-moment trip had gone down in that freak Colorado storm.

And if that crash hadn't happened, you would never have met Jessie, he thought. *And Luke, precious Luke, would never have been born.*

The sense of loss he felt at the very idea startled him. It still had the power to shock him sometimes, how that tiny little boy had already wrapped him around his finger. He'd clung to him at first, when he'd thought Jessie dead, because Luke was the only part of her he had left. But it hadn't taken long to see himself in the child, as well. And soon he was enamored with Luke himself, amazed at how the baby was already showing individuality and personality.

He'd never before understood the fascination with having children. He'd always known what was expected of him, that he would have to provide an heir to the throne, it had been hammered into him from his own childhood. And on the rare occasions when he'd thought about it growing up, he'd thought little about the woman who would bear those children. He would make, he assumed, a suitable match when the time came, hopefully with a woman he could like and respect. When his parents had chosen a British woman he'd never met, daughter of some earl or other, he'd accepted it as inevitable, eventually.

He'd also known he would only have to be as involved with his future children as he wanted to be—there would always be nursemaids, nannies and, later, governesses to deal with them. It was expected in many circles.

But now, he couldn't imagine handing his son over to a string of caretakers. And he suddenly understood why his parents, who had been considered quite odd in royal circles, had insisted on being so directly involved in their children's lives.

And now, instead of that phantom woman he only hoped he could reach an accord with, he'd had a child with a woman he loved.

And not only that. He liked and respected Jessie, as well. He admired her, was sometimes even in awe of her, something he was unused to with any woman other than his mother.

In fact, Jessie was the first woman he'd ever been serious about that he was certain wouldn't crumble in the face of his mother's strength. He doubted she would tremble in the face of his father's power, either.

He tried to picture it all, tried to envision Jessie in his world. Doubt assailed him, but he shoved it aside. She was the woman he loved and the mother of his son.

He let out a long breath. He'd tried to put the future out of his mind for this time of respite. More important, he'd kept himself from broaching the subject with Jessie, because he was sure he already knew what her reaction would be. But he couldn't put it off much longer. He had a finite amount of time he could spend here, no matter how much he wanted to stay and give her all the time she needed.

A chill overtook him, and the bay shifted restlessly. He reached out and patted the horse's neck. Jessie loved this place as she did nothing else; it was in her bones, her blood. And now it was working its magic on her. It, and baby Luke—the bond between them grew stronger every day, and Lucas guessed it would soon be as limitless as if they'd never been separated on the day he'd been born.

In the time they'd been here she'd grown stronger, healthier, and he could see color in her cheeks once more. As she put the nightmare further and further behind her, that old sparkle in her eyes returned, joined now by a new joy—joy in the baby they'd created here in this place. Would Montebello bring her joy, as well?

Reluctantly, he reined the bay around and sent him toward the barn. He felt the cold of the night air against his face, reminding him winter was bearing down on them, a winter unlike any his island home would ever see. There was something exhilarating about the cold, crisp air of

ese mountains. Taking a deep breath was like a drink
crystal-clear, icy water. There was also a certain appeal
being snowed in, he remembered. A dangerous appeal,
thought, remembering the long, cold nights when Luke
ad been conceived.

Heat flooded him then, and the chill of the night was
othing against the inner fire. His body tightened fiercely
the hot, sweet memories. They'd kept each other warm,
and Jessie, during those mountain nights. They'd kept
ch other warm, and she had kept him sane.

Now he was going crazy, sleeping every night under
e same roof but knowing he had no right to join her in
at big, old brass bed. Knowing that Joe would have had
e right, but Prince Lucas Sebastiani did not. Odd, how
e position that had gained him easy and welcome entry
so many places around the world had shut the door
gainst him in the one place he truly wanted to be.

Back at the barn, he took his time rubbing down the
g bay even though it was after midnight. He gave the
g horse a ration of extra grain as thanks for the unsched-
led late-night excursion, and at long last, he made his
ay back to the silent, sleeping house.

At least, he'd thought it was silent. As he crept past
ssie's closed door, he heard a murmuring sound behind
. He stopped, listening. The murmur sounded almost like
whimper, and that was enough to have him knocking
n the door. When no answer came, he pushed the door
pen.

Jessie was just sitting up in bed, shoving tangled blond
ocks out of her face, blinking owlishly.

"Jessie? Are you all right?"

"I...think so," she said, staring at him somewhat
azedly. "It must have been a dream."

"A nightmare?" he asked softly, stepping into
e room.

After a moment she nodded. "Gerald. It was Geral and he'd come for Luke...."

Her gaze shot to the small crib beside her bed. Tl baby slept on, peacefully. Unable to resist, Lucas walke over and sat beside her on the bed.

"It's all right, Jessie. You're safe now."

That strength he'd seen building back up since they come here asserted itself. "I know. It was just a dream.

"Do they happen often?"

"Not as much as before. And I know they'll go awa eventually."

The admiration he'd been acknowledging before surge to the forefront now. Jessie Chambers was the gutsie woman he'd ever met, possibly excepting his mother, th teacher who had become a queen.

For a long, silent moment he sat there, aching to tak her into his arms, aching to bury himself in her, find th comfort the lost soul called Joe had once found.

"Jessie," he said hoarsely, and was a little startled the heat he heard in his own voice.

She looked up at him as if she'd read his thoughts. ' know," she whispered. "But I can't. Everything's too ta gled up, too confused."

He reined himself in. He hadn't really expected an thing different.

"If you were Joe," she began, then stopped.

And not for the first time, Lucas envied that man he' been, with no memory, no past, and no life to get in th way.

This was so awkward, Jessie thought.

She had finished changing Luke's diaper—she was ge ting better at it, she really was, she told herself—and p him down for his afternoon nap, then wandered down the kitchen for a snack. She'd lost enough weight durin her ordeal that she could afford a couple of Mrs. Winstead's wonderful, sinful chocolate-fudge cookies.

Now, with the sweet taste of the chocolate lingering, she leaned against the counter and stared out the windows, not really seeing the barn or the paddock beyond where Brat was kicking up her heels.

She hadn't really thought about what it would be like to have him under the same roof, when their circumstances were so changed. But that night last week, when he'd come in after she'd had that nightmare again, it had been pounded home to her that if he indeed had been Joe, she could have sought solace in his arms. She could have let his body and what it could do to hers drive away all the nightmares, all the horror of it. She remembered so well those long nights, so cold outside and so hot with passion inside. She remembered so well the way he had loved her, the way his clever fingers had played upon her nerve endings, the way his mouth had teased her to a frenzy, how the slow, huge invasion of his body had sent her soaring.

But that had been Joe. This was a man she didn't really know, a man with a past that was the stuff of history books, a present that was in the news and a lifestyle she couldn't begin to comprehend.

She supposed she should be grateful that he hadn't pressed her, that he hadn't come back to the ranch assuming they would pick up right where they left off.

Then again, maybe he hadn't because he didn't want to. She'd been good enough for Joe, but a prince?

"You're frowning again, girl," Mrs. Winstead said as she came into the kitchen. "What are you worrying about now?"

"Not worrying," Jessie said. She licked the last of the melted, gooey chocolate from her fingers before adding, "I was just being silly. Wishing Lucas was still just Joe."

"Do you, really?"

"Well, not if it meant he never got his memory back. That would be too cruel. I guess I just wanted—still want—Joe to be...real."

"Feel you've lost him, do you?"

"I feel as if I never really had him, because he never really existed."

Mrs. Winstead clucked and shook her head. "He's just hidden behind all that princely stuff," she said with a sniff.

Was it possible? Could her Joe still be there, amid all the changes she saw?

She walked outside thoughtfully, then smiled as Brat whinnied the moment she set foot on the porch. She walked across the yard to lean on the fence, and the mare raced over and skidded to a flashy stop in front of her.

"Show off," Jessie said, but her voice made it clear she was teasing.

The horse bobbed her head, making her black forelock dance. Jessie reached out to rub the velvety nose and leaned forward to puff a soft hello at the horse's nostrils, something she'd learned early on the animal liked. After a moment she heard footsteps behind her. She didn't turn to look; she knew that steady, long stride.

"She's quite a horse," Lucas said.

"Yes, she is."

"I'll never forget that day you cut that sick little white-faced calf out of the herd, and momma came after it."

"Neither will I." Jessie meant it; the herd had been at one angle, the cow had been coming at her from another angle, trying to get to her calf on yet another. Brat had been puzzled at first, but had apparently decided her job was to keep them all apart no matter what, and had put on a show of cutting, darting and spinning unlike anything Jessie had ever seen, let alone ridden.

"I'm thinking of breeding her. A foal next year would be just about old enough for Luke when he's ready to ride on his own."

Lucas didn't answer, and when she glanced at him she was startled at the grim look on his face. She wondered what had brought it on, and could only think of one thing.

"You don't believe in starting a child riding that early?" she asked.

"Of course I do. I was three."

"Oh. Well, good then." Another possible explanation for that look came to her. "Are you thinking you won't be here when he's that age?" she asked gently, knowing how it would hurt her to have to live a life without that child who had already become so precious to her.

He went very still. "I won't be far away from him, Jessie. Ever."

She sighed. "How can you not be? Your life is half a world away."

"Yes." He took a long, deep, audible breath. "And so is Luke's."

It was her turn to go still. "What?"

"He's coming back with me, Jessie. He's the heir to the throne of Montebello. He belongs to us."

And just like that, the man she'd once loved—or rather, this man who looked like him—managed what Gerald had never quite accomplished.

He'd terrified her.

Chapter 6

"No," Jessie said.

Lucas was already cursing himself for the blunt way he'd put it. He hadn't meant it to come out like that, he'd had the words all worked out, the words to explain to her, but he'd somehow lost them. Since the first moment he'd seen her holding their baby, he'd had trouble holding on to the reality he knew was coming.

But when he'd heard her making plans for an idyllic life for herself and the baby here on the ranch, apparently without him, he'd known it would only get worse if he waited any longer. He had to return home, and he had to bring the heir to the throne with him. There was no choice. Even if the life she'd been planning aloud made him ache inside with longing.

With an effort, he gathered his scattered thoughts. "I shouldn't have said that. I'm sorry."

She gave him a look so chilly he nearly shivered. "Am I supposed to be honored? I suppose not many get an apology from a prince."

"Jessie, please, don't. Do you think that this is easy for me?"

"I don't know. Because I don't really know you at all, do I?"

He let out a compressed breath. "I suppose you don't. So will you let me tell you? Who I am?" She looked a bit startled, as if she hadn't expected that. He pressed his advantage. "Come ride with me," he suggested, knowing she was at her most amenable on the back of her beloved Brat, riding the land she loved. "Let me tell you everything."

"Nothing you tell me will make me let you take my baby away from me," she warned him.

He didn't tell her he had no intention of taking the baby away from her. He had another plan, one she wasn't ready to hear. Not yet. "Just ride with me, listen. Then we'll talk."

But when they were at last heading out, Brat prancing a bit, as if she sensed her rider's edginess, Lucas still wasn't sure where to start.

"Let me tell you about my home, first," he finally said. "What do you know about Montebello?"

"I've read the stories," she said, her voice so flat it told him volumes about how hard this was going to be. "I know it was an English colony, and only became self-governing in eighteen-something."

"Eighteen-eighty. And England never left, not really. They've been part of Montebello forever, and now we're so intermingled they always will be. Besides, it was wise of the first king to keep in favor with Britain, with Tamir on our doorstep."

"The first king. Your great-times-something grand-father?"

"Yes. Augustus."

He knew she was thinking of Luke and the ancestral

name he'd been given, he could see it in her face, but she said nothing about that. Instead she asked, "I read about some sort of feud or something from back then."

"Yes. All the melodrama you could want, an arranged marriage for political reasons, a dowry of a large piece of Montebellan land, the mysterious death of the groom-to-be." His mouth quirked. "We do nothing in a small way."

"With the crown prince crashing a plane in America and disappearing for months, turning up later having had amnesia, just in time to help the FBI break up a terrorist stronghold in the U.S.? Yes, I'd say you don't."

He would have been able to handle it better if her tone had been sarcastic, but it hadn't. It had still been as flatly neutral as before. As if the tale didn't matter to her, didn't affect her in any way.

As if she'd already cut herself off from him, and from his world.

For the first time Lucas felt a twinge of desperation and doubt. He quashed it, but it took more effort than it ever had before. Perhaps, he thought wryly, because he'd always been arrogant enough before to assume that he could resolve any problem he came up against, that he could make anyone do what he wanted, eventually.

He wasn't at all sure he could make Jessie do a thing.

He tried another tack. "My family has ruled Montebello since the day Britain gave us self-rule. We *are* Montebello, the people of our country are our responsibility, and one that we take very, very seriously. Unlike other monarchies, we aren't just figureheads. We govern, and every decision made is made because we truly believe it's for the good of the people."

"Noble," she said, again with no trace of sarcasm, no emotion at all.

Despite his concern over that lack of feeling in her

voice, Lucas smiled inwardly at her choice of words. Someday he would tell her that in Montebello, that word had a special meaning because of a group of very special men who had become part of Montebello's history over the years. The story of the Noble Men and their firstborn sons would appeal to her, he thought, and not only because they were Americans. He knew Jessie would appreciate their quiet heroics.

And, he admitted honestly, the fact that they were heroes in Montebello couldn't hurt when it came to swaying her toward acceptance of the inevitable.

But first he had to convince her to come.

"Not really," he answered. "It's simply that we understand that we rule by the grace of our people. We serve at their pleasure, not the other way around. It's been that way since Augustus."

"Unusual king," she said, and he noted with relief that there was at least a spark of interest in her voice.

"So is my father. He has a long legacy to live up to, and he knows it."

"As does his only son?"

"Yes." There was really nothing more to say, so he left it at that. He thought she was going to let the conversation die there, but after a long moment she finally spoke.

"You have sisters, don't you?"

"Three. Julia, Christina and Anna. Every one of them as strong-willed in her own way as our mother." He cast her a sideways glance. "So Luke has three aunts to spoil him."

He saw the flicker of pain in her eyes, and knew she was thinking of Luke's other aunt, the wicked, vicious Ursula. Quickly, he leapt into a spiel about Montebello, things about which he was most often asked about his homeland.

"We have three hundred days of sunshine a year. You never need anything heavier than a sweater, or a light jacket when it rains in the winter. San Sebastian is an international trading center, and we host leaders from all over the world on a regular basis. We have a variety of plant life to make a botanist weep, orchids and lilies of the field growing wild, side by side, and over three hundred and fifty species of birds, not to mention a rare species of goat that can only be found there."

"You sound like the Chamber of Commerce."

He grinned. "I know. And in a way, I am. Since my father is king, and he's healthy as your Brat there and likely to rule for many more years, I've got nothing more important to do than extol the merits of Montebello to the world."

He thought he saw a flicker of a smile curve her lips, but it didn't last.

"The Sebastianis *are* Montebello, because we've always stood for the rights of the people, and because they've granted us the right to rule. We've fought for them, and occasionally died for them, and they for us. Our history is inextricably linked, and our destiny is with the people. It always has been, and it always will be."

"And that," she said, "sounded like a speech."

"Perhaps it was, at some point," he said, not reacting to the slight edge that had come into her voice. "My father, and his father before him, and all the Sebastianis who have worn the crown believe those words."

"And you?"

"And me. When my turn comes, I will do the same."

She abruptly reined Brat to a stop and sat there looking at him intently for a long, silent moment.

"And Luke?" she whispered finally.

He drew in a deep breath, knowing the moment had

come. "He is my designated heir. One day, he will assume the throne of Montebello."

"He *will?* Just like that, no choice?"

"He has no more choice than I have," Lucas said flatly.

Something hot and determined flashed in Jessie's eyes. "That," she said, her voice sharp-edged now, "is what you think."

She put her heels to Brat's flanks, and the mare leapt away as if catapulted. Lucas lifted his reins and the bay's ears shot up, but before he sent the horse rocketing after her, he hesitated. Jessie didn't get angry often, but when she did, there was no moving her. He'd do better, he thought, to let her go, let the far reaches of her beloved ranch and the steady, rocking-chair gait of the leggy buckskin calm her down.

So instead of pursuing the rapidly departing black-and-gold horse, he reined the bay around and sent him slowly back toward the house.

When Jessie reached the flats along the river, she gave Brat her head and yipped her up to a full, mad gallop. It had been a long time since the horse had had the chance to run free, and the mare leapt forward gleefully. Jessie leaned over her neck, concentrating on the ground-eating stride and the smooth, sweet action of the beautifully put together animal, marveling at her steady strength and her quickness. The horse's mane whipped back in the wind, and in her mind's eye Jessie could see her tail flying. On and on they ran, the pounding four-beat rhythm balm to her soul.

She knew the horse would literally run her heart out if asked, so when they reached the curve of the river she signaled Brat to ease up with a slight tightening of her fingers on the reins. Beyond the curve was broken ground anyway, where there was too much danger of the horse putting a foot wrong, or into a critter hole, to keep up such a pace. Reluctantly the mare slowed.

Jessie turned toward her favorite place, a small, grassy clearing on a bluff overlooking the river; a place she called the lookout. It was where she always went when she had heavy thinking to do. Or when she needed to escape. She'd spent many hours up here after her parents had died five years ago. More when she'd discovered she was pregnant. And after Joe had left her that cold winter night, she had lived up here for two days, until fear that she would become ill and endanger her child had sent her back down to the ranch.

When she reached the lookout she dismounted, loosened Brat's cinch and sat for a long time, staring out over the landscape.

The time had finally come. She had to fight for her son as hard as she'd fought for her own life. Harder, if need be. And she had to fight something that was so foreign to her she didn't know where to begin.

Calmer now, Jessie mounted up and turned the mare toward home, letting Brat pick her own path and pace. She knew she was not heading back to the ranch house for the hearty meal and peaceful evening she'd been hoping for. Instead she was facing what could be the biggest fight of her life, bigger even than the battle she'd fought to stay alive in poor, mad Gerald's clutches.

When they got back to the barn, Jessie took her time grooming Brat. She knew she was only stalling the inevitable, but she did it anyway, grooming the mare to a glistening shine, combing mane and tail, even clipping the bridle path atop her head, although it didn't really need it yet.

Finally the horse nickered in protest at the delay in the expected grain, and Jessie knew she'd dragged her feet as long as she could. She put the buckskin in her stall, dumped a portion of sweet feed in the trough, added an extra dollop of molasses by way of apology, and washed her hands at the tack room sink.

She could soap and oil her saddle, she thought, looking at the racks she'd replaced them on. That would take a good hour, maybe two if she did a real thorough job.

Coward, she muttered to herself. *Quit stalling.*

She came in through the side kitchen door, intending to head straight up to check on Luke, who should be awake by now. Instead, she found Lucas sitting at the table, as if waiting for her. As he probably was, she realized.

"Feel better?" he asked.

"I feel fine," she said, not stopping but heading toward the door that led to the stairs.

"Luke is with Eliya and Mrs. Winstead. And Lloyd is outside."

She stopped in her tracks, then turned to face him. "On your orders?"

"We need to talk."

"Maybe," she said. "Or maybe you need to listen."

"Maybe," he agreed, surprising her. "So talk to me."

Slowly she walked back over to the table, pulled out a chair that was safely on the other side from him, and sat down. Now that she was face-to-face with him again, all the things she'd worked out on her long ride seemed to skate right out of her brain. It took her a few minutes to gather them together again.

When she spoke at last, she started with the most important one. "No one," she said firmly, "is taking my baby from me again."

"No," Lucas agreed.

She blinked, feeling as if he'd already taken the wind out of sails she'd only now run up the mast. But she forged onward.

"Besides, this whole thing of your role in life being chosen for you at birth—even before birth!—that's... it's...well, it's...."

"Un-American?" Lucas suggested.

"Unfair," she countered. "How can you look at that baby and tell him he has no choice?"

Lucas winced, and she knew she'd hit a nerve. But he didn't say anything, so she went on.

"I'll admit Americans have a hard time with the concept of hereditary leadership in general. We were built on an opposing principal, after all."

"Do you think I haven't thought that myself? That I, and all the Sebastianis haven't questioned the concept? Believe me, we have. But we also know no one has the best interests of our country at heart more than we do."

"Fine. Good for you, and good for Montebello. But Luke is an American by birth."

"And he's Montebellan by blood," Lucas said. "He's a citizen, simply because he's my son."

She wasn't budging Lucas, she could see that. But she wasn't going to give in. Too much was at stake here.

"He can visit, then. But he's growing up here, in America, on this ranch, where he can be free to decide his own path."

"He isn't free. He's in line for the throne of Montebello. That can't be changed."

Something about the implacability in his voice set her off. "Because he's unfortunate enough to be your son?"

Lucas drew back, and she knew she'd drawn blood that time. She told herself she couldn't care, that her son's very life was at stake, as much now as it had been when he'd been taken from her at birth.

She had to fight for him. Even if she had to fight his father.

* * *

It had reached the point where he dreaded each morning. For now, not only did he spend long nights aching for the woman across the hall, he spent his days fighting with her. Fighting over the tiny child they had created out of love, who had somehow become the crux of the entire dispute.

This morning, up with the sun, he walked reluctantly into the kitchen, knowing Jessie was probably already there with Luke, because both her bed and the crib were empty. He found her giving him his bottle in the big rocker beside the woodstove in the corner of the homey kitchen. It was a picture that made his heart ache with a sensation he wasn't sure he'd ever felt before, a sort of longing that made him feel hollow inside.

Her hair was loose this morning, falling forward like a blond veil over her and the baby. He'd almost forgotten just how long and lovely it was. He stood, simply watching them, until that ache in his chest became a pressure almost too great to bear.

Jessie looked up then, saw him and went still. He braced himself for the adversarial expression he'd almost grown to expect to come over her face. But instead, after looking at him for a moment, she smiled. A soft, warm, inviting smile that made him think that at least something of what he'd been feeling must have been showing in his face, despite his practiced facade.

Encouraged, he walked toward them. He crouched beside the chair, and looked from her face to the face of his firstborn child, and the ache inside eased a little.

"He's so beautiful," he said softly. "Sometimes I just stare at him in awe."

"So do I," she confessed.

They lapsed into silence, watching their son as he fed. He wondered if they were both afraid to speak, afraid to start the battle again. He felt the undercurrent of tension that marred what should have been a perfect moment, and he knew until it was resolved they would have no real peace. Still he waited, not wanting to spoil this precious time with them both.

"He's so precious. Fragile yet strong. I spend hours looking at him, wishing I could guarantee he'll never be hurt, never be disappointed, never be treated unfairly."

"I understand," Lucas said, meaning it. He had more than once looked at his son and thought that he would kill anyone who tried to harm him. He'd wanted to kill Ursula. If Gerald hadn't so clearly been simpleminded, he'd have wanted to kill him, too.

Jessie looked up at him. "Then how can you possibly want him to live the life you're talking about? You should want your son to have the choices you never had."

So there it was, out in the open, simmering between them again. And the worst part was that Lucas had no argument against what she'd said, because he knew she was right. He stood up, jamming his hands into his pockets.

"I wish it could be that way," he said. Her expression changed slightly, as if she'd heard the genuine longing in his voice. "I really do understand how you feel, Jessie."

"But?"

"But it wasn't for me, and can't be for Luke, either. Montebello comes first. His life and path are set, just as mine were."

"If you never had any choice, you should understand why that's so wrong."

"I never felt like I was deprived. It was just something I knew, from childhood. Like having blue eyes."

"You didn't have anything to say about the color of your eyes. That really is a matter of no choice. What you do with your life shouldn't be."

"I never felt I was missing anything."

"What if you'd wanted desperately to be a…a lawyer? Or an airline pilot? Or—" she gestured toward the window "—a rancher?"

He smiled at her. "Actually, I am. In a way. I studied a lot of law in college, and although I didn't go for the degree, I can hold my own with most lawyers. I am a pilot, and a better one than my recent record might indicate. And I'm also a rancher. We raise purebred Arabians on our ranch near the palace."

She was staring at him, looking a little stunned. He wondered if she hadn't realized this aspect of his life, this benefit of his family's wealth and position. Whatever he wanted to do in life, he was pretty much free to do as long as it didn't conflict with the well-being of his people.

"Luke will have those same advantages," he pointed out. "Whatever he wants to do, he'll have the resources."

Jessie went very still. "I know you can give him more than I ever could. But material things aren't that important to me, and I don't want my son growing up thinking they are."

Lucas pulled a chair out from the table and straddled it backward, crossing his arms over the back before he said earnestly, "I know that, Jessie. I'm not trying to buy him. Believe me, he'll work hard for every privilege."

"He's just a baby. Let him enjoy his life. When he's old enough, he can decide what he wants."

"That will be too late. He has so much to learn, about our history, the needs of our country. He'll have to learn about business to address the economics, world affairs to understand our place in that world. He'll have to know how to deal with ambassadors, prime ministers and presidents. And the even more intricate protocol of dealing with other royal houses. He'll have to learn how to speak in public, for at all times he'll speak for Montebello. It must be ingrained, so deeply he never misspeaks. He'll have to—"

"What if he just wants to live his life?" Jessie burst out. "I don't want my son fettered and duty-bound, with no life of his own!"

"It's a good life," Lucas protested, sitting up straighter on the chair. "Yes, there's duty, and a great deal of responsibility, but that's not all. He'll have the world to draw on for whatever interests him. He can play as hard as he works."

"Another Playboy Prince? No, thank you."

Lucas winced. "I'm not proud of that nickname, or the reputation that hung it on me. All I can say is I know better now. I know what's really important, and it's not how I was living."

"Then how can you ask me to send my child into that life?"

"Because there is no other option. But I promise you he's going to learn that nothing is more important than family and caring about people. He's going to learn that he's entitled to have fun, but not at the cost of worrying those who love him. He's going to learn that his rank is a privilege, not a right. You'll have to help me teach him all that, Jessie."

Her head came up, and he saw the fire of determination glowing in her eyes once more. "I know nothing about that kind of thing. I can teach him about life here, about the beauty of a mountain sunrise, the joy of a newborn foal, the reality of a world where you get the work done or pay the price, the satisfaction of a job well done and the pure peace of a simple life in one of the best places on earth. Those are the values I want my son to treasure."

"They're good values," Lucas agreed. "But not the only ones that are worthwhile. And you can learn, you know you can. You're smart, you're quick, it will come easy, once you get started. There are many obligations, and the social etiquette will probably drive you crazy. But there's a certain comfort in following traditions that are a century old.''

"Ranching is an older tradition than that. I'm happy with it, thank you.''

She was closing off, he could sense it. He got up and paced the kitchen as he fought to keep his emotions in check. He had to be fair about this; he had to convince her honestly, not trick her or force her in any way. She'd been through too much already. With an effort, he kept his voice business-like and unemotional.

"The next queen of Montebello will have a tough act to follow. My mother is incredible, and the people adore her. She is tireless in her pursuit of anything she feels will benefit them. She's charmed aristocrats and politicians the world over, but she exerts that same charm for the average person on the street. And they know it. They know they are as important to her as any world leader. My father may be the head of Montebello, but my mother is the heart.''

"She sounds extraordinary,'' Jessie said, sounding a bit calmer now.

"She is. And another like her is what Montebello will need, when the time comes.''

"Exactly,'' she agreed, as if he'd just proved her point. "A long time from now, I would hope,'' she added. "Your mother is still young.''

"Yes. And that's for the best. There's plenty of time to learn what's needed to continue in her tradition.''

"I'm not sure that can be learned,'' she said.

"It can. She did. She wasn't raised a royal, after all.'' He took a deep breath before continuing. "I know what I'm asking you to sacrifice, Jessie. And I don't do it lightly. I know this is a huge step, because it's a huge job. Your place would be unlike my sisters, for example, and not just because they were born to it and you weren't.''

Her brow furrowed as she looked at him. He tried to explain it more clearly.

''My sisters are princesses, they aren't looking at ascending to the throne.''

''You mean they can't?'' she asked, her voice suddenly sharp. ''Because they're female?''

Oops, he thought. *Bad move.*

''My father's working on that,'' he promised. ''But it's going to take some time.'' He hurried on, not wanting to get hung up on the issue of a woman's rights in the succession. ''What I mean is, that succeeding my mother isn't going to be easy. I know that. And it will be harder for someone who hasn't grown up in that world, who hasn't had the traditions drummed into them since birth. But you can do it. I know you can.''

Suddenly the crease in her forehead vanished, as her eyebrows shot upward. ''*I* can do it?''

''Of course you can. As I said, you're smart, you're quick. And you have a good heart. It won't be hard for you to come to love my people, just as my mother did.''

She was staring at him, so incredulously that he stopped the flow of words that he knew had begun to sound like a desperate sales pitch. It was a moment before she spoke, and when she did her voice was tight, each word enunciated carefully and precisely.

''Somewhere in that job description you just presented me, was there the suggestion that this paragon who's going to succeed your mother is…me?''

Lucas's brows lowered in puzzlement. ''Who else?''

Luke held tight in her arms, Jessie got to her feet, still staring at him. ''Correct me if I'm wrong, but wouldn't that require a marriage?''

He blinked. "Well, of course."

"*That* was your idea of a marriage proposal?"

As Lucas looked at her, saw her slender body quiver as she clutched the baby to her, he knew he'd made the biggest mistake yet.

Chapter 7

Jessie knew she would have said yes to Joe in an instant, never mind that he had had few prospects and no idea who he really was or where he'd come from. None of that would have mattered beside what she felt for him. She knew what really counted.

But this formal, frightening man, who spoke of nothing but duty and responsibility, she didn't know at all.

Without another word, she quickly retreated from the kitchen, deciding abruptly that it was time to take Luke upstairs for his bath. Lucas, with more perception than she wanted to credit him with at the moment, stayed silent and remained where he was.

When Eliya appeared to lay out towels and clean clothes for the baby, Jessie seized the opportunity to speak to the quiet, unobtrusive woman.

"Tell me, Eliya. Are you from Montebello?"

"I was born there," the woman said. "I lived in England for a short while, but I was terribly homesick. I will not live anywhere else again."

"Is it so wonderful, then?"

The woman's eyes lit up. "It is the most beautiful place on earth. You will see, as soon as you get there, you will think so, too."

Jessie eyed the woman warily. "What makes you think I'm going there?"

The woman's eyes widened. "But of course you will. Prince Lucas wishes it."

She couldn't have said anything more likely to make Jessie angry. "And *Prince Lucas,*" she drawled, her voice dripping sarcasm now, "always gets what he wants?"

The woman's forehead creased deeply, as if she were trying to figure out what she had said that could possibly have irritated anyone. "Perhaps not always, but any woman would consider herself most lucky to become his wife, and someday queen of Montebello."

"Not any woman," Jessie said grimly. "Not this woman."

"But you are Prince Luke's mother. Of course you will wed him. Prince Luke must have his mother with him. Besides...what woman would not want to be a princess?"

"One who's perfectly happy where she is."

Eliya frowned. "But surely you would not turn down Prince Lucas. You would one day be queen. It is such an honor."

It just wasn't love, Jessie thought. "Is it?" she asked. "It sounds to me like a life full of duty and etiquette and not much else."

"But of course it is an honor. Although you are right, the royal family does take its obligations very seriously," Eliya agreed.

There are many obligations....

Was proposing to her—in that cold, emotionless way— simply another obligation? Had he come to her only because she was the mother of his child? Or only because she was the mother of the heir to the throne? It certainly wasn't because he needed her to take care of Luke. He could afford a herd of nannies as efficient as the competent Eliya.

Or worse yet, had he come to her under orders, perhaps from his father the king, to bring his heir home to Montebello no matter what it took?

She shivered, and rubbed her arms. She tried to distract herself with more questions.

"Are you married, Eliya?"

"I was. My husband died some years ago."

"I'm sorry."

"He had been ill for some time. It was sad, and I miss him still, but he was ready to go." She gave Jessie a sideways look. "I would have been in a very bad way had it not been for King Marcus. My husband was in his service, and when he died, the king made certain I was taken care of. And when Prince Luke was brought to us, he did me the great honor of entrusting his grandson's care to me."

Jessie ignored the rather obvious attempt to sway her. "Did you love your husband?"

"Yes. Very much."

"It wasn't a marriage of...duty?"

To Jessie's surprise, the woman blushed. Her dark eyes sparkled as she answered, "Oh, no. It was a marriage of passion. As yours will be."

It was Jessie's turn to blush. She opened her mouth to deny the woman's statement, but realized the very presence of Luke would make her words suspect.

But while there might be traces left of that passion that had sparked between her and Joe, there had certainly been no love in that business-like presentation that Prince Lucas Sebastiani had apparently intended as a marriage proposal. It had been as juiceless as granite.

It wasn't until later, when she put the baby down for a nap, that it struck her.

She'd been dwelling entirely on what was to her an impossible dilemma—how could she say yes to such a dry, heartless proposal? It was worse than no proposal at all. She was a simple Colorado rancher, and the entire idea of a royal life scared her to death. A royal life without love would be the proverbial fate worse than death.

And then she realized that the question wasn't just how could she possibly accept a proposal tendered as dryly as a job offer. There was more to it than that. Much more. She wasn't sure she could accept even if the offer had come with a passionate declaration of undying love. Because even if it had come that way, it didn't change her fear of the whole idea. Life in a fishbowl, always under observation, always having to be mindful of every action, every word, because it might reflect upon king and country.

Not to mention that the idea of living under a monarchy rankled. Britain, where the monarch was mostly ceremonial, was one thing; a king who actually ruled by right of hereditary succession was something else. Even though it appeared King Marcus was devoted to his people, it was still utterly foreign to her American psyche.

Then again, there had been some real prizes elected to the highest office in the United States, she thought wryly, so who was to say the odds of getting a good one might not be about the same?

With a sigh, she pulled a lightweight blanket up over her son's tiny form, then tucked it around him carefully. And for a long time she stood looking down at him, soaking in the pleasure of simply having him, while at the same time trying to envision this tiny little boy as, someday, the man who would be king. She couldn't do it.

...there is no other option.

Lucas's words echoed ominously in her mind. She felt panic welling up inside her, and quickly stepped out of the room, stopping only to let Eliya know to keep an eye on the baby as he slept.

She ran downstairs to the kitchen, intending to retrieve her boots and heavy sheepskin jacket from the rack in the mudroom and take a head-clearing ride on Brat.

Mrs. Winstead was standing at the large center island, kneading a large lump of bread dough with intense concentration. She looked up when Jessie came in and gave her a smile.

"The little one's napping?"

Jessie nodded. "Eliya's with him."

"She seems like a nice enough sort. And she has a way with the baby."

"Yes."

"She's been taking care of him since they got him?"

"Yes," Jessie said again. "But she told me Lucas has been quite involved." Her mouth twisted up at one corner. "It was part of her campaign to convince me the Sebastianis are unique among royals, I think. They don't believe in handing their children over to others to raise, as most royal families do. Queen Gwendolyn has strong feelings about that."

Mrs. Winstead frowned. "But he's not all theirs."

And there it was, Jessie thought. She sank down into her mother's old rocker. The thought of being separated from her child again was unimaginable, but....

...*there is no other option.*

"They'll never give him up," she said, almost to herself.

"But you're his mother. You have rights."

Jessie laughed, and it was a melancholy, almost bitter sound. She'd been trying not to think about this, but now the words burst from her.

"Do you have any idea what kind of custody battle it would be, me against the entire royal family of Montebello? With their resources? Not much of one, and I know who would lose."

Mrs. Winstead paled, and Jessie knew the kindly woman was quite aware of what losing her baby all over again, even to the luxury of a royal life, would do to her.

She might as well have died at Gerald's hands.

He'd blown it.

Lucas had never proposed to a woman before; that had been the problem, he decided. The arrangement for him to marry the daughter of a minor British royal had been made by his parents, and it hadn't survived the revelation of Luke's existence. Not surprisingly, the lady hadn't wanted this child to precede any she might have in the line of succession.

At least he hadn't had to deal with that, he thought. He'd never proposed to anyone before, but therefore he'd never broken off an engagement, either. He imagined it wouldn't be pleasant, no matter what the circumstances. But his father had dealt with it, somehow managing to soothe ruffled feathers in the process. It was one of those times when he'd despaired of ever having his father's diplomatic talent.

He could have used some of it when he'd presented the facts to Jessie, too. But now that he'd done it so badly, the problem was how to undo the damage.

For one of the few times in his life—his life as Lucas, anyway—he wasn't sure what to do. His instinct said to give her time to calm down, but his heart wanted to rush all fences, for fear she would slip away. He'd tried so hard to be fair, tried to let her know what it would really be like. Hadn't he lived with the ups and downs all his life, minus those precious months when he'd been simply a man called Joe? Taking on the kind of life he lived was no simple proposition. He knew that.

But now he wasn't sure if it was his presentation that had sent her running, or simply the fact that she truly hated the idea of his kind of life.

"Problem, Your High—Mr. Sebastiani?"

Only when Lloyd's quiet query stopped him did Lucas realize he'd been pacing the living room floor. He turned to look at the man who had been in his father's employ for years, just as Lloyd's own father had been.

"Yes," he said bluntly. "Americans."

He thought he saw the man's mouth quirk slightly. "They are a unique breed, sir."

"Arrogant."

"Sometimes," Lloyd agreed.

"Stubborn."

"Often."

"Ethnocentric."

"That, as well."

This time Lucas's mouth quirked. "Independent," he said.

"Incredibly."

"Generous."

"To a fault."

"Able to laugh at themselves."

"Delightfully so."

"Admirable."

"In countless ways."

Lucas's tone softened as he said, "Brave."

"Oh, yes." Lloyd smiled. "Most definitely brave."

Lucas sighed. "So how can I change the mind of one particular brave, stubborn American?"

Lloyd frowned. "Change her mind, sir?"

Lucas noticed Lloyd had no doubt who he was speaking of, which didn't surprise him. He almost wished he hadn't started this, but he figured Lloyd had a better view of things, since he wasn't in the middle of the forest, as it were.

"She doesn't like the idea of...a royal life," Lucas said. He wasn't about to admit to the man that in his effort to be fair he'd made a royal hash out of asking her to marry him.

"Perhaps she simply does not wish to leave her country," Lloyd said. "Americans are notoriously loyal, after all."

"She wouldn't have to leave, not really. She could return for extended visits anytime, and there's such a thing as dual citizenship."

"Is it...." The man paused, coughed delicately, and didn't go on until Lucas made a prodding gesture with his hand. "Is it the idea of a monarchy, perhaps? Americans do tend to believe in the rule of the common man."

"'Of the people, by the people, for the people' and all that? I know. But she's never met my father, or she would know that's exactly how he rules."

"Then does she have some objection to Montebello in particular?" Lloyd asked in a tone that made clear he didn't see how that was possible.

"She's never been there, so how could she?"

"Hmm. And you've discussed all this with her, and she still won't see reason?"

Lucas felt himself flush slightly. "Well... No."

"I see."

And so, suddenly, did Lucas. He'd blundered this from the very beginning.

"May I dare to suggest you do so, sir? And slowly, if I might add. Miss Chambers does not seem the type of woman to be rushed."

"No, you're right. She'll just dig in her heels even more."

"Precisely."

Encouraged at last, Lucas started toward the door, eager now to go find Jessie. He had his hand on the knob, then stopped and looked back over his shoulder.

"Thank you, Lloyd."

"My pleasure, sir."

Ironic, Lucas thought. After all his flings, all his casual affairs, the first time he seriously, genuinely cared about a woman, he couldn't do a thing right. Or perhaps because he seriously, genuinely cared.

As he stepped outside, he wondered if his father had chosen the perceptive, wise Lloyd to accompany him for more than just security reasons. Perhaps, Lucas thought wryly, his equally wise father realized his idiot son was going to need other kinds of help to avoid making a botch of everything.

She'd given up on sleep, and after checking to be sure Luke was sleeping peacefully and that Eliya was within earshot, Jessie went out to the barn. Brat seemed surprised, but more than willing to allow her to run the soft finish brush over her already gleaming hide. Jessie guessed if she dragged out the hoof pick or started thinning the mare's thick tail, her mood would change rapidly. So she settled for the rhythmic brushing that was a balm to both of them.

When Lucas showed up after barely five minutes had passed, she knew he'd been watching her. She'd seen little of him since that horrible business proposition, and she would have preferred to keep it that way a bit longer. But now that he was here, she decided a quick departure would betray how frightened she was, which in turn would show him just how much power he had over her.

As if he doesn't already know, she told herself sourly. As Lucas or Joe, he had never been stupid.

"I've been thinking," she said quickly, before he could speak.

"Oh?" He sounded wary, cautious, and somehow that pleased her.

"Maybe we could work out some sort of joint custody. Luke could come to Montebello for summers. Of course, not until he's older, but eventually."

Lucas looked at her steadily, and she knew before he answered what he would say. "I'm sorry, Jessie. That won't work. This is a process that takes a lifetime. Luke must be groomed for his future from the very beginning."

"You mean, the indoctrination starts before he's even old enough to talk?"

Her tone was acid, but she couldn't help it. That his was so gentle only made it worse.

"I know this is very different to you, but—"

"Different? No, we see it all the time here." She was intimidated by this Lucas, this man with a much-loved face but a very different soul. But this was her son she was fighting for, she had to be strong. "Parents who decide they want the next prodigy of tennis, or golf, or whatever, and force their child onto a path they never would have chosen for themselves. Do you know how many lives, how many families have been ruined by that kind of thinking?"

"This is different. This is what Luke was born for."

"That," Jessie snapped, "is the biggest load of hooey I've ever heard."

"What about Brat?" he asked, gesturing toward the horse made restless by the agitated voices. "I think you'd be the first to say she was born to be a cow horse."

"Yes, she was," Jessie fired back. "But I never *assumed* she was. We let her grow up like all the horses do, and found out naturally that she had the talent. And if she hadn't, nobody would have forced her to do it!"

He had the grace to at least look as if he'd lost that point, so she pressed on.

"Besides, Luke is a child, not a quarter horse. What if he has a knack for numbers, or science, or even medicine? What if he could be the doctor or researcher who cures cancer, but he never gets the chance because he's locked away in some moldy palace somewhere?"

"My parent's home is *not* moldy."

That he seized on that idiocy to respond to only irritated her further. "Then it's their thinking that's moldy. Luke should be able to choose his own future. Every child should have that right."

"I can't do that to my family. Not after what they've been through."

Jessie's tenuous hold on her temper snapped. "What about what *we've* been through?"

The look that came across Lucas's face then made her anger drain away as quickly as it had risen. For the first time she realized she wasn't the only one under pressure. Lucas was also under tremendous strain. And right now he looked incredibly, devastatingly weary, and when he spoke, his voice echoed the look.

"Sometimes I think I'd be happier if I'd never gotten my memory back."

Chapter 8

It was a long, sleepless night for Jessie. Lucas had re-covered quickly from that moment of what she was sure he would call weakness, and had gone on to give her yet another sales pitch on how life could be, the possibility of dual citizenship, how she would love Montebello, how she would see his father ruled wisely and well, and how she could also visit here anytime she wanted.

As if that would be enough, occasional short visits to the place where her heart, where her very soul, lived, she thought wearily.

She spent the morning with baby Luke and trying to avoid Lucas however she could. She feigned sleep when he knocked on her bedroom door; she peeked into the kitchen to be sure it was clear before she went in; and she dodged into her father's study when Lucas came in through the front door as she was heading out the same way.

Finally she escaped him long enough to gather some

things and get to the barn. Quickly she saddled Brat and
sent the buckskin off at a gallop. As if sensing her ur-
gency, the mare put her head down and ate up the distance
with her long, smooth strides.

Again Jessie headed for her favorite thinking spot. She
knew it was going to take her a very long time to work
through her tangled emotions, so she had prepared for a
long day and possibly evening, with food, water, her
heavy jacket and a thick roll of blankets tied behind her
saddle. Once she was out of sight of the house she let
Brat pick the pace, and since the mare's blood was up,
she ate up the distance with a ground-covering lope most
of the way.

When Jessie arrived at her bluff-top lookout, she set up
camp with more concentration than was really necessary
and settled down on the thick blankets. She waited for the
peace she always felt here to flood her, but she soon realized that even this special place couldn't help her with
this decision. That there was no help to be had with this
decision.

It was impossible. She couldn't, wouldn't, give Luke
up. She'd thought she'd lost him once; she could never
go through that again. Nor could she surrender him to a
world where his life was laid out like a route on a map
he had no choice but to follow. But how could she fight
an entire royal family? And one of the wealthiest royal
families in the world? How could she, with her only re-
source this land she loved—free of debt only because of
her father's financial cleverness—ever fight such a powerful family?

Because she had little doubt the entire Sebastiani family
would rise up against her with the cadre of lawyers they
no doubt had.

And all she had was a mother's love.

She would like to think the court would find that more

valuable than wealth, but it had been proven too often that in America, you could buy your version of justice. Slick lawyers could manipulate the system until fairness was just a memory.

And what if his lawyers found a way to have the case moved to Montebello? It didn't seem possible, but again, vast wealth could literally move mountains. And in Montebello, she had even less faith in her chances.

Sometimes I think I'd be happier if I'd never gotten my memory back, Lucas had said.

She couldn't argue with that. She'd be happier, too. She and Joe would have had at least a fighting chance. She and Lucas seemed to be floundering in a morass there was no escape from, and the more they struggled, the deeper and deeper they sank.

How had something so beautiful become something so painful? How had things gotten so confused, so ugly?

She sat for hours, watching the light shift and change across this land she loved, this land that was in her blood. She barely moved until the afternoon shadows drove her to pull on her heavy coat and to light a fire.

When night fell, she was still there, huddled before the fire, thinking. She finally admitted she couldn't see any way out of this, short of taking the baby and running away. Even as the thought formed, she admitted that it would be defeating the purpose, and hardly true to what she wanted for her son. She wanted him to know the life she'd known, clean and simple and honest, before he had to go out and face life in a world that too often wasn't that way.

But how could she fight the Sebastianis? And how on earth had it become so muddled that she had to fight the father of her son, the man she'd fallen in love with when she—and he—hadn't known who he was?

She thought of all the long, lonely nights after he'd

gone, when she'd ached for him, when she'd cried out at the loss of his touch. She thought of the nightmare time in that cellar, feeling terrified and alone as the only piece of Joe she had left was stolen from her.

She thought of the shock that had filled her when Ursula had tossed that newspaper down in front of her and ordered her to look at the photograph of the face that was so familiar and yet so strange. And she thought of the nights since they'd come back here, nights spent in an agony of need as he slept just across the hall, yet she couldn't—wouldn't—go to him. He'd made it clear he still wanted her, and God knew she still wanted him, but things between them were too confused, too complicated, and she didn't know if, let alone how, they could ever be straightened out.

The sound of someone calling her name yanked her out of her painful reverie. She glanced at her watch, had to tilt it until she could see the tiny glowing hands pointing nearly to midnight. After a couple of minutes the call came again, and this time there was no mistaking the source of the booming voice.

Lucas.

She didn't want to see him. Not yet. She was far from any kind of decision, and facing him would only make her feel more coerced. Right now she was angry at life, fate, the world, and whatever else had conspired to put her in this impossible position.

But she knew sooner or later he would see her fire, it would be impossible to miss that beacon in the night, so she tried to brace herself. At last she could see him riding toward her, on the big bay gelding he'd always ridden before. As Joe.

And for an instant she was back in that sweet, breathless time before the ugliness had closed in. The time when she'd reveled in falling in love, truly in love, for the first

time in her life. The time when she'd been able to dismiss
her lover's lack of memory, lack of a past, as a mere
annoyance, of no importance when compared to his love.

Too bad she couldn't dismiss the return of that memory
as easily.

But she couldn't. He was who he was, who he had
always been. He rode through the night with the same
easy grace that had always made her stomach knot, but
now, instead of looking eagerly forward to his presence,
instead of anticipating the wildfire that would leap in her
at his touch, all she could think was that he had likely
learned to ride by playing polo. Didn't all princes learn
that way?

He called her name again, and then again, and finally
some undertone in his voice penetrated her mood. He
sounded…worried, she thought. In fact, there was an edge
in his voice that sounded almost like panic, were such a
thing possible in the self-contained, polished Prince Lucas.

For all her confusion about him, it wasn't in her to let
anyone worry needlessly. She'd been through too much
of that herself. Reluctantly she rose to her feet. In the
moment before she could call out in answer, she saw the
big bay spring into a lope. Lucas must have spotted her
fire.

For a moment she admired his skill in the saddle. No
matter how or where he'd learned, he was a magnificent
rider. And then the bay came to a skidding, dirt-throwing
stop she hadn't known he was capable of. Lucas leapt off
the animal and hit the ground running in a single flying
motion. He covered the few feet between them in two
long strides, but before he even stopped moving he had
grabbed her shoulders and was yelling at her. It took her
a moment to make sense out of his tirade.

"—doing? Do you know how long you've been gone, and what time it is?"

"I—"

"Do you realize we've all been in a panic for hours? Mrs. Winstead has been calling everyone in Shady Rock. Lloyd has been driving all over, searching. And Eliya is so upset even Luke started to cry."

She was glad it was dark so he couldn't see her blush. The hands were used to her occasional trips up here, but the others weren't. Even Joe hadn't been, because while he'd been on the ranch, she'd never wanted to wander any farther than her bedroom. With him.

"I didn't mean to worry anyone," she said meekly.

"Well, you did! We were worried sick. I thought something had happened to you, a fall, a snake, who knows what. I thought I'd lost you all over again."

And in that instant, by the light of her fire there on the bluff, she saw Joe looking at her out of Lucas's eyes. Her Joe, with all the love he'd felt for her burning bright in his gaze. Her breath caught, and in that instant he grabbed her and pulled her to him.

"I thought I'd lost you," he repeated, his voice broken. And he held her as he had before, as Joe, as if she were the center of his world. As if he were desperate. As if he needed her as much as she needed him.

His hands moved over her urgently, as if he simply had to touch her to be sure she was indeed alive and well. Jessie's heart was pounding with elation, with pure joy as she realized there *was* something of Joe's love for her left in this man, somewhere.

She wasn't sure when it changed from concern to something hotter, wilder, she only knew that here in this place that was so important to her, it felt so right she couldn't, didn't want to resist. And once he kissed her, the old familiar fire leapt as if it had been merely banked all these months and had never truly gone out.

He tasted so wonderfully familiar, yet after the long, lonely time without him, exotically new. He deepened the kiss, probing, teasing, and she opened for him, welcoming him with an eagerness that surprised her even as it swept over her. But she should have known, she realized in some part of her mind that wasn't yet swamped by the sudden onslaught of sensation. She should have known, because Joe had always been able to do this to her, as no man ever had.

His mouth was hard, demanding, insistent on hers, but unnecessarily; she wouldn't—couldn't—refuse him. Not now, not here in this place. That same part of her mind that was still functioning pointed out that this was no longer Joe but Lucas, but it was the last gasp of common sense before, as his hands began to move over her body, a wave of pleasure pushed out every logical thought.

At last he broke the kiss, and she nearly cried out at the loss of that sweet touch. She pressed herself against him, mutely begging him not to stop.

"Jessie," he said, his voice low and harsh.

"Please," she whispered.

"You do remember. You do remember what it was like between us."

"I could never forget," she told him.

She kissed him this time, reaching up and slipping her hands behind his neck to pull him down to her. Again the fire sparked, blazed to life, and the chilly night air was nothing against the heat they generated. The campfire she'd built was needless, forgotten.

"Please," she said again, and Lucas groaned.

He took her down to the blankets with exquisite care. Jessie clung to him, giving herself silent permission to let go all her reservations for this one last, glorious time. Her hands began to move, stroking, caressing, his face, his hair, his chest, his belly, and the already rigid flesh behind his zipper. She gasped in anticipation, remembering how that flesh filled her, stretched her, made her whole again.

Soon Lucas would go back to his world, she would be left in hers, and this would be all she had, so she had to make it strong enough and powerful enough to last that lonely lifetime.

Lucas groaned deep in his throat, hardly able to believe what was happening. He'd worked so hard at not pushing her, not rushing her that now, with her hands all over him in a way he'd not been touched since the night he'd walked out on her, he was nearly dizzy with the power of it.

But there was something desperate in her touch, in the way she held on to him. He didn't understand exactly what it was, but on some deep level he knew what he had to do. He had to remind her so completely of how incredible it was between them, that she would never, ever, want to give it up. With his memory intact he knew now, more than ever, how special what they'd found together was.

Now he had to convince her of that; convince her it was worth any sacrifice.

He set about doing so with full intention, stroking, caressing, kissing until she was writhing beneath his touch. Her body had changed, he thought. She'd already put some much needed weight back on, but it was more than that. Her body had a slight roundness, a fullness that hadn't been there before. That the change had happened because she'd borne his child made her even more enticing, and he had to stifle another groan.

By the time they hastily shed their clothes, they were both so hot the chilly night air and the hard ground had little impact. Still, he pulled one of the blankets up over them; he didn't want her distracted by anything, wanted her to think only of how good this was.

His plan backfired. In working to arouse her to a fever pitch, he brought himself to an agony of readiness. When at last she cried out, begging him to take her, he'd never been so achingly hard, never shuddered with the sheer effort of maintaining control.

He slid into her welcoming body, and her name broke from him as her slick, hot flesh clasped him so tightly, so perfectly. His control snapped, and he drove hard and deep, wanting to be so deeply inside her he could never be lost again.

She called out again, his name this time, and that it was Joe instead of Lucas didn't bother him; he knew that inside him Joe still lived, treasuring this life and the woman who had saved him. He lost track of what he'd meant to do as his senses spiraled out of control, every slumbering nerve leapt to life and blazed with the heat he'd found with her, only with her.

He barely hung on long enough. The moment he heard her cry out, felt her body convulse around his, squeezing him with an unbearable sweetness, he let go and plummeted after her. Their exultant cries were swallowed by the vast silence of a Colorado night, and when they lapsed into silence only the moon watched over them.

Jessie sighed and stretched. At this moment a couple of blankets spread over hard ground was the most luxurious bed she'd ever slept in. And it was all because of the man beside her, the man who had driven her wild beneath a winter night sky. Her body had blazed to life as if it had been just yesterday that he'd touched her like that, as if the intervening months alone and scared had never happened.

She savored his heat as he held her close. With him pressed tightly to her, she could feel tiny ripples going through him, like the pleasant aftershocks going through her body that were only now beginning to fade.

Finally, Lucas let out a long, compressed breath that held a note of awe. She wondered if he, too, was stunned by how quickly and completely they had rekindled that old passion, by how swiftly it had raged anew as if there had never been any time or distance between them.

He reached over and tugged the blanket over her bare shoulder. For a long time they simply lay there, looking up at the stars, but eventually Lucas spoke softly.

"We have to work this out, Jessie."

She sighed, wishing she could have had just this one night without the intrusion of reality. "The only thing that's changed is that we know…it's still as good as it was."

"The sex? Yes, it is. But that's only part of why we can't let it slip away." He lifted himself up on one elbow to look down at her. "You've always been fair-minded, Jessie. Be fair about this. You haven't even seen my home, met my family, yet you're making a life-impacting decision about them."

What he said made sense, but she was certain there was nothing that would change her mind about this. "I can't let my son grow up like that."

"Be honest, Jessie. You don't really know what it's like. And it's not like you to be judgmental. If it was, you never would have hired me when I didn't even know my name, let alone anything else. You gave me, Joe, a chance. It's only fair you give Montebello a chance, too."

He had, she had to admit, a point. As if he'd sensed her uncertainty, he pressed on.

"If you won't give that chance to me as Lucas, give it to Luke's father. I deserve that much."

She felt buffeted, helpless. "What do you want me to do?"

"Come home with me, just for a visit. See Montebello, meet my parents, my people."

She didn't know how to tell him that royal assumption, "my people," had just quashed any hopes she might have had that something could be worked out. There was simply no way, no middle ground as long as he refused to compromise on Luke's future.

But she couldn't deny one thing. As Luke's father, as the man who had brought her son home to her, he did deserve at least that much.

"All right," she said at last, reluctantly. "I'll come. For a visit. But that's all," she warned.

"Thank you," he said, accepting her grudging offer in a voice so fervent she knew she'd done the right thing. For now, at least. Even though she knew she could never surrender her son to such a life.

And when Lucas made love to her again, this time with a gentle passion that warmed her to the soul, she ached with the wish that it could last forever.

Chapter 9

Lucas was very aware that Jessie wasn't happy about the decision she'd made, but he himself was delighted. Acceding to her wishes, he'd set a departure date of next Monday, although he was eager to go now. He just knew that once he got her to Montebello, his home would work its own special magic. She would see that all her fears were groundless, and they could begin to plan for their—and Luke's—future.

Jessie, meanwhile, was running from dawn to dusk, determined to make sure the ranch was well taken care of during her absence. He thought concern about the ranch was all it was, this forced busyness, until he caught her with Brat in the buckskin's stall, weeping against the horse's satin neck. Then he realized just how unhappy she was. He went to her and pulled her into his arms. He was about to ask what was wrong, but realized he didn't want to hear the answer. He was afraid it would be that she'd changed her mind and refused to go with him, and he didn't know how he was going to deal with that.

So instead he just held her, and she seemed to come back to herself.

"I'm sorry," she finally murmured. "I don't usually dwell on a decision once it's made. But the last time I left home, I was terrified I'd never see it again. I guess I'm still a little edgy about leaving."

"That's understandable, after what you went through," he said, relieved this was all it was, and thankful for her honesty. But then, Jessie had always been honest. "But it will be all right. You'll see."

She let out a sigh, but said nothing. Worried that she wasn't going to be able to give his home a fair chance, he impulsively asked, "Do you want to bring Brat? We could have her flown, easily."

Jessie backed up and stared at him. He let her go. "Halfway around the world?" she asked.

"We do it all the time, when someone buys one of our horses. One of the planes can be refitted for horse transport in a matter of hours."

"You have a plane just for your horses?"

"We're an island," he said with a shrug. "It's only practical."

"Oh." She ran her hands up and down her arms as if chilled, although the barn wasn't cold.

"I can call and have them send it for her, if you want to bring her."

It was a long silent moment before Jessie slowly shook her head. "No. No, that won't be necessary."

The formality of her words and tone bothered him, but he wasn't sure why.

"You're sure?"

"Yes." She turned and walked to the door of Brat's stall. When she got there, she looked back at him. "I won't be there long enough for it to be worth it."

She left him there, deflated, wondering what he'd really gained by getting her to agree to come with him.

Jessie clung to Luke as if the baby were her only link to reality. And that's how it felt to her—this entire morning seemed surreal.

Leaving the ranch had been bad enough, but somehow the luxurious limousine had made it worse, as if she'd already crossed the line into a different world that wouldn't let go. This time Lloyd rode up front with the driver, and Eliya either dozed or pretended to. Jessie occupied herself with making Luke giggle, pretending she didn't notice Lucas watching them intently, a soft smile curving that luscious mouth of his.

She had settled in for a long drive, so when they turned off at the small county airport she looked up in surprise. Then she realized she'd been foolish, thinking they would have to get to a commercial airport. Of course the Sebastianis flew whenever and wherever they pleased, and their personal planes waited at their beck and call.

The limo came to a halt beside a sleek, twin engine jet parked near the edge of the small airport's single runway. Painted in a red and gray pattern she found nicely subtle, the plane looked bigger—and faster—than she would have imagined.

The door was open, and a gangway was down. At the bottom of the stairs was a man in a uniform she didn't recognize, but judging from the black, white and gold color scheme, the same as the Montebellan flag, she guessed he was employed by Montebello or the Sebastianis.

"If there's any difference," she muttered to herself.

Lloyd exited the front seat, came back quickly and opened the limo door. Lucas stepped outside, then leaned back in and reached to take Luke from her. For an instant she hesitated, and she saw something pained flicker in Lucas's eyes, as if he thought she didn't trust him with the baby.

"It's just hard to let go of him," she said softly.

Lucas's face changed then. He reached out and touched her cheek with the backs of his fingers. The gentle touch sent her mind rocketing back to that night at the lookout, the night that had brought her to this.

She'd made her decision then, she thought. And she had promised him to give this a fair chance. It wasn't fair to hold back.

She held Luke out to him. He took the baby gently, yet with assurance, with none of the fumbling of the brand-new parent. In fact, she thought wryly, he handled Luke more easily than she did, which reminded her painfully that Lucas had had him much longer than she had.

She got out of the vehicle, and followed Lucas to the foot of the gangway. She stopped, doubt assailing her as she looked up the steep stairway.

"It will be all right, Jessie."

Lucas's voice from behind her was soft, coaxing. She'd heard that tone before, when Joe had been soothing a restless horse. She turned to look at him.

"I'm not a horse and I'm not going to bolt," she told him. "I just need a moment to resign myself."

Again pain flickered in his eyes. "I'm delighted to be going home, and you have to resign yourself."

She hadn't meant to hurt his feelings. "I'm sorry," she said. "I shouldn't have said that. I agreed to this, so I should at least not be sullen about it."

"I suppose it's too much to ask you to look forward to it? People do, you know. They come from all over the world to vacation in Montebello. San Sebastian is one of the most visited capitals in the world."

Perhaps she could do that, she thought. Consider it a

vacation, of a kind thousands of people dreamed of all through long, cold winters. Besides, all vacations had an end, and when it came, you went home. If she hung on to that, maybe she could relax about this whole thing.

"I'll try," she said.

"That's all I ask, Jessie. That's all I ask."

She walked up the steps with that determination firm in her mind.

And almost lost it the moment she stepped into the plane.

She had never seen anything like this. This wasn't a plane, she thought, it was a flying five-star hotel suite. The carpet was plush, in a deep, rich burgundy bordered in navy blue, as was the upholstery. The trim was some rich, dark wood that she had no doubt was exotic and expensive. To one side was a large table of the same wood, polished to a high gloss. Judging by the large leather chair behind it, it served as a desk.

All of the seats had a view of small video screens placed throughout the main cabin. At the back of the cabin was a wet bar, and even from here she could see the warm, gold glow of the fixtures. *Real gold? Probably,* she thought.

The only sign they were in a structure that moved were the discretely same-colored seat belts at every seat.

"The Wright brothers never imagined," she said as she finally stepped into Wonderland.

"It's a beauty, isn't it?" Lucas said. "Redstone makes great planes. We could almost make it without refueling, if we pushed our luck."

"Let's not," she said dryly. "How far is it?"

"About sixty-seven hundred miles. We've got a range of over six thousand, if we hold it down to Mach point eight."

"Hold it down?" she nearly yelped.

He nodded. "If we push it up to over Mach point eight-five, we drop about a thousand miles in range."

"Mach point eight-five," she echoed faintly. Mach was a word she'd always associated with fighter jets and space vehicles. Not private planes, and certainly nothing she'd ever intended to be in herself.

"All the necessities, too. Full head with a shower. A fully furnished stateroom, plus bunks for support personnel. Galley's fully equipped, too, and Mareta is an excellent cook if you want something."

"No, thank you," Jessie said, reeling a little from all this. How on earth had Joe ever thought her ranch house warm and cozy, when it was nothing less than shabby next to this? Of course, Joe hadn't remembered this, but still, surely some part of him knew her scarred wood floors and slightly worn furniture weren't what he was used to?

For that matter, she thought as she sank into a luxurious chair he directed her to, Lucas hadn't ever remarked on the condition of her home. He'd never said anything about the lack of amenities, even though he was obviously used to the absolute best. She should give him credit for that, she supposed. At least he'd been tactful enough not to mention whatever he thought about it.

The amenities weren't the only difference, she soon realized. In addition to Eliya and Mr. Gallini, there was the man who'd been at the bottom of the steps, and a woman in a variation of the same uniform, who were clearly the private version of flight attendants. And they fluttered around Lucas as if he were.... As if he were royalty, she finished in silent chagrin.

But what truly flustered her was the fact that they catered to her in the same way. It seemed every five minutes one or the other of them approached her offering food, drink, a blanket and pillow, or to put on a movie out of the amazingly huge collection on board, practically begging to be "of service" as they put it.

But it wasn't until Lucas finally gave in to temptation and made his way forward to the cockpit that she discovered the full reason behind their actions.

"Please," she said to the man when he approached her yet again, this time with an offer of wine, "I don't need anything, I'm perfectly comfortable. Relax. You must need a break by now."

"It is no hardship to serve our future queen," he said fervently.

Jessie blinked. "What?"

"It is an honor, truly," chimed the woman in uniform. "All Montebello awaits your arrival. And of course, your wedding. It will be a joyous occasion."

Jessie stared at them both. Did the entire world know about her? How? And did they all assume she was going to not only marry Lucas but be delighted to do so, no questions asked?

She was tempted to clarify matters for them, to tell them in no uncertain terms she would not even be living in their precious Montebello, let alone be queen, but realized it would likely be a futile effort. They would never understand, even if they did believe her, which she doubted. Who wouldn't want to marry their precious prince? Didn't little girls all over the world dream of such a thing?

Not this little girl, she thought. Her dream had always been of a man who wanted to live the life she loved, who would be content with its simplicity and stick with her through the frequent hard times, just for the love of it. A man like Joe. Not a prince used to living in the proverbial lap of luxury. Like this plane.

She did eventually get up and make her way to the bathroom. It was as ridiculously luxurious as the rest of the craft, and so far from the standard airplane lavatory that she could barely stop herself from laughing out loud.

When she returned, Lucas was back from the cockpit, which surprised her—she'd figured he would be there for hours. Instead, after he took a peek at Luke in the specially designed crib that was bolted to the aircraft floor— a modification, she was sure, to the plane's design, and one she couldn't deny made her more comfortable flying with the baby—Lucas took the seat next to hers and strapped himself in.

She sensed a tension in him she hadn't noticed before, and unease filled her. They were on a very small plane, after all, in a very big sky.

"Is there a problem?"

He gave her a sideways look, and her heart jolted into her throat, because the answer was obviously yes. Instinctively she looked out the window, wondering if they had an engine on fire or something.

"No, no, it's nothing like that," he said quickly. "I'm sorry, I didn't mean to scare you."

Jessie let out a sigh of relief. "What, then?"

"They got a news report up front."

Her mouth tightened. Was this the answer to what she'd been wondering, how everyone from Montebello apparently knew about her? Had he said something to reporters? Had he arrogantly assumed she couldn't possibly say no and announced it as a done deal?

"And?" she said, not trusting herself to say anything more. If he had—

"Gerald was committed to a state hospital. No jail time."

It took her a moment to make the switch to the unexpected subject. "What?"

"I had them call my friend in the FBI for details. He was deemed criminally insane and committed."

"Oh."

He looked at her for a long moment. "You don't seem upset that he got off so easily."

"I'm not. Not really. I can't quite hate him."

"After what he put you through?"

She shrugged. "It was horrible, but…he didn't kill me, even when he was ordered to. I sort of owe him for that, even if his reasons were crazy."

Lucas looked thoughtful for a moment. "I guess I was so angry at him I never thought of it that way." He hesitated, then said, "There's word on…Ursula and Gretchen, too."

She supposed he'd hesitated about calling Ursula her sister. As if she no longer deserved the title. Jessie smothered the pang that always arose when she thought of the girl she'd once adored and looked up to, who had turned into a bitter, vicious woman she didn't even know anymore. She wondered if she would ever reach any equanimity about it, if she would ever resolve her horribly confused feelings about Ursula.

"What?" she finally asked, when she was sure her voice would be steady.

"They were denied bail. Apparently the judge thought anybody who would try to murder her own sister in order to steal her baby, on top of murdering a former lover, or anyone who'd help her with full knowledge, like Gretchen, is a flight risk. They'll be awaiting trial in jail."

She waited to feel something, a pang, a qualm, anything, at the thought of her sister in jail. But nothing came. And somehow that made her feel worse.

"Do you want to see her? Speak to her?" Lucas asked.

"I…feel like I should want to. But I don't." She stared at her hands. "I think I'm afraid I'm hoping there was some other reason besides pure greed, bitterness and viciousness for what she did."

"There isn't."

"I think I know that, deep down. But having to face it..." She shook her head. "Maybe someday. But not now."

"She's not worth your worry or your concern, Jessie," Lucas said quietly. "I know it must be hard, she is your sister, but after what she did, she doesn't deserve even a passing thought."

"I just feel badly for what was," she said. "We were close, once."

"Which makes what she did even more reprehensible."

"I know. But it's still hard."

He reached out and took her hand, squeezing it comfortingly. "It's hard because you're a good, decent person, and you don't easily write anyone off."

She wondered if there was a message for her from him in those words, but when she looked up at him, she saw only genuine concern. That warmed her, and the knot inside her loosened a little.

She didn't pull her hand from his, and eventually, lulled by the distant hum of the engines and the comfort of the luxurious seat, she dozed. And dreamed. Dreamed of purple robes and a glittering crown, lifted from a velvet pillow and placed on her head.

It didn't fit.

And after a while, it slid down and ended up a heavy, choking weight around her neck.

Chapter 10

Lucas watched her, glad of the chance to simply look. When she murmured in her sleep, an undertone of distress noticeable even though the words were unintelligible, he wondered if he should wake her. But then it subsided, so he let her sleep.

She would need even this restless sleep—flying this far into tomorrow, jet lag was practically unavoidable. And he was under no illusions about the strain she would be under once they arrived and the inevitable chaos surrounded her. He would try to protect her as much as he could, but he could only do so much. Too many people had learned their story, too many people already knew her face, and knew their prince had gone to America to find the woman who had borne him—and them—a royal heir in line to the Montebellan throne.

He was used to his goldfish-bowl life—not that he liked it—but Jessie was not. And in her way, she was a very private person. Many Americans, especially those from

the West, were, when compared to the open gregarious-
ness that was typical of Montebellans.

Perhaps it was the more tropical climate there than, say,
Colorado. Montebellans never had to hole up alone while
a blizzard blew through. The weather was always good
for socializing, for being outside, soaking up the sun and
balmy breezes.

He sat musing for a while, his gaze occasionally shift-
ing from Jessie to the video screen to his left, which he'd
keyed in to show the cockpit instruments, a special feature
that he'd requested and Redstone Aviation had had designed just for him. The head of the company, Josh Redstone, being a pilot himself, had understood perfectly what
he'd wanted. And why. In fact, the man had wondered
why he hadn't thought of it himself, for his own plane.

And periodically Lucas rose and walked over to look
down at his baby son. He couldn't describe the emotions
that filled him, he only knew he'd never felt anything like
them before. He'd known love at first sight existed, his
parents proved that, but he'd never expected it to happen
to him. Yet the moment he'd looked into Luke's wide,
innocent eyes, he'd fallen and fallen hard. That at the time
he'd thought Jessie dead, and baby Luke the last precious
bit of her on this earth, had only made the feeling more
powerful.

Looking at that child was like staring into the future,
and he felt the weight of it as never before. Not even
standing in the palace picture gallery that housed paintings
of every ancestor of his for generations could inspire this
kind of feeling in him.

Jessie's words echoed in his mind. *Luke should be able
to choose his own future. Every child should have that
right.*

He knew he was right, knew that Luke had to be raised
as he had been, knowing his future was set, that the throne

of Montebello was his destiny. It would take that long, a lifetime, to train him properly for the job. It wasn't something you could learn in a short time, it had to be ingrained, until it was instinctive, until you reacted without thinking in the way that was best for your position and your country.

Her impassioned plea hadn't fallen on deaf ears. He understood her feelings, completely. But she didn't realize that when you were raised with the knowledge of what you would become, when you learned at an early age that it was unchangeable, you adjusted. He had. Not that he'd ever had a burning desire to do otherwise. His parents had indulged his need to experiment with any field he found of interest, but at the core he'd always known it was just that, experimentation, because his course lay elsewhere.

He wondered, had he not grown up with his father's sterling example, if he might have been more restless, felt more constrained by his lack of choices about his future. But King Marcus had always found such joy in leading his people wisely that Lucas had grown up assuming he would find the same fulfillment when it was his turn to rule. And he had, in the duties he'd already assumed as the invested crown prince. So surely Luke would, too, as long as he was brought up in the same tradition.

But Jessie's words lingered in his mind, provoking the tiniest of doubts. And when Luke opened his eyes, so much like his own, looked up at him and smiled Jessie's smile, he suddenly understood her need to make sure the boy had everything his way in life. He didn't ever want to look in that little face and see pain or disappointment.

He touched the baby's soft, silken cheek, which reminded him of Jessie's soft, silken skin. He quashed his reaction once more, as he'd been doing frequently of late, knowing he didn't dare push her, despite that incredible night at her lookout.

After a few minutes Luke went back to sleep, and Lucas began to pace the length of the main cabin, trying to walk off his restlessness. Finally he sensed the plane beginning to descend in the moment before the pilot announced it to him over the intercom. They would be on the ground only for refueling, not long enough to deplane. Someday, he thought, he was going to test the promised range of this beauty and try that flight without refueling.

Then Luke made a tiny, cooing sound, drawing his father's gaze.

On second thought, Lucas amended silently, *maybe I won't push that envelope.*

The old Lucas would have done it. The reckless, sometimes feckless Lucas. *The Playboy Prince,* he thought ruefully. *Now that would be a great way to convince Jessie you're not that man anymore—pull a fool stunt like that. You walked away from one plane crash, just how golden do you think you are?*

His ears popped in adjustment to the loss of altitude. In that moment Jessie stirred, then opened her eyes. For an instant she just looked at him, then a soft, sleepy smile curved her mouth and his heart seemed to skip a beat and then rush to catch up.

Then she seemed to realize what had awakened her. She sat up straight and looked toward the window. Then she glanced at her watch. He winced inwardly at the troubled expression that changed her face.

"We're not there yet," he told her. "We're just stopping for refueling."

"Oh."

The troubled expression eased, and he felt that pang again, that she would be dreading so much what he was so anxious for. He told himself that it was only because she hadn't seen his home yet, but deep down he wondered if he had lost this battle before it had really begun.

* * *

The first thing that struck Jessie as she steeled herself and stepped out onto the gangway was the brilliance of the sun. The next was the warmth. Heat, she mentally corrected. For a body used to and already preparing for a Colorado winter, this wasn't just balmy, it was downright hot. If she had to guess, it was at least seventy degrees out, although she admitted she might not be the best judge, having just come from fifty-eight-degree Colorado.

Lucas had told her Montebello was ten hours ahead of Colorado time, so she guessed that coupled with the long flying time, it was the next day here. It felt odd to have missed an entire day, but she didn't have long to dwell on it. Not when she saw the crowd of people standing near the bottom of the gangway, next to a limousine even longer than the one Lucas had hired in Colorado, this one with darkly tinted windows and two small black, white and gold flags on the front fenders.

There was a much larger crowd on the other side of a chain-link fence several yards away. In that group larger Montebellan flags were prominent, waving in the sun-warmed air. She heard calls and shouts, but couldn't tell what was being said. She wasn't sure what she had expected, but they sounded friendly, even warm, which was reassuring.

At the foot of the gangway was, she saw with rueful surprise, a red carpet. An honest-to-god red carpet. And she had a feeling this was going to be just the first of many such moments, when her American sensibilities collided with royal ceremony. And the first of many incidents that would pound home to her just how impossible this all was.

After that moment everything seemed to blur. Her nap on the plane hadn't made up for the sleepless night before, and she felt suddenly exhausted. And buffeted by the barrage of greetings that began the moment Lucas, carrying the baby, urged her to start down the gangway steps.

She concentrated on every step as if she expected it to slide out from under her feet. The calls from the crowd were clearer now, and she realized they were calling Lucas's name. And Luke's. She even thought she heard her own name once or twice, and she was positive she heard one woman call out "Marry me, instead!"

Now there's a plan, she thought wearily. And then quickly took it back when the thought of him doing just that, marrying some other woman, stabbed her more deeply than she ever would have expected.

When they got to the bottom, she realized the rear door of the limo had been opened by a man in the same uniform as the flight attendants on Lucas's jet. An imposing man with a mane of white hair and a neatly trimmed beard got out, turned, bent, and held out an arm. A lovely woman with golden hair, barely touched with silver, and clear blue eyes took the proffered arm and stepped out of the long, low car with exquisite grace. And finally Jessie realized who they must be. Lucas's parents. They were, she thought, regal. It was ironic, but it was the only word that truly fit.

And belatedly she realized she was in the presence of a real, genuine king and queen. And she didn't have the slightest idea what to do. Why hadn't Lucas told her? Was she supposed to bow, or curtsy or something? Or as an American, was that somehow wrong?

As it worked out, she had to do neither. King Marcus took her hand, smiled in a way that put Jessie in mind of his son, and said quietly, "My son understated your beauty."

Jessie blushed, but before she could say a word the queen murmured a soft, "Welcome to Montebello, dear," and gestured her into the limo.

"We should go," Lucas said when she hesitated. "So the airport can clear the crowd."

She acceded to his request. Once they were inside the thankfully cooler vehicle, he handed her Luke and took up a seat beside her. He'd indicated what seat she should take, which meant they were facing forward, leaving the back-facing seat for his parents. She wondered about that, since they'd gotten out of the seat she was now in, but guessed they wanted her to have the best view of their precious Montebello.

She supposed she should be flattered, but she was too nervous to feel anything positive just now.

She watched the crowd as the older couple were getting in, then leaned over and asked Lucas quietly, "Is it like this whenever you go somewhere?"

"Like what? Oh, you mean the crowd. No. I mean, only lately. Since I got back. Before, the only people I had to dodge were the media. Looking for a photo of my latest escapade," he finished in such a wry tone she couldn't help but smile.

The moment the king and queen were seated, the man holding the limo door closed it and quickly walked around to get in the passenger-side front seat. Almost immediately the vehicle began to roll.

Jessie found herself staring down at the baby, this time not only because she loved to look at him, but because she was too nervous to look at anyone else. But with her peripheral vision she saw the king grasp his son's hand in a firm handshake in the same instant the queen reached out and laid a hand on Lucas's knee.

"I'm fine," Lucas said softly, his tone gently reassuring. "It's all right."

She stole a peek then at the stately couple opposite her. What she saw in their faces registered sharply—they adored their son. She could see echoes of the grief they must have felt when they had thought him dead etched into their faces, and in the way they clung to him now, as if they had feared he would once more not return to them after a flight.

She was surprised by the obvious genuineness of their emotions. Then she chided herself. They were human, after all, and there was no reason that being royalty precluded loving your children. At least they weren't afraid to show it, as she guessed other monarchs might be.

The limo had reached the fence, and while the airport personnel, with the help of a couple of people in that same white uniform with the gold and black trim that she now supposed was for the royal staff or whatever they were called, did their best to control the group, it still surged forward. For a moment Jessie felt a jolt of fear, but the next thing she knew Lucas had rolled down the window beside him and waved to the crowd, who responded with a joyous cheer.

Once they were clear, Lucas powered the window back up and sat back in his seat. Jessie didn't look at him or speak. She was feeling a bit overwhelmed, and couldn't think of a thing to say anyway. Luxurious private jets, uniformed attendants, red carpets, mile-long limousines and throngs of cheering admirers....

She smothered a sigh. Despite the obviously real feelings she'd seen between parents and son, Jessie knew that if she had to decide this instant, she would get right back on that plane and go home. She could never be part of this spectacle, this kind of glitter and pomp. It just wasn't in her.

The size of the airport surprised her, as did the sleek, gleaming, and clearly state-of-the-art terminal. She'd known Montebello was wealthy, but somehow it was different seeing it in person. She would even admit it was beautiful, at least what she'd seen from the air of the

island surrounded by Mediterranean waters glistening
with more colors of blue and green than she'd ever realized existed in nature.

She didn't really know how long the drive took. Lucas's parents—she found she was less nervous if she
thought of them that way—tactfully chatted, putting no
pressure on her to join in. At least, she assumed that's
what their intent was, rather than an attempt to exclude
her. She wasn't that paranoid. Not yet, anyway.

This gave her a chance to look out the window at the
passing landscape. Which, she admitted, was as beautiful
as it looked from the air. And as varied as Lucas had
promised her.

The airport appeared to be on a large plain, but she
could see mountains rising in the distance. Off to one side
on a separate airfield adjacent to the airport, she saw what
appeared to be military airplanes. She was startled for a
moment when she saw the insignia they bore and realized
they were American planes. Then she recalled the em-
phasis in the articles about Montebello on its strategic
importance to the U.S., and the frequent mention of the
military base that had been there for years. The sight of
this little piece of home caused both a pang and a smile.

From the airport they followed the coastline, and Jessie
stared out the window, rapt. She'd thought Lucas had
been exaggerating when he'd talked of "orchids and lilies
of the field growing wild," but it was clear he hadn't
been—that exotic-looking flower over there, just growing
along the side of the road, had to be an orchid.

As the coastline curved into a lovely, large, sweeping
cove, she saw on the far shore the first buildings of what
appeared to be a sizeable city. San Sebastian, the capital,
she thought, remembering the maps she'd looked at when
she'd first discovered who Lucas really was.

She barely had time to soak in the natural beauty before

they were in the midst of a place that could have been any cosmopolitan city on the globe. The buildings soared, glass and concrete and steel, the outward manifestation of the wealth of this small nation. Only the occasional touch of distinctive architecture betrayed they were in the Mediterranean, on the doorstep of the Middle East rather than any other similar-sized city.

As they reached the other side of the cove, the road began to climb as the land changed from rolling hills to steeper terrain. The buildings they passed became older, more classical in style, and if she'd been told she was in an old Italian village, Jessie wouldn't have argued.

They reached an open area amid the buildings that made her think even more of photographs she'd seen of Italy. A piazza, she thought, complete with tourists, cobblestones and pigeons, or whatever the local version of the ubiquitous bird was. And the requisite romantic horse and carriage or two to convey tourists to the local attractions.

Of which they seemed to be one, she noted with some amusement as people turned to stare as they passed slowly through the crowded piazza. Some of them waved, some nodded, some even saluted in one way or another. She supposed those last were locals who knew who the big limousine belonged to. And again she thought what a strange way this was to live.

Around the edge of the expanse were several shops and restaurants that fairly reeked atmosphere. *And high prices,* Jessie thought. There were even a couple with no visible signs to show what business they were in, which to Jessie had always meant if you didn't already know, you couldn't afford to shop there.

She supposed Lucas knew them all, and patronized them. She had the feeling she had only seen the tip of the iceberg when it came to his wealth.

"—Jessica?"

It took her a moment to tune in to the quiet female voice and realize she was being spoken to directly for the first time on this strange journey.

"Jessie, please. Or Jess," she said automatically, as she always did whenever anyone used her detested proper name. Then she caught herself, blushing, as she realized she had just corrected a queen.

But Queen Gwendolyn responded with pure grace. "Thank you, dear. I'm honored. I was just saying that we were going to have a welcome dinner for you at the Glass Swan—" she gestured toward an elegant-looking restaurant overlooking the harbor "—but we were afraid it would be too much too soon. So we'll do it another day."

"I…thank you. Yes, it would have been too much. It's been a very long day."

"I'm sure it has," she said kindly. "So we'll just get you home where you can rest until tomorrow."

"Thank you," Jessie repeated, this time with heartfelt gratitude, and the queen smiled.

The car began to slow, and Jessie looked out. There was a gap in the buildings around the piazza where there stood only a tall, wrought-iron fence. In the center of the fence was a pair of even taller, ornate iron gates. There was an elaborate pattern in the center, and it took her a moment to realize that it was a crest of sorts, with a stylized "S" at the center.

In the instant she realized the letter probably stood for Sebastiani, the gates began to open, confirming her guess. Yet no one seemed inclined to bother them—apart from a family of obvious tourists, clad in loud clothing and with cameras in hand, trying to peek into the tinted windows as they slowed to go through the heavy gates. They passed a guardhouse where a man in uniform bowed, then waved.

"No crowds?" she asked, wondering if that was due to fear, or respect.

"Not usually," Lucas said. "Most people know they're allowed in to tour the house on specific days, with few questions asked." He smiled. "A tradition we borrowed from your White House."

Respect then, she decided.

She turned to watch the huge gates swing closed behind them. Then she returned to facing front.

And realized they'd entered Oz.

Chapter 11

She truly did feel like they'd entered another world once they'd passed through those gates. They'd gone from the quaint, bustling piazza that could have been in any crowded city, to expansive grounds that were like a huge park, with great swaths of green lawn, patches of profuse, exotic—to Jessie at least—flowers, which she guessed weren't nearly as casual in planting or maintenance as they were in appearance.

Once they were out of sight of the gates, she never would have guessed that the city they'd just passed through even existed, let alone that it was so close. She remembered from the map she'd seen that the royal palace was on one tip of the island of Montebello, and she guessed that had to be where they were headed now. She'd just had no idea the grounds surrounding the palace would be so expansive. It wasn't home, but she didn't feel cramped or hemmed in, either.

The drive rounded a small hill, and she could see the

sparkle of the Mediterranean at the bottom of the cliff. Each turn revealed another spectacular vista. It put her in mind of some of the high mountain roads back home, where every curve in the road brought you a different view.

At last they turned slightly away from the sea, and the road rose as they headed up a slight grade. And then nothing could draw her attention from the amazing building that came into view.

Here was the pure Mediterranean feel, two stories of sunwashed marble gleaming in the midst of all the greenery. A long, wide circular cobblestone drive wrapped around a large fountain, beautifully landscaped with flowerbeds and inviting benches. Across from the fountain was what appeared to be the main entrance to the large building.

Palace.

It suddenly struck her that this was the right word. She was about to enter a palace. Smaller than, say, Buckingham, but then, Buckingham didn't have this kind of view. Few places on earth had this kind of view.

But she didn't get much chance to take it in. The limo pulled to a halt in front of that main entrance, and within seconds the man from the front seat had the back door open. The next thing she knew she was being guided up the massive front steps and into a marble-floored foyer with an exquisitely painted ceiling that soared so high it nearly made her dizzy to look up at it.

Directly ahead was a wide, grand staircase that led to the second floor. Off to the left was a balcony that looked down on the foyer where they stood. She glanced around, but it seemed impossible to take it all in, all the marble, gilt details, and paintings. She would have thought the place would feel dark, heavy, but it was instead amazingly light.

"You'll get the big tour tomorrow, if you want," Lucas said to her. "But now, I think you need to rest."

"Rest sounds wonderful," she said gratefully.

Sleeping for about a week sounded wonderful. She shouldn't be so exhausted, Jessie thought. All she'd done was fly on a plane. For many hours, of course, but she'd slept a bit during the flight. It didn't seem to make any difference, though; she felt as if she were about to drop. Stress, she supposed. Unfortunately, even if she slept for that entire week, when she woke up she would still be here in Montebello, and thus still under stress.

But she couldn't even begin to articulate her feelings, and Lucas wouldn't understand even if she could. He was home, and happy to be here, she could see it in his face. She, on the other hand, was wishing she'd never decided to do this. Still she told herself she was just tired, that she'd agreed to this and it was time to stop whining about it.

She hesitated when Eliya came to take the baby, but rationalized that the woman had taken care of him before and he'd come to no harm. Her exhausted brain tried to make up some nightmare scenario where she never saw Luke again, and this was all a plot engineered by the imperious Sebastianis to get rid of her, so there would be no dispute over who would raise Luke. After all, if her own sister could do what she'd done, what was to stop these total strangers, with all their wealth and position, from securing their royal heir however they had to? Who would question them if she disappeared, never to be seen again? She had no one left, no one who would care.

Lord, you're pitiful, just get off it, she snapped at herself inwardly.

Because of her silly thoughts, she followed Lucas rather meekly up those stairs. She wondered if her weariness was why the place seemed to expand with every step she went up, or if it was some strange optical illusion. At the top Lucas seemed to hesitate for a moment, then turned left.

They went through a large room she guessed was a sitting room of some kind, or a common area for the upper floor. It was furnished in bold colors that could have overpowered the room were it not for the many tall French doors in the far wall, opening out onto a lovely terrace with a gasp-inducing view of the sea. As they continued, she saw a balcony that she recognized as the one she'd looked up at from below.

But then Lucas was opening a door and gesturing her through. She stepped into one of the most incredible rooms she'd ever seen, decorated in luscious tones of blue and green, furnishings a bit ornate for her taste, yet fitting in this gilt-edged setting. The bed was a huge four-poster such as she'd only seen in pictures, so tall there was a three-step stool beside it. Each post of the bed was swathed in rich fabric of a deep royal—of course, she thought—blue, while the windows were draped in equally rich fabric of green patterned with the same blue. The matching bedspread had the unmistakable sheen of silk, and inanely Jessie wondered if anybody ever dared eat in bed around here.

Beyond the windows she saw that she had a terrace of her own, with the same breathtaking view as the large parlor they'd come through. The thought of stepping outside to that view in the morning—or perhaps at night, since it would be so much warmer here, the novelty of that attracted her—was enticing, and she smiled.

She realized that her bags were already here, placed neatly on the carved mahogany bench, upholstered in the same silk, at the foot of the huge bed. She wasn't sure how they'd managed that, and wondered if everything at the Sebastiani palace worked so quietly and efficiently.

"I'll have someone unpack and press your things," Lu-

cas said, "but for now why don't you lie down for a
while? We'll have lunch in a couple of hours."

"Lunch? What time is it here?"

"Ten *a.m.* On Tuesday," he added, with the ease of
one long used to crossing more time zones than he had
fingers.

She shook her head; another thing she could never get
used to. "I would like to sleep for a while," she agreed.
"And," she added, "I can unpack myself."

"Of course you can," Lucas said easily.

He turned as if to go, then turned back to her. He gave
her a look she couldn't quite define. And then he leaned
over, cupped her face in his hands, and kissed her. With
exquisite care, yet so deeply and thoroughly that she was
reminded of those days back on the ranch when she and
the hand named Joe had fallen so totally and completely
in love.

When neither of them had known who he was. When
the idea of this place, and him belonging in it, would have
been the height of absurdity.

He left her reeling, without saying a word. And she
rather dizzily wondered why he'd put her in here, instead
of his own room.

She snapped out of her pleasurable haze. What on earth
was she thinking? Did she really want to stay with him
in this place, with his parents, knowing her private life
would be public knowledge, and no doubt the subject of
gossip from the moment it was learned she was sharing
Lucas's bed? Not that it wasn't obvious by Luke's very
existence, but it was one thing on her ranch, where everybody minded their own business, and something else
here, where from everything she'd seen and heard, these
people lived in a goldfish bowl. And she wasn't about to
provide any entertainment for the fish watchers.

That decided, and with a sense of relief that Lucas had

had the sense to put her here, she slipped out of her travel-wrinkled clothes. She dug her nightwear out of the smaller suitcase, and with a sense of wicked glee at sleeping amid silk and satin in a faded T-shirt bearing the image of Taz, pulled it on and climbed up the steps and fell into the sumptuous bed. She was asleep in moments.

"She's lovely, Lucas," his mother said.

"Yes. She is."

Lucas continued his pacing across his parents' sitting room. Even the much-loved view of the gardens and the sea beyond, including the yacht harbor where his parent's luxurious, hundred-and-twenty-five-foot *Sophia* was docked next to his own smaller sailboat, were unable to hold his gaze for long.

"Why don't you sit, son?" his mother asked.

"Can't," he said briefly, making a turn and going back the way he'd come. He knew if he tried to be still, he would quite simply fly apart. He wasn't sure why, he should be feeling relaxed now that he had Jessie under his roof, but that wasn't how he was feeling at all.

He saw his parents exchange glances, and wondered what they were thinking. They'd been married so long they could communicate without speaking, an oddity he'd accepted but never quite understood.

"She seems quiet," his father put in.

"She's nervous," Lucas said, stopping for the space of two breaths before resuming his back-and-forth treks. "I had a devil of a time convincing her to come at all."

"Is she angry with you?" his mother asked. "Surely she doesn't believe those tabloid stories."

Lucas winced. He'd been unaware of the flurry of stories and rabid, wild speculation that had appeared in the trashy papers, but his personal secretary had placed a pile of them on the desk in his office downstairs, by way of

warning and preparedness. He'd dreaded it, but he'd
looked at them. The first ones were full of the news that
he was alive, and later the news of Luke's existence had
broken.

The stories had ranged from the merely sensational,
playing up his part in the breakup of the U.S. cell of the
terrorist Brothers of Darkness—which had consisted
mostly of trying to stay alive while in their hands—to the
utterly lurid, focusing on the innocent, naive American
he'd seduced and abandoned, with frequent mentions of
his "alleged" amnesia. Those stories managed to plant
the idea that he'd really known who he was all along, and
had just chosen to dally with "a commoner" out of arrogant ennui, because his old thrills had palled.

"She doesn't read them, thank God. If she did, I never
would have gotten her here, not because of what was in
those stories, but because they even exist. The idea of
living in a glass house open to the world doesn't appeal
to her."

"Then why was it so hard to convince her to come
here?" his father asked. Lucas had to smile inwardly at
his borderline indignant tone. His father believed whole-
heartedly there was no better place in the world than Montebello. He liked, respected, even admired the United
States, but Montebello was still his pride and joy.

"Because she has some crazy idea that Luke—" he
began, then stopped. He had to be fair, he told himself.
Jessie had valid concerns, and he wouldn't belittle them
by speaking disparagingly of them to his parents.

So with an effort, he explained to them in some detail.
When he'd finished, his mother nodded in understanding,
while his father looked bewildered.

"But the boy will have every advantage!" he exclaimed.

"She knows that. She just doesn't think it outweighs freedom of choice."

"But he is the heir. How can she possibly—"

He broke off when his wife gently touched his arm. "I understand perfectly," she said softly. "I'm British, and I've learned what happens when someone who doesn't want it is forced to take the crown."

Lucas gave his mother a grateful look. But it turned into a frown as he realized she had just validated part of Jessie's argument. He'd have to tell her not to mention that view to Luke's mother, if she wanted her grandson here to continue to spoil.

"But it's hardly like that here," Marcus protested.

"How is she to know that?" Gwendolyn said soothingly.

Grumbling somewhat, Marcus subsided. Lucas wasn't truly worried about his father. He might take affront at the implication anything in his beloved Montebello could ever be bad for his grandson, but once he was face-to-face with Jessie, his powerful sense of fairness would kick in and he would be just that with her, fair.

But it was going to have to wait, Lucas thought later as he inched open her door after she didn't respond to his light knock. He saw the small shape under the covers of the bed and moved quietly into the room. She was sound asleep, looking so weary he didn't have the heart to wake her.

He used the intercom—a system he had introduced when he'd grown tired of the ancient bell-pull system— to speak to the upstairs maid who handled the guest rooms, and asked her to please notify him when Jessie was awake and ready to go downstairs.

Lunch came and went. She never called.

Later, Lucas headed purposefully up the stairs from his office. He understood that Jessie had been tired and wary, and reluctant to face his parents under those conditions. But he'd let her rest for six hours now, and if she didn't get up for a while, he told himself, her sleep patterns were going to be hopelessly confused. So he headed for the guest wing to wake her up.

When she didn't answer his knock, he became concerned; the maid said she'd peeked in twice to find their guest still sleeping. Perhaps the woman had mistaken the situation, maybe Jessie was ill, or something else was wrong. She'd been through a horrible ordeal, after all, and wasn't that long out of the hospital.

Determined now, he reached for the ornate door handle. He let out a tiny breath of relief when he found she hadn't locked it; she didn't feel that threatened, apparently. He pushed it open and stepped inside, his mouth open to call her name when he spotted her out on the terrace.

She was wrapped in the guest robe from the bathroom, and leaning on the stone balustrade. The slight breeze lifted strands of her hair, which gleamed gold in the afternoon sun. There was something about the sunlight here in his homeland that was unlike anywhere else, he thought.

He crossed the room quietly, enjoying simply watching her as she looked out to the sea. She looked entranced, and he hoped she was. It was the first step toward falling in love with Montebello.

"Jessie?" he said softly as he reached the French doors that led outside. He didn't want to startle her. She turned to look at him. She didn't seem surprised by his presence, and in fact looked almost as if she'd expected him.

"I'm sorry," she said immediately. "I must have been more tired than I realized."

"That's all right," he said, going to stand beside her. He noticed then that tendrils of hair around her neck were damp, and realized she must have showered and come out here before dressing.

Before dressing.

Which meant she was likely naked under that damnably thick robe.

He swore silently. He'd tried not to pressure her. After that night on the ranch when she'd agreed to come back with him, he'd walked so carefully that whole eggs wouldn't have broken beneath his feet. He had never assumed he was welcome in her bed, and indeed had spent a couple of achingly lonely nights alone when she'd been so exhausted from pushing to get done everything she wanted to before they left.

He'd been so careful then because he didn't want anything to interfere with getting her here, and he was desperately afraid he'd somehow say something to make her change her mind. It had been a very strange feeling for him. He was a man who hadn't spent much time worrying about how he dealt with people; as Prince Lucas Sebastiani, people worried about how they dealt with him. And never was he afraid that he might repel someone he didn't want to. People went out of their way to spend more time with him, not avoid him.

He'd never thought much about his assumptions before, and how ingrained they were. And this added to the niggling uncertainty he now felt regarding things he'd always been positive about. Jessie Chambers, he thought, had truly rattled his cage, as his American FBI friend was wont to say.

And never more than at moments like now, when all he could think about was how soft and sweet she was, how luscious she tasted, how her body could coax his to heights he'd never believed existed, again and again.

Her expression slowly changed, telling him that his must have also.

"Lucas," she began, and he didn't miss that she took the tiniest of steps backward.

"I see," he said tightly.

Jessie looked suddenly flustered. "I know this is a huge place, but it is your parents' home."

"Yes, it is. And I would never do anything they wouldn't approve of here."

"You do that elsewhere?" she asked, and he supposed he'd asked for that one.

"The Playboy Prince did," he admitted. "But I gave up my 'elsewhere' the day I came home from America, because I knew I could never be that man again."

For a long moment Jessica just looked at him, and he wished he knew what was going on in that quick mind of hers. Did she not believe him, not believe he'd truly changed? Or was she thinking about the way he'd walked out on her?

He had the fleeting thought that she might have seen, or someone had told her about, the tabloid stories, but he didn't know when that could have happened. And certainly none of his staff or the palace staff would have been foolish enough to say anything. Most of them had been with the Sebastiani family for years, and were utterly loyal. Treating people well was a philosophy his father carried through down to the lowliest of employees.

He opened his mouth to plead with her to believe him, that he was no longer that kind of man. But he knew Jessie wasn't a woman who believed in talk, she believed in actions. He couldn't tell her, he would have to show her.

But at least she was here, so he had a chance.

Somehow he doubted that ignoring her reservations about being in his parents' home and jumping her here and now, as he so much wanted to do, would convince her. The allure of her naked, still damp body was nearly overwhelming, but the thought of driving her away by proving he thought of nothing but pleasure gave him the tiny edge he needed to tamp down the fire that threatened to break loose.

He made himself back up a step. "My mother has ordered dinner served in the breakfast room." Jessie looked puzzled, and he explained. "It's where we eat on informal occasions, or when it's just family. It's much more relaxed, and she thought you might be more comfortable there."

"Oh. Thank you." Then her brow furrowed. "What should I wear? Not that I have a lot of choice," she said rather ruefully. "Not much call for dressing for dinner on the ranch."

He resisted the temptation to tell her just the robe, and said evenly, "Informal means casual. I admit jeans aren't my mother's first choice for attire, but she's had to surrender since all her children wear them."

Jessie looked suddenly panicked. "Are they here? Your sisters?"

"Not at the moment. But even if they were, I promise you they don't bite. Julia is quite regal these days, since marrying Rashid, but she's still her generous self. Christina is brilliant, but Jack keeps her in line. And Anna is still adorable, and leading her new husband a merry dance. Both she and Christina are expecting."

"Sounds…active." Jessie looked a bit overwhelmed.

"It is, but it's also fun. They've all found a happiness that practically glows."

He didn't add that he wanted to see that glow on her face; he knew she wasn't ready to hear it. But he did want it, and the only thing he wanted more than that was to be the one that put it there.

Chapter 12

Jessie was starting to feel smothered with kindness as she walked along the terrace outside the first floor of the palace. It wasn't oppressive, not really, but definitely unrelenting. It made her feel as if everyone was under orders to make her welcome, which took some of the spontaneity out of it all.

On the other hand, she couldn't deny that the imposing King Marcus and the lovely, charming Queen Gwendolyn positively doted on Luke. And the baby already responded to them with happy familiarity, so she knew this was not simply a show put on for her benefit. They also made it clear they would welcome her into the Sebastiani family graciously, but, Jessie suspected, it would be as much because she was Luke's mother as anything else. More, probably.

Of course, once the king and queen made it clear she was accepted, the rest of the family—and probably the country, if what she'd heard about the high regard the populace had for the royals was true—would follow their lead. Were she crazy enough to accept this loveless bargain, her life would not be difficult in that regard, at least. In the beginning, anyway. She seemed to recall a couple of British royals who had married into The Firm and had been welcomed at first....

But as determined as everyone was to make her feel welcome, she couldn't miss the fact that everyone here apparently considered her marriage to Lucas all but accomplished, nothing left but the paperwork.

Jessie stopped to peer through a tall window into the huge grand ballroom, remembering then how she had even been asked by a cheerful woman who identified herself as the queen's junior secretary where she thought she might like to have the ceremony, inside in the grand ballroom, or perhaps out in the royal gardens, since the weather was always lovely in Montebello. Jessie had honestly blanked for a moment before realizing the woman meant wedding ceremony, which earned her a very startled look.

The fact that they all seemed to think that her marriage to Lucas was a sure thing made her feel even more determined to make her own decision, in her own sweet time. And if her choice turned out to be no—as, of course, it would—wouldn't they all just feel a bit silly, for thinking their precious prince was irresistible?

The problem was, Lucas darn near *was* irresistible. She'd proved that a time or two, she thought ruefully. He had only to touch her, kiss her, and she was ready to give in. In that way he was still Joe, able to leave her breathless and longing for more with a single kiss.

But she had to be strong, no matter how she might ache for his touch. She had to make this decision with a clear head, and clarity was the first casualty of Lucas's touch;

thinking much at all through the golden haze of pleasure
he could rouse in her was impossible.

"Ready for the rest of the tour?"

Jessie sighed as Lucas came up behind her, as if she'd
conjured him up with her thoughts.

"I'm not sure," she said frankly. "I've already seen so
much, and it's all jumbled together in my mind."

"It is a big place, and a bit confusing. And you've only
seen a fraction of it."

She knew that, since he'd so far only shown her the
top floor, the family's residential area and the other guest
rooms. She'd found it curious that he began with the private part of the residence rather than the public areas, but
she supposed it was part of his campaign to make her feel
as if she were already part of the family, and therefore as
if she belonged in that part of the house.

While escorting her back to her room in the guest wing
after dinner last night, he'd given her a brief glimpse of
his parents' quarters, which occupied an entire wing beyond the guest suites, and of his sisters's rooms, empty
now that the princesses had all married and moved on,
but still kept in readiness for visits. Apparently, Princess
Anna and her husband, Tyler, stayed in the palace often.
And Princess Julia, Sheikh Rashid and their young son,
Omar, were frequent visitors. Christina lived in Montana
with her husband and travelled to Montebello less often,
but a room still waited. Lucas had shown her the music
room, and the private screening room where they watched
movies at their leisure. And the billiard room, which was,
she noted wryly, directly adjacent to his personal quarters.

And that, she guessed as he headed back in that direction, was where they were headed now. Which of course
put her on edge, yet at the same time she was very curious
to see what his rooms were like.

He didn't make a production out of it. He merely

opened the door for her, and as she stepped in pointed out the parlor, a rather formally decorated room where he told her he met with friends.

Then came what he called his retreat, a room done in an English-library style, with a leather sofa and a couple of richly upholstered wing chairs, bookcases filled to overflowing with everything from leather-bound volumes with gilt-edged pages to dog-eared paperbacks. There was a desk in one corner, with a computer on another table behind it, which he said was linked to his computer downstairs in his official office.

She knew what the next room had to be, and steeled herself for stepping into his bedroom. When she did, she was startled; a less royal-looking room she'd never seen. There were no formal draperies on the terrace windows, only simple pleated shades, nothing to interfere with the view of the water. The four-poster was of dark wood in simpler lines, but even bigger than hers. Lucas had no need of the steps, she noticed.

The linens were as rich as the ones in her room but simpler, in an attractive dark green and cool blue plaid. There was another bookcase near the bed, as full as the other one had been, telling her that Joe's love of reading at the ranch had been real and long established.

Above the bed was a painting that looked to be of a sheltered cove in a turquoise sea, somewhere here on Montebello, she guessed. Her chest tightened a little when she saw, next to a comfortable chair beside the bed, a small table that held a single framed photograph. Luke, smiling a baby grin into the camera.

And then she turned slightly, and saw the wall opposite the bed. Saw what would be the first thing he saw upon waking. And it took her breath away. For on the wall was a panoramic, scenic photograph, enlarged to great size, of her own beloved Colorado. It was a view of the Rockies that almost could have been taken on the ranch itself.

Instinctively her head snapped around and she stared at him in surprise.

"I found it online. Once I saw it, I had to have it."

The idea of Prince Lucas of Montebello personally ordering a photographic print online was almost disconcerting enough to overshadow the fact of the print's subject. Almost.

"It was my way of hanging on to Joe, and what he learned there."

She turned to face him then. "You could have just come back."

"And I inevitably would have brought all this with me," he said, gesturing vaguely around him as if to include everything. "I've been front-page news ever since the media discovered I was alive. I knew if I went to you after my memory first came back, I'd bring all that with me."

"So you decided not to give me the opportunity to decide for myself," she said, giving voice to the real crux of the matter for her.

"I knew you would hate it," he said, apparently not seeing her point at all. "And before I could even come home, I was..."

She let the other go for now, and finished it for him. "You were off breaking up terrorist groups."

"Just one."

"Still...." She owed him this, she thought, because it was how she really felt. And not everyone would have been willing to do what he'd done, and most certainly not every royal. "It was a heroic thing to do. Those people shouldn't be allowed to exist in a civilized world."

"I don't know about heroic. It had to be done, for the

sake of that civilized world, not just my country or yours."

"Exactly," she said, still smiling as he made her point for her.

He shrugged. "Anyway, after that the media followed me everywhere. Everywhere outside of Montebello, anyway. Here they at least acceded to my father's request to back off, for the most part."

Jessie couldn't help thinking of all the presidents who would have liked to do the same thing, not that it would have done any good in the U.S. But apparently it did some good here, such was the king's power.

"Then," Lucas said, and there was a world of echoed pain in his voice and in his eyes, "I was told you were dead. My cousin Drew tried to break it gently, but it didn't matter. I felt...shattered. Because now I could never go back, it was too late."

Jessie stared at him. Surely such pain meant he had cared, didn't it? Her hopes wanted to soar, but she knew she couldn't afford that, so tamped down her emotional reaction. Of course he cared, he'd loved her as Joe, and it was likely some feeling had survived his metamorphosis back to Lucas. But apparently it wasn't love. Or at least, he wouldn't admit to it.

And suddenly she wondered if perhaps he wanted her to be the bad guy, wanted her to turn him down, and that was why he'd made sure not to mention the one thing that would make her want to say yes, that he still loved her as much as Joe had loved her. Maybe she was supposed to say no, and thus free him to go back to his life as it had been.

"That started the worst time of my life." His voice softened. "Until they brought us Luke."

His words brought her out of her thoughts, and reminded her of the real reason she was here—because she was the mother of a prince's son. He had only come back to her after he had Luke, and for all his reasons for not coming back when his memory had first returned, she wasn't sure she believed them.

For that matter, even if she did believe his reasons for staying away, she wasn't sure they were good enough, not to her battered heart.

Lucas seemed to sense her change in mood, because he quickly suggested they move on, and he would show her the rest of the palace. The afternoon became a jumbled collection of impressions as they went down the grand staircase and into the ballroom she'd been looking into from outside. She held her breath, waiting for him to make some suggestion about a wedding being held here, but he said nothing beyond pointing out the main chandelier, an incredible waterfall of crystal teardrops.

From there he showed her the library and two drawing rooms, one decorated in red, one in gold, which connected by sliding doors that could be opened to the large banquet room. She marveled at the huge tapestries on the wall and how the rich cherrywood of the furnishings blended well with the burgundy of the walls and draperies. With a fireplace at each end, the room inspired her to imagine what an incredible setting it would be, with dignitaries dressed in their finest clothes and jewels, glittering by firelight.

She liked the more subtle, smaller dining room better, cream and gold accented in dark green, and liked the pastel-hued, light-filled breakfast room best of all.

He took her to the picture gallery and archive room next. She had expected something of the sort, but still the string of portraits of Sebastianis down the years was fascinating. Old King Augustus bore a startling resemblance to Lucas's father—or the other way around, she supposed. In fact, the family resemblance through the years was strong; she could see traces of that stubborn jaw and fierce intelligence in almost all the portraits that hung there.

Next to the big oils of the king and queen there was a portrait of the current family, with Lucas and his three sisters gathered around the royal couple, but no individual ones of the children were present.

"None of you or your sisters?"

"Not yet. The traditional portraitist unfortunately passed away a couple of years ago, and mother hasn't chosen a new one yet. She's rather particular."

Jessie glanced back at the painting of the queen in full regalia, noticed the way the artist had, while not being fawningly flattering, captured the essence of her beauty and personality, the genuine smile that curved her lips, the twinkling glint in her blue eyes. "I can see why."

"And this," he said, gesturing to the next room, "is the archives."

"Amazing," Jessie said, more used to the idea of love letters kept in a shoe box than anything like this.

"Family documents, letters dating back centuries, marriage agreements, treaties, declarations, you name it, it's all here."

This brought something to mind that she'd been meaning to ask. "Including the famous feud?"

"Especially that," he said, with a grin that belied the seriousness, to her at least, of the subject.

"Is Luke in danger here?" she asked bluntly. "He's been kidnapped once, because of who he is. I won't let him become a target again."

"Do you think I will?" Lucas said, an edge in his voice. "I can't deny that anyone high profile isn't always safe in this world. But Luke will have a cadre of protectors, willing to die for him if necessary."

She frowned. "That's not my idea of reassurance."

"There's little threat from Tamir any longer. Julia and

Rashid ended the feud, then our friends began to marry into the families, and now the Sebastiani and Kamal families are all either friends or in-laws. We have to get along, whether we like it or not.''

Now that did reassure her. ''Sounds...confusing.''

''I'll lay it all out for you, if you like.'' His smile was a bit crooked. ''Or maybe Mother should. So much of it happened while I was gone, I'm not up to speed myself.'' He gestured at the room they stood in. ''But you could say this is where the feud between my country and Tamir came to an end.''

She blinked. ''In here?''

He nodded. ''This is where Julia and Rashid discovered the truth about the murder that started that feud all those years ago.''

''They themselves?''

''Yes.'' He grinned. ''They had to resolve it, or Julia never would have married him. And believe me, those two *needed* to be married.''

''Because she was pregnant with his child,'' Jessie said, remembering the news stories.

''No,'' Lucas said, his voice suddenly tense. ''Because they were crazy about each other. Let's go.''

She followed him silently. She'd hit a nerve, it seemed. Because her question had pointed out the difference in their situations? Because she'd inadvertently reminded him that he felt forced to marry the mother of his child, a woman he no longer loved?

She wished she could believe he'd corrected her because he loved her in that same way, but nothing could erase the cold, business-like presentation that had been more job offer than proposal. There had been nothing of love in it, nor had it been spoken of since, not even the night they'd shared at the lookout. She told herself she shouldn't be surprised; why would a man who lived this life want a plain, ordinary woman like her?

And there certainly hadn't been love in the actions of the man who had walked out without even giving her the opportunity to make a choice about her future. Just as he wanted to take away Luke's choices. Which she could not and would not let him do. No matter what it cost her. Her son's entire life was on the line here, and she had to fight for him while he was helpless to fight for himself. Even if it meant she lost his father.

Lucas came to a halt at a huge pair of the most ornately carved and gilded doors she'd ever seen—and she'd swear the gilt was real gold. There was something about the warmth and sheen that screamed it.

"You might as well see the heart of it, then," Lucas said, and from his edgy tone she gathered he was still tense. She was about to ask him for an explanation when he reached out and gave the doors a shove. They swept open automatically, and she guessed they had to be powered somehow.

And then she was staring into a room that matched those doors, a huge expanse of glitter and gleam, with soaring columns, tile mosaics along one wall that portrayed what looked like historical events, portraits of the kings along the other wall. Then she saw the roller of thick, red carpet beside the door, and then the raised dais at the far end of the room, behind which hung a huge, exquisitely detailed map of Montebello.

You might as well see the heart of it....

The throne room. This had to be the throne room, she realized with a little shock.

Never in her life had she ever thought she'd be standing in a throne room. Any throne room. The closest she'd ever been to seeing one at all was in television documentaries on Great Britain. She had to admit it had her a little awe-struck.

"My father was crowned here, and his father before him, back to the beginning," Lucas said, his voice softer now. "On an ordinary day, it seems too much, almost a gaudy display. But on a state occasion, it befits the mood, the tradition, the importance."

She was moved by the solemnity of his words; he felt deeply about this, she realized. "And you will be crowned here?"

"When the time comes," he agreed. "But that's a long time away."

"I hope so," she said, meaning it. "I quite like your father."

"Really? He intimidates most people."

"I can see how. But when I see how he loves your mother, I can't be too scared by him."

Lucas smiled then, and a tightness in her chest she hadn't even realized was there lifted.

"It will be a long time," he repeated. "As I told you, he's as healthy as the proverbial horse, thank goodness. Speaking of which, let me show you what I'm sure will be your favorite place."

Curious, as much at the sudden gleam in his eye as wondering what place could be more special than this, she followed his lead and was surprised when they stepped out through a side door she hadn't realized was there. Parked just outside were a couple of small vehicles that looked like golf carts, and he walked her over to one.

"I usually walk, but I don't want to wait to show you this," he said.

She got in, he went around to the driver's side, and they were quickly off. The vehicle was silent, and she realized it must be electric.

She looked back as they pulled away, realizing anew

how huge the palace was, yet at the same time understanding that as palaces went, it was fairly modest. One of the maids had told her—part of that unrelenting campaign to impress her—that the royal family had repeatedly rejected plans to expand, using the housing budget only for repairs to the existing building, saying such an expenditure was unjustified when there were still things to be done for the people of Montebello.

The cart wheeled easily along a well-groomed path that made a curve to the right around a rise a hundred yards or so away from the palace. When the building went out of sight, she turned back to face forward again. And gasped.

Below, in a small valley still within view of the sea, was an expansive set of buildings and structures that could serve only one purpose, and one very dear to her.

Horses!

It was the most luxurious, well-kept stable she had ever seen. A sudden image from some long-ago-read children's book popped into her mind, of stables with marble mangers, and horses's names on brass plaques above each stall. It was that kind of place, worthy of the finest blooded animals, Kentucky derby winners or the Lippizaners of Austria.

"Brat would have been well housed," he said.

The thought of her lovely but rough-and-tumble little buckskin in this setting made her smile. "She would love it, for a while, but I think she'd be longing for the mountains before too long."

"Like horse, like rider," Lucas said, letting out a breath that sounded almost like a sigh.

"Yes," she said honestly. "I can't deny that. But I said I would be fair, and I will."

She meant it. And she couldn't say this wasn't fascinating, or that she was sorry she'd come. At least, as far as seeing this piece of the world was concerned; Montebello was beautiful, fascinating, and she could understand why some thought it paradise. If it wasn't for her mixed emotions about Lucas, and the intense pressure she felt because of why he'd brought her here, she would be having the time of her life.

But only because she knew she'd be going back home soon.

It wasn't that the luxury of this life wasn't amazing. She was constantly looking around and marveling that people actually lived like this. But for a country girl, used to the simplicity of life on her ranch, it was often overwhelming. And only proved to her what she'd already known; the expensive trappings of this kind of life weren't very important to her.

But this, she thought, looking eagerly ahead as they continued toward the stable, this she could get used to.

The main barn was a long, low building with at least twenty stalls on each side. Each stall had a long run outside, and she imagined they opened onto a large center corridor inside.

"There are fans in the attic, every fifteen feet, to make sure the barn doesn't get too hot in high summer," Lucas said. "Each stall is fifteen by fifteen except the broodmare stalls, which are twenty by twenty."

"I can't wait to see the inside," she said, leaning forward to peer at the circular corral, which back home they called a bullpen. A larger paddock was beyond that, and in it on the far side was a black horse.

It was the horse that drew her attention most of all. From here she could tell little except his color, a gleaming black she was willing to bet was pure, unlike most horses called black who were really a very dark brown, as evidenced by lighter brown in areas on the flanks and nose.

Lucas whistled, a piercing sound that made Jessie glad

her head was turned. The black's head came up sharply, he looked their way and trumpeted an answer that made her heart beat faster. Stallion, she thought.

And then the animal started toward them. First trotting in a high-action way that put her in mind of those Lippizaners she'd thought of earlier. And then he broke into a smooth, sweeping gallop that sent his heavy mane and tail flying. He was at the fence waiting for them when Lucas maneuvered the cart to a halt alongside the paddock.

Jessie got out without waiting and took one look at the horse's classic, dished Arab face and whistled lowly.

"He's beautiful," she breathed.

"Meet Pitch," Lucas said. "As in 'black as.' Pitch, be polite now."

Knowing the propensities of stallions, Jessie approached cautiously.

"He's a gentleman," Lucas said, "but you're wise to go slowly."

She lifted a hand but didn't touch, just let the animal sniff. He stretched his neck out farther, and on instinct she did as she did with Brat, puffed little breaths against his nose. The horse snorted, but didn't move, and after a moment nudged her hand in a signal that it was all right to come closer. In his way, she thought, the horse was as royal as his owners.

Then she was stroking and patting the powerful neck, feeling the play of taut muscle beneath sleek hide, and there was room for nothing in her mind but the joy of being near horses again.

She could have stayed admiring the stallion for much longer, but she was also eager to see the rest. The barn was everything the spruce-and-tidy exterior promised; a horse lover's dream. He showed her the tack room with a varied array of gear, the office with its modern computer to track feed, vaccinations, veterinary info, shoeings, and then let her wander from stall to stall to her heart's content.

Each occupant was unique to her, from the delicately boned white yearling filly to the heavier built four-blood bays used to pull the royal carriage on state occasions. She introduced herself to all of them, savoring the beautiful lines, the intelligent eyes, and the immaculate conditions.

"If I'd known this was what it would take to enchant you, I would have brought you here first," Lucas teased.

"Well, you should have known," Jessie retorted without thought.

"Yes, I should have," he answered, his voice very quiet.

She glanced at him then, but his expression told her nothing. She hated that polished, practiced facade. She'd never seen it on Joe; Joe's face had been open to her, readable. With Lucas, she never felt sure of what he was thinking.

And she couldn't help thinking that that was because Joe had loved her, so he'd let her see.

And Lucas did not.

Chapter 13

"It wasn't easy," Gwendolyn said in heartfelt tones. "If I had let things out of my hands, those children would have been spoiled absolutely rotten. Our people seemed to feel it was their duty to shower gifts of all kinds on each child as they came along. Lucas most of all, because he was the heir."

Jessie had been surprised when the queen had invited her, alone, to her personal parlor. She'd arrived, after dressing hastily in her nicest linen pants and a pale yellow cotton sweater, to find Gwendolyn dressed in a light-weight dress of nearly the same shade of yellow. Somehow that made her able to relax a little.

She'd been here a week now, long enough to see that the easy, close relationship between Lucas and his parents was a real one of long standing, not just one engendered by the near escape they'd been through. After a few awkward moments spent wondering if she was holding the proffered cup of tea correctly, or sitting in a ladylike manner, Jessie had asked about raising royal children.

"I tried to raise them as normally as possible, keep them in touch with the real world despite—" the queen waved in a regal way that encompassed all of their surroundings "—all this. I'd seen what happened to royal children who grew up thinking this was their just due, who knew nothing of the real world. Fortunately, Marcus agreed with me."

Jessie seized the chance to ask a question that had been lingering in her mind. "Lucas said you've been married thirty-seven years."

"Close enough," Gwendolyn agreed. "I love Marcus more now than I did then. And I loved him a great deal then," she added with a smile.

"Yet you told him no? Often?"

"I see my son has been busy spilling the family history," she said, sounding so amused that Jessie knew she hadn't offended her. "Yes, I did, at first. Five times."

Jessie's eyes widened. "May I ask why?"

Gwendolyn gave a shrug that somehow managed to be elegant. "Everyone else did. I was supposed to be swept off my feet by the simple fact that I was being courted by a prince. But I was a teacher to the British royal family. I had seen that life from the inside, and was certain it wasn't for me."

Jessie's breath caught. It could have been her speaking those words. And by the way the queen was looking at her, she suspected the woman knew it.

"Besides, I didn't want to leave my home. I grew up in the English countryside, and I loved it there. I couldn't imagine leaving it."

"But you did," Jessie said, watching the woman's still beautiful face intently. Hearing her own misgivings voiced by this regal woman was one of the oddest sensations she'd ever experienced.

"Yes, I did. Because, you see, in spite of my resistance,

I fell quite in love with Marcus Sebastiani. And realized he truly loved me. And once that happened, there really was no choice but the one I made.'' Gwendolyn returned her intense regard levelly. ''And I have not regretted it, not once in those thirty-seven years.''

The queen's words echoed in her mind as she walked through the royal gardens a while later. Gwendolyn was a very smart woman, so Jessie had little doubt her answers had been planned to alleviate Jessie's worries. But the queen was missing one important detail that made Jessie's situation different than that of herself and Marcus.

Marcus loved her. He had chosen and married his queen for love, not duty. He had not been forced in any way— she had noticed the dates of their marriage and Lucas's birth, and there were months to spare.

Once more that lost feeling swamped her. Why couldn't Lucas love her as Joe once had? Had that nasty tabloid story been true, once his memory had returned, had he realized he was too far above a mere American ranch woman?

Unbidden, a memory of that night at the lookout flooded her mind with images and her body with heat. Could that really have been a man who didn't love her?

Don't be a naive fool, she told herself. *You know perfectly well that for a man, sex and love are often two totally different things.*

For Joe, they hadn't been, she protested silently. But Lucas wasn't Joe, not really. She had always believed a person was the sum of many parts. It wasn't just who you were inside that made you the person you were, but how you were raised, what you were taught and what you believed. And there couldn't be two men further apart in that than an itinerant ranch hand and a crown prince.

It was Joe who had loved her. And it was Joe she had loved. Lucas, she wasn't at all sure about.

Her head began to whirl with it all; it seemed no matter which way she looked at it, it was an unsolvable conundrum. The only thing she was positive of was that she didn't want her son to grow up with no choices about his life's path.

She decided to do the one thing that always helped her think—be around horses. She ran to her room, changed into jeans, and headed for the stables. She took the path on foot, figuring the exercise wouldn't hurt her; she was used to long, work-filled days, and she hadn't had that here. Maybe she could ask if there was something she could do around the stable; she felt useless and lazy with no work to do.

She began to trot in her eagerness to get to the horses. She rounded the curve and started down the hill, then looked up to see if the stable complex was as wonderful as she remembered. And saw that someone was riding the black Arab in the paddock.

Lucas.

She couldn't really see the rider's face from here, but nevertheless she knew it was him. There was simply something about his easy, graceful way of riding that was obvious to her practiced eye.

She slowed to a walk, watching the duo work, first in long circles along the fence, then in an elongated figure eight across the middle of the enclosure, with the stallion doing a graceful, perfectly executed flying change of leads at the cross point. She stopped a few yards away, not wanting them to see her and stop. Because for a moment, one sweet, precious moment, it was like watching Joe again.

But then reality took over the image, and she saw the English-style saddle that looked tiny next to the Western stock saddles she was used to, and the refined riding attire he was wearing, so unlike the jeans and Western shirts Joe had worn, and that she was used to.

The stallion moved with a grace and power to match his rider. The two together were an overpowering picture, and when the image blurred, it took Jessie a moment to realize her eyes were brimming with tears.

She didn't know what to do. The choice before her seemed so ugly—risk losing her son, or spend her life in a marriage of convenience that was convenient for only one of them.

She couldn't deny the physical attraction between them. It would be foolish to. But neither could she convince herself of what she'd hoped after that night they'd spent making love under the Colorado sky, that there was more to this than a simple business proposition, that he didn't just want to marry her because she was the mother of his child and it would make things—the succession in particular—so much simpler.

She tried not to kid herself that it was anything else. And she had all those long, lonely nights when he could have come back to her but hadn't, to convince her it wasn't.

If it hadn't been for Luke, she thought, she wouldn't even be here. Lucas would have kept the clean break, never to walk back into her life again.

She blinked to clear her vision. When the swimming stopped, it seemed she had cleared it in more ways than one. As she looked down at the richly appointed stables, at the pure wealth demonstrated there, she saw that Lucas truly belonged here. He was part of this picture, as Joe could never have been. This was his life, his way of life, and it was no wonder he wouldn't trade it for the quiet, laborious life she lived. It was the life she loved, but she couldn't see someone who had grown up with all this—

Her thoughts broke off as she realized he'd seen her.

He had the black horse sidling up to the gate in the fence, nudging it open. Just as she'd taught him to do back at the ranch, where opening and closing gates was crucial.

She wondered if she had time to turn and get away, and avoid this encounter. But he sent the black toward her at a lope, and she knew she might as well stay here, since the horse would eat up the short distance between them in a matter of seconds. With a sigh, she stayed put. Her horsewoman's eye automatically focused on the black.

He was as beautiful as she remembered, she thought as they neared her. She'd always thought of Arabians as flashy, showy, but delicate. This horse made that a lie; he was fit, strong, and looked as if he could run forever and then start over again. He looked light after the bulky, brawny cow horses she was used to, but he was no less powerful. It was simply a different kind of power, designed by nature for the long haul, not the short, dramatic explosions of power of the quarter horse.

"Come for a ride with me?" were the first words out of Lucas's mouth. "I'm sure we can find a horse you'll like."

Being alone with him was not high on her list of things she wanted just now, not with the tangle of emotion and reality and longing she was feeling. But the temptation of being on a horse again was more than she could resist.

So a few minutes later, the black tied and patiently— for a stallion—waiting outside, they were walking into the huge, airy barn. And within less than a minute, a uniformed groom skidded to a halt in front of them.

"May I help you, Your Highness?"

The royal appellation still rattled Jessie, but Lucas merely nodded. "We need a second horse, Mario."

The groom nodded. "For the lady? There's that lovely little bay mare, or—"

The man stopped when Lucas held up a hand. "She's been riding since before she could walk, Mario. I don't want to bore her."

A wide grin flashed over the man's face. "Ghost?"

Lucas smiled. "That's more like it. She will do nicely, thank you."

As the groom trotted away, Jessie gave him a sideways look. "Back home, when a new hand shows up, we give him the toughest horse in the stable to try out."

He grinned. "I know. I carried the bruises from that big piebald of yours for days."

The boys had indeed put the newcomer through his paces, graining up Buddy until he was nearly coming out of his skin before they led the big paint out for Joe to climb aboard.

"But you won everybody's respect. You had old Buddy stepping out like a dressage champion."

"After getting thrown three times," Lucas said wryly.

"That's why they respected you," Jessie told him.

"I promise you this horse won't throw you. She's got the spirit of her sire," he said, gesturing toward where the black was tied outside, "but the loving nature of her dam, who sadly died giving birth to her."

The minute she looked at the lovely dapple-gray mare with the intelligent, gentle eyes, delicate face and flowing mane and tail, Jessie fell in love. It went against everything she believed in, all the years of finding the best horses in some of the most unlikely—and unprepossessing—packages, to fall in love with a pretty face, but nevertheless, she did.

And it seemed, after a few moments of inspection, the feeling was mutual. The mare sniffed at her hand, then her hair, and pronounced her acceptable with a soft whicker. By the time Jessie finished rubbing beneath the horse's jaw, and puffing air at her nose, the bond was complete, and Ghost nuzzled Jessie eagerly.

She wasn't used to the English saddle, but she'd ridden on them a few times in her life, and the adjustments necessary came back quickly. It felt odd to have a groom beside her, adjusting stirrup length and checking the cinch—or girth, she supposed, on this rig—for her, but simply being astride a horse again was worth just about any price.

For one used to the wilds of Colorado, this ride over exquisitely groomed grounds on carefully maintained paths seemed tame. But when they reached a straight stretch and Lucas signaled this was a good place to let them run, she gloried in the gray's smooth, effortless stride, and the pure joy in running the horse transmitted to her through the reins. The black loped alongside them, but she was fairly sure Lucas was keeping him in check to keep from outpacing them. The mare was fast, but Jessie doubted she could match the black.

When she felt the all-out charge begin to slow, Jessie gradually reined the mare in. Lucas slowed the black, as well, and although the stallion made a brief protest with a toss of his head, he gave in and settled into a walk easily enough.

Exhilarated, Jessie smiled broadly at Lucas. "Thank you," she said, meaning it with all her heart.

"It's not good for you not to be on a horse for too long," he said.

"Thank you, doctor," she said with a laugh. "I like your medicine."

For a moment it looked as if he was going to say something serious, and she held her breath, waiting for him to ruin this special moment by bringing up what she didn't want to talk about just now.

He didn't do it. Instead, he led the way toward the sea.

When they reached a narrow, less defined trail along the cliffs, she couldn't deny the vast panorama of the sparkling Mediterranean before them, as breathtaking in its own way as her beloved Rockies. A salt-tanged breeze blew up the cliff face toward them, stirring her hair and the gray's mane.

"Is this all your land?" she asked, gesturing toward the cliffs, then back in the direction of the palace.

"Yes. This entire tip of the island. It's been part of the palace grounds since it was built. So while we don't have your acreage, we don't feel cramped, either."

"Does being on an island ever seem...."

"Isolated?" he asked when she didn't finish. "Sometimes. But that's as often a good thing as bad. We avoid some problems other countries can't. And we can be in a major hub of the world in a fairly short time, so no, it rarely bothers us."

She wondered if he was aware he'd answered in the plural, as if he spoke for all Montebellans. And then she realized that he probably did. As their prince, if he was the kind of leader his father seemed to be, he would know how the people felt.

"Now that you've seen the palace and most of the grounds, I'd like to show you the rest of Montebello," Lucas said.

This was what she'd come for, what she'd agreed to, so Jessie made herself nod and say, "All right."

"And tonight," Lucas said, "you'll get the chance to meet Julia and Rashid. They're flying in for dinner."

Panic flooded her at the thought. It was too much. Dinner with a king, a queen, two princes and a princess? She was plain old Jessie Chambers, of Shady Rock, Colorado. She had no business sitting down with royalty.

That this was hardly the view of an egalitarian citizen

of the U.S., who supposedly shouldn't see anything special about royalty at all, didn't escape her.

But it did nothing to ease her panic.

She was as skittish as a newborn foal with a predator circling, Lucas thought.

He'd tried to tell her no one in his family had bitten anyone in decades, tried to calm her by saying it was not a formal occasion but just a small family dinner in the breakfast room that she liked so much. It didn't seem to help much. And just when he'd almost gotten her calmed by telling her anything she wanted to wear was fine, Rashid's helicopter buzzed the palace and settled on the lawn, setting her off again.

Finally he left her to dress, figuring he was only making things worse by hovering. So instead, he went downstairs to greet his sister and brother-in-law.

Julia looked radiant. So radiant, Lucas wondered if perhaps his sister was pregnant again. His nephew, Omar, was ten months old now, and the way she and Rashid still acted like newlyweds....

He stopped his own thoughts as a rueful realization struck him. He'd always looked upon displayed marital bliss with rather smug amusement, certain such a thing would never happen to him, that he would never become so besotted with a woman. And yet he had flown over twelve thousand miles to get Jessie and bring her here, and he was about out of his mind with worry that she wasn't ever going to change her mind.

Perhaps, he thought wryly, this was his payment for all those years of finding amusement at the expense of others.

"And what, dear brother, is on your mind to make you look so serious?" Julia asked gaily.

"Payback," Lucas muttered.

"Spoken like a man getting his just desserts, I think they call it," Rashid said.

It still took Lucas a bit of adjusting to remember this man was no longer the enemy. Coming home had been shock enough, coming home to find the ancient feud ended and his sister married to Rashid Kamal had almost been more than he could fathom. But his parents had insisted Julia was deliriously happy, and the first time he'd seen her after his return, it had only taken one look at her to know it was the absolute truth. And for that alone, Lucas welcomed the man in the beginning, but he'd come to like and respect Rashid in his own right as he'd gotten to know him better.

And now he saw a devilish glint in his brother-in-law's dark eyes, and knew Rashid had guessed the trouble was female.

"We shall talk later, eh, my brother-in-law? Perhaps I can help."

"Help?" Lucas asked.

Rashid looked at his wife, and the emotion that leapt between them was almost palpable. "I had to propose to Julia many times before she finally saw the wisdom of saying yes."

"Then perhaps," Julia said archly, "my brother should speak to *me,* to learn why I changed my mind."

"Right now," Lucas said frankly, "I'll take whatever help I can get. She is one stubborn American."

"There are those who would say that is a redundancy," Rashid replied. "Among them your very own sister and the two Dukes Sebastiani."

"Not to mention two of your own siblings, as well," Julia pointed out to her husband.

Lucas chuckled despite his worry. It was true, the Sebastiani and Kamal families were now as intertwined with Americans as they were with each other, and had been with the British before. They had truly become multinational. And he couldn't deny the energy and fresh viewpoints the new family members had brought with them. And they had reached an accord—even the people of Tamir, who had a greater mistrust of the West, had eventually accepted the changes.

"Perhaps I should speak to them all," he said ruefully. "It may take advice from everyone to convince this woman."

"Any woman worth winning is worth fighting for," Rashid said pointedly. And his sister's glow redoubled. Perhaps, Lucas thought, he could do worse than get advice from his new brother-in-law.

"Have patience, big brother," Julia said. "As long as she knows you love her, she will come around." She glanced at her husband before adding, "She *does* know you love her, doesn't she?"

"Of course," he said impatiently. "She knows I fell in love with her when I was on her ranch. That's not the problem. The problem is Luke."

"Luke?" Julia was startled.

"Yes. She's worried about his future."

"But what is there to worry about?" Rashid asked. "He is your heir, is he not? He will be king."

"Exactly," Lucas said. But before he could explain, Julia put a hand on his arm, and he looked up to see her watching the doorway. He turned his head, and sucked in a breath at the sight that met his eyes.

She was wearing a simple blue dress he'd never seen her wear before. It made her eyes look the color of a Colorado summer sky, and her body look both slender and richly curved. A thin gold chain gleamed at her throat. Her hair was down, not in its usual tail or braid, and the golden shimmer of that sleek mass that fell over her shoulders made his fingers curl with the need to touch.

Rashid nodded appreciatively.

"Definitely worth fighting for," he said.

Chapter 14

Jessie had never been so wary of simply going to dinner. She'd changed her clothes three times, finding something wrong or unsuitable about every outfit she tried on. She had finally settled on a blue linen dress that she knew fit her well, even though she was afraid the best from Sally Tucker's dress shop in Shady Rock would be too simple for the royal company she'd be keeping tonight. But it was one of her best, and it would just have to do. She wasn't royalty, but a simple American rancher, and she wasn't going to pretend to be anything else.

At least she would blend well with the room, she thought wryly, guessing that Queen Gwendolyn had decided to have this meal in the informal breakfast room for her sake, since she was more comfortable there than any of the other, more ornate rooms dedicated to the intricate process of formal meals.

Just two more people present shouldn't have made that much difference, Jessie thought as she hovered in the doorway, hesitating. But they did. Because these two, Lucas's sister Princess Julia, and Prince Rashid Kamal, were a very dramatic pair. Knowing their history, and how they had resolved the ancient feud between their two families, she'd been curious to see them. But now that she actually had, she felt a bit overwhelmed.

What was it about these people? What gave them this presence, this air of…well, of regalness? Did it come from being raised to think they were different, special? Or was it somehow born in them? Her brow creased at that thought, because it skirted too close to what Lucas had been saying, that Luke was born to this life.

And then the woman she knew had to be Julia, tall, with thick dark hair, a porcelain complexion and blue eyes like her mother's, swept forward.

"You must be Jessica," she said, reaching out and taking Jessie's hand. "It's so good to meet you at last. Welcome to Montebello."

Julia wore a simply cut silk dress, rich-looking but not flashy, in a pale peach that set off her dark hair. Nothing that made Jessie feel her own attire was either inappropriate or shabby.

"Thank you," she answered automatically. "But call me Jessie, please. Or Jess."

"I will, thank you. This is my husband, Rashid."

The dark man smiled graciously, then bent over her hand and kissed it in a way that should have seemed pretentious but didn't; she'd be willing to bet his ancestors had probably invented the extravagant gesture.

"It is my pleasure indeed, Jessie, to meet at last the woman who has managed to bring such consternation into Lucas Sebastiani's life."

Jessie blushed at the outrageous words, but before she could become too embarrassed, Julia was chatting away to her as if they were old friends.

"I hope you're having a wonderful time. Has Lucas shown you everything? No, wait, you've not been here long enough to see all the wonders of Montebello. You can't even have begun."

"Is everyone here a walking travel brochure?"

Jessie nearly gasped as the words slipped out of her mouth. She knew she never would have said it if she hadn't been feeling so pressured. She held her breath, afraid to look at anyone.

And then, suddenly, she heard a chuckle. It broke loose, and she realized Rashid Kamal had lost a tremendous battle to stifle his laughter.

"I am sorry, but she is so very right," he managed to choke out.

Julia frowned. Or rather, she tried to, but Jessie saw the corners of her mouth twitching. And then she, too, was laughing out loud, a lovely, silvery sound.

"I'm afraid it's true," she said. "We do all sound like that. To us, there is no better place in the world than Montebello."

"You have my sympathies, my dear," Rashid said to Jessie, "if you have been subjected to the constant chorus of the glories of this island." He gave his wife a quick sideways glance before he added with a grin, "You will have to come to Tamir, where you will truly find the best place in the world."

Julia laughed again. "Even I must admit it is not the wretched place I was always told it was."

Only then did Jessie risk a look at Lucas. He wasn't laughing. Julia seemed to notice his lack of amusement at the same moment, and proceeded to take some sisterly license with him.

"And what has you so glum, brother mine? Are you feeling guilty because you've been barraging poor Jessie with your sales pitch?"

To Jessie's amazement a hint of color tinged Lucas's cheeks. "I haven't been barraging her."

"Oh?" Julia looked at Jessie, her eyes twinkling, telling her she had an ally.

"Oh?" echoed Rashid, and when she glanced at the tall, exotic-looking man she saw a grin that invited her to join in the fun.

She turned to Lucas and said, "Oh?"

Both Julia and Rashid burst into open laughter again, and this time, after a moment, Lucas chuckled along with them, albeit ruefully.

"All right, all right," he said. "Maybe I've been doing a small sales pitch."

"I don't want to see your big sales pitch, then," Jessie said, relieved that he wasn't angry, and more relieved that she hadn't completely humiliated herself with her unthinking outburst.

"Good evening."

The strong male voice came from behind them, and Jessie turned quickly, just in time to see the king and queen enter. She let out a sigh of relief to see they were also dressed simply, although nothing could rob them of their glamorous impact. Even the simple clothes they wore looked elegant, with Gwendolyn's blond, English rose beauty and Marcus's silver-haired, dark-eyed, aristocratic good looks.

The pair greeted Julia and Rashid first, and if there was any reserve on their part toward their former enemy and now son-in-law, it certainly didn't show. Jessie supposed the fact that the ancient feud had been discovered to have been founded on a false assumption had gone a long way toward resolving the situation.

"You've met Jessie, I see," Gwendolyn said. "We've been delighted to have her here."

"I can see why," Julia said, and Jessie felt somehow

flattered. "I'm hoping she'll let me sneak upstairs and take a peek at my nephew after dinner," Julia added.

"Of course," Jessie said, glad to be able to repay Lucas's sister for her support after her faux pas.

As nerve-racking dinners went, this one wasn't as bad as she'd feared. Gwendolyn was clearly a practiced hostess, and had also taught her daughter well. They both made sure Jessie was included in the lively talk, and whenever anything was discussed that she wouldn't be familiar with, they made certain someone explained.

Jessie had just begun to finally relax when the conversation turned on her, and again she felt as if it were her own fault, although she hadn't meant to open the subject that soon yawned before her.

"You're so like your mother," she told Julia. "Not so much in looks, since she's blond and you're dark, but in your grace, and movements. Even your smile."

"Since my mother is still considered the most beautiful woman in all of Montebello, I'll take that as a compliment," Julia said.

"Ah, but you forget the way in which she is most like her mother," Rashid said.

"What's that?" Jessie asked.

"She made her husband propose five times before accepting him."

Jessie blinked. "You, too?"

Julia laughed, as she did so readily. "Yes, I did."

"So you see, Jessie," King Marcus said with a devilish grin that gave her a glimpse of the dashing young prince he'd been when he'd been in pursuit of a spirited and smart young Englishwoman, "you shall fit right in. You've already shown you have the backbone required to be a Sebastiani, to keep this one—" he gestured at his son "—dancing on a string."

Jessie blushed furiously. "I'm not— He isn't— That is not my intent," she finally got out.

"Oh?" Lucas said, in an exact echo of her tone earlier, when she'd joined Julia and Rashid in their teasing.

Jessie knew from that tone he was teasing, but for her this was no matter for lightness. "No! My concerns are for my son," she said adamantly, finding that when Luke was the subject, she was no longer intimidated by anyone. "And I have every right to them," she added with a determination she felt down to her very bones.

"Well spoken, dear," Queen Gwendolyn said approvingly, surprising her.

"Don't mind the Sebastiani men," Julia said lightly. "They tend toward blind stubbornness, you know."

"But our women forgive us," the king said, looking at his eldest daughter. "And for that," he added softly, "we are most fortunate."

Something passed between father and daughter, and Jessie had the oddest sense it was both an old pain and a new peace. She glanced at Lucas for an instant, but if he'd caught the exchange and understood it, it didn't show in his rather mutinous expression.

"And don't you dare say you're not stubborn, Lucas," Julia said, "because your expression alone will make a liar out of you."

"Indeed," the queen agreed mildly, but with a smile that made it clear she looked upon the foibles of her men with a certain fondness.

Lucas grimaced, but in the face of the united front of mother and sister, he wisely said nothing.

The rest of the meal and the talk passed comfortably enough, but when Julia suggested Jessie take her upstairs for a look at baby Luke, she acceded gratefully. And when she was out of the room, she felt a knot of tension inside her ease slightly. Something must have shown in her face, because Julia put a gentle hand on her arm as they started up the stairs.

"I know it's hard, Jessie. It's hard for me sometimes, and I was born to it." She smiled. "And my parents are quite something, aren't they? They were just my parents tonight, but when they're in regal mode, they even intimidate me."

Just that quickly the rest of that tension let go, and Jessie let out a long breath of relief. "They intimidate me all the time."

"They shouldn't, really. They like you, I could tell. Especially the way you stand up for your son. And speaking of that cutie...."

"He's in my room, with Eliya," she said.

Julia didn't seem to find it odd that the baby was in a guest suite rather than in the well-equipped nursery the palace had. And if the knowledge that she and Lucas were not sharing his luxurious apartments surprised her or even registered, that didn't show, either. Julia simply turned left at the top of the stairs, toward the guest wing.

"I'm sure it's better that you keep him close to you, especially just now. It must be very hard to let him out of your sight."

"Very," Jessie said, thankful she understood.

"I know how hard it is to leave my boy for even this evening," Julia said. "I can't imagine how I'd feel if he'd been taken from me for so long."

Jessie's throat tightened at the woman's graciousness, kindness and understanding. She didn't know how to thank her, couldn't think of any words, didn't know how you thanked a princess anyway. And then, almost unbidden, the right words came to her. Putting herself in Julia's place, in the place of any young mother, they came to her.

"Your son must be beautiful. I would love to see him sometime."

Julia's smile lit up her face, and Jessie knew she'd said the right thing.

"Oh, yes, you must see him. He's the most beautiful child. I will bring him the next time we come. Or better yet, you must come to Tamir, as Rashid suggested." Her smile became mischievous. "It is not as nice as Montebello, of course, but it has its good points. And if you've never been to a place like it, it's quite fascinatingly exotic."

"I'd like that," Jessie said, and found somewhat to her amazement, that she meant it.

"We'll arrange it, then. Soon," Julia added as they stepped into Jessie's room.

Eliya rose as they entered, smiled at Jessie, but bowed respectfully to Julia. "Your Highness," she said.

Jessie wondered if whoever did marry Lucas would get the same treatment. The thought of him marrying some other, faceless woman in the future caused her a pang, which she banished by thinking decisively that if she was good enough to get bowed to after a marriage, she should have been good enough before.

"Good evening, Eliya," Julia answered the nurse. "How are you?"

"I'm well, thank you. It is very nice to have a little one to look after again."

Julia smiled. "I still wish I'd been able to convince you to come to Tamir and take care of Omar, but now I am glad you refused, so you were here for Luke."

Refused? Jessie wondered. Was it possible for a mere commoner to refuse a request from the royal family? Apparently so, since here Eliya was.

The woman smiled and at the princess's nod, made a discreet exit. Julia walked to the crib, and immediately exclaimed, "Oh, he's as adorable as I remembered."

Immediately pleased, Jessie smiled as the other woman

cooed over her son. And gave a quick nod of permission when Julia asked if she could hold him.

"My, he's grown so, and it's only been a few weeks since I've seen him."

"Has he?" Jessie said, feeling rather silly. "He still seems so tiny to me."

"I'll bet he didn't when he was born," Julia said jokingly.

"No, he didn't," Jessie agreed quietly. She would never forget the agony of those hours, when she'd fought to bring her son into the world with no one but her mentally unstable kidnapper to help her.

"Oh, no," Julia exclaimed. "Oh, Jessie, I am so sorry, that was unforgivably thoughtless of me, after what you went through when Luke was born."

"It's all right."

"No, it's not. I just didn't think."

Jessie managed a smile. "Neither did I, before I accused you all of being travel agents in disguise."

For a moment Julia just looked at her. And then, the warmest smile Jessie had ever seen curved the woman's lips. "You know, I was determined to like you for Lucas's sake, and for Luke's. But now I see I don't need to worry at all, I simply like you. And I hope we'll be friends."

Never had she been so sweetly complimented by an offer of friendship. Nor had she ever wanted so much to accept. She didn't know how to tell this charming, generous woman that she wouldn't be staying.

"May I ask you something?" she said instead.

"Of course."

"Something personal."

"Oh, even better," Julia said with a grin. She put Luke carefully back in the crib, plopped down on the bed and patted a spot beside her. "Girl talk. With Christina off in

America and Anna off who knows where with Tyler, I've missed it. Come, what do you want to know?''

She was so warm and welcoming Jessie couldn't resist the invitation. She sat down and curled her legs up under her. She drew in a breath to steady herself before finally asking what she knew had to be a very personal question.

"Did you ever regret being…who you are? With your place in life determined probably even before you were born?''

Julia got very quiet. "You don't start with the easy ones, do you?''

Jessie lowered her gaze. "I started with what matters most to me just now.''

"I see," Julia said.

And Jessie thought that perhaps she did. And she appreciated the fact that Julia didn't give her some quick, glib answer, but instead thought for a few moments before speaking.

"I can't deny," she said finally, "that there were times when I yearned for what I used to think of as a normal life. Times when I envied Christina for her independence and her life in America, free of the fuss and feathers of our lives here. But at the same time there was a sort of comfort in this life, in knowing no matter what, I would always have a place to be, a role to fill.''

Jessie had never thought of it in quite that way. But now that Julia had said it, she could see where it made sense. It didn't change her mind, but she understood.

"Is that what your concern is, about Luke?'' Julia asked softly, glancing at the baby in his crib.

"Yes.'' She met Julia's gaze levelly. "My country was founded on the idea that anyone can become anything they want. Any kid can become president, or a doctor, or a mechanic, if that's where his talents lie.''

"It is the same here," Julia said.

"Unless your last name happens to be Sebastiani," Jessie retorted.

"Even if it is. My sister Christina is a brilliant scientist. Anna does as she pleases. And to a certain extent, so do I."

"So it's only Lucas—and Luke—who are...." She stopped herself when she realized she'd been about to say "doomed." No matter how understanding Julia was, Jessie doubted she was *that* understanding.

Julia gave her a long, intent look, as if she'd heard what she hadn't really said. "Their destiny is set more than ours, yes."

"And that is what I can't do to him. I can't give my son to a life where he has no choice."

Julia frowned. "But he will have many choices. And the freedom to do whatever he wishes."

"Except choose his own career."

"But he will be able to, for a good long time. Unless, God forbid, something else happens to Lucas, it will be many years before he is called upon to wear the crown."

Jessie hadn't really thought of that, either. But before she could ponder it, Julia was speaking again.

"But really, Jessie, does anything else really matter besides the fact that you love Lucas, and he loves you?"

Jessie laughed, a sad, almost bitter sound. "But he doesn't. Joe loved me. Lucas doesn't."

"Joe?" Julia asked. "Wait, that was the name he went by, after he was injured, wasn't it, when he didn't know who he really was?"

"Yes. It was Joe I fell in love with, and who fell in love with me. Lucas just needs the mother of his son."

Julia stared at her. "What?"

"It's a tidy package, isn't it?"

"But...he has proposed to you, has he not?"

"If you want to call it that. He outlined my duties in

detail, and the advantages as he saw them, and then offered me the position.''

Julia grimaced. "Men. They can be such fools. Believe me, I understand what you are saying."

Something in the other woman's expression caught Jessie's attention. "You do understand, don't you?" she asked quietly.

"Yes. Rashid was much like Lucas, although there was a time when such a comparison would have infuriated them both. But he had to be shown the error of his ways, before I finally said yes to him."

"Lucas hasn't made an error, really. It's not his fault he's not Joe anymore."

Julia eyed Jessie for a moment before asking, "And you do not love him, now that he is no longer this…Joe?"

Jessie wished she could say yes and mean it. It would make things easier when she had to go. But she was very much afraid she did still love him, as Lucas. Still, she wondered if she would spend most of the time looking for traces of Joe in the man who would be king.

"I don't know," she said softly.

Chapter 15

Jessie headed down the stairs, wondering if she'd ever really learn her way around this place. And then she stopped dead mid-staircase, in shock that she'd even in passing thought she would have any need to learn this palace. She would not, of course. This was merely a strange interlude, a brief pause in her life.

Even as she thought the words she knew they weren't true. Knew this was no mere pause. Her life had changed forever, because of the baby she'd just finished bathing. He had brought such joy to her, but he'd also brought some incredible complications with him. But it was hardly his fault; he hadn't chosen his parents.

She'd had to change her clothes when she'd finished his bath, since Luke had enjoyed the small tub Eliya had provided so much that he'd splashed as much water on her as he had on himself. Just seeing the simple, honest cheerfulness of the child had done much to ease her mind, but now all the troubles she'd pushed aside had come rushing back as she admitted to herself, standing there on the grand staircase of a place she could never have imagined herself even visiting, that nothing had been resolved.

Lucas had been very careful about not pressuring her. But neither had he given any indication he'd changed his mind at all, about anything. In fact, she'd come to realize that he was right, you'd have to be born and groomed to this life, with all its ins and outs and protocol. She wondered if he expected Montebello and its beauty to cast a spell on her, to make her forget all her reservations and hand her son over to this life without a second thought.

She could almost see why. It was a beautiful place, and she found she loved being able to look at the sea from almost any vantage point, anytime she wished. She also found the weather pleasantly different, always warm, and she'd read in a book conveniently left on her nightstand that the winter low temperatures here were higher than the average highs she was used to in Colorado.

She'd been told she could take Ghost out any time she wished, and once she had learned her way around she had ridden whenever she could escape. It was the only thing that kept her sane, other than Luke. She missed her mountains. What passed for mountains here didn't hold a candle to her Rockies. Of course, she admitted, few mountains did. But she also missed that brisk hint of winter in the air, and the wonderful contradiction of a sunny fall day where she could stand still and feel the warmth of the sun and the chill of the breeze on her face at the same time. It was one of her favorite things about her home.

And Colorado was her home, in a way this place could never be.

She shook herself out of her reverie, wondering just how long she'd been on this stairway, and grateful no one had happened along to see her standing and staring into space. And she'd been here long enough now to realize how lucky she'd been; there were always people around the palace. There never seemed to be a quiet moment, or a spot that stayed quiet for long, and she knew that would drive her crazy after a while.

She could barely remember all the people she'd met— Eliya, the Sabinas, Josie and Rudy, who had been in King Marcus's service for decades stuck in her mind. As did Nathan Winters, the gardener, remembered as much for his obvious love and knowledge of the plants and flowers he tended as for the unexpected story of his daughter Serena and her marriage to the queen's nephew.

The Sebastianis were not, she had to admit as she finally continued down the stairs, an exclusionary bunch. Their family members married commoners without concern, it seemed. Which made the idea of royal blood a little more confusing. Except that none of the others were in the direct line of inheritance for the throne. And she couldn't help wondering how those commoners felt, once they were face-to-face with the reality they now had to live with.

The massive front doors began to swing open just as she reached the bottom of the stairs, and she stopped abruptly for a second time, this time because she heard voices. Male voices, several of them. And lots of hearty laughter. She hadn't heard about any visitors, but also didn't want to stick around to see who they were. Or have them see her.

She dodged to her left, into the gold room she vaguely remembered, ready to run before she intruded on some high-level private meeting. This place, she reminded herself, was also where a lot of government business was done. And the last thing she wanted was to be the focus of a bunch of male eyes as she was introduced as…as what? Lucas's one-time lover? The mother of Lucas's son? Broodmare for the heir?

The drawing room was fortunately empty, and she drew a breath of relief. She could cut through the banquet room, she supposed, trying hard to remember the layout of this part of the palace. Then go through the—

She stopped for a third time, this time because the voice she heard next from the entry foyer next was unmistakably Lucas's.

"—rest assured. Montebello is as solid as ever. My father is, as you have seen, in excellent health, I have suffered no ill effects from my little adventure, and the succession to the Montebellan throne is assured through yet another generation with the birth of my son."

"Our investors will be glad to hear that," another voice said, but Jessie barely heard a word.

…my little adventure.

Was that what it had been to him? A "little adventure" that was over and done with, and now only something to be chuckled about with business acquaintances?

The rest of what he'd said rang in her head like some bell tolling for a funeral. *…the succession to the Montebellan throne is assured through yet another generation with the birth of my son.*

As if her concerns were meaningless and already set aside by royal decree. As if it were all settled, and it was a given she would quietly and docilely hand her helpless baby over to the Sebastianis to raise in the manner they saw fit. While she had no doubt that he would be well taken care of, and in fact smothered in attention and caring, she also knew she could not take away her son's choices before he even knew they existed. She simply couldn't.

Nor could she stay here, knowing so little was thought of her rights when it came to Luke.

A shiver went through her. What *were* her rights, in Montebello?

She had to lean against the nearest wall to stay on her feet. What if this was one of those utterly patriarchal places where the father had all rights, the mother none? Or where she had no rights at all, simply because she was a woman? What if the Sebastianis were not exceptions to a harsher rule over women? Considering what part of the world they were in, she realized belatedly, she should have thought of that before.

She had to find out. But she didn't want to betray her hand, in case her worst fears proved true. The library, she thought. Surely there would be information there. Now if only she could manage to find it....

It was off the grand ballroom, she remembered that much. But the only route she remembered, that she was sure would get her there, was through the foyer. So she crept closer to the doorway and listened. The voices had faded, and continued to fade as she stood there. Wherever they were going, it was away from her, and toward the back of the palace. She waited until she'd heard nothing for several minutes, then risked a peek to make sure the coast was clear. Then she darted for the doors to the grand ballroom.

Thankfully, she found it was empty—amazingly, she thought, since she guessed maintaining it was a constant chore. She turned right and found the library doors standing open. She stepped inside, wondering if she dared close them to hide her presence here.

She had to, she decided. She couldn't risk being caught here reading about women's rights in Montebello, they would quickly guess she was getting ready to fight them. And who knew what they might do then—the Sebastianis were used to winning, she was certain.

"May I be of assistance?"

Jessie yelped and whirled. She'd been so focused on not being seen from outside it hadn't occurred to her that someone might already be inside the library. But here she was, face-to-face with an older gentleman—it was the only word that truly fit—looking at her imperturbably from behind wire-rimmed glasses.

"I'm Arthur," he said by way of introduction. "I'm the palace archivist."

"Oh." Still flustered, she decided she should introduce herself. "I'm Jessie Chambers."

"I know, miss. Welcome to the palace library and the Montebello archives."

She wasn't sure she wanted to know how he knew who she was. And was sure she didn't want to know who he'd been told she was. "Thank you," she said hastily.

"Is there something I could help you find?"

She thought quickly. "There must be a section on Montebello. You know, history, laws, geography, that kind of thing?" She hoped by dropping the one thing she really wanted into the middle he wouldn't fixate on it.

"Most certainly." He said it calmly, but there was a spark of appreciation in his eyes, and she wondered what kind of thing he was usually asked for. "Right over here, if you will please come with me?"

She followed him over to a rather alarmingly large corner of the room. The shelves were clearly labeled, however, so she supposed she would be able to find what she needed, given enough time.

Not, however, if he was hanging over her shoulder, making her nervous. "I think I'll just browse, if that's all right," she said.

"Of course, miss. Make yourself at home." He gestured toward the back of the large room. "I'll continue with my cataloging, so if you need anything just call."

She would have preferred to have been left alone, but realized it would hardly be productive to draw his attention by asking him to leave when he obviously had work to do. So instead she picked out a naturalist's book on the plant and animal life of the island, another on the history of the royal family, and after some searching, pulled out a very dry-looking book on civil law and slid it in between them.

She carried the books over to a large leather wing chair that was placed, conveniently, with its back to where the man named Arthur was working. She glanced through the naturalist's book first, spotting first the familiar eucalyptus and cedar trees, then the less familiar jacaranda and arbutus. When she was fairly certain Arthur was paying no attention to her, she slid the civil law book out and opened it.

She knew after scanning twenty pages of dense, small print that it was going to be difficult to get what she needed. She didn't have the background—or right now the time—to translate all this legalese into plain language.

What I need is some scandal rag or something, the kind that documents celebrity divorces and custody battles, she thought. And had to stifle an ironic, miserable laugh that she would ever be personally involved in anything like that, the kind of thing she shook her head over when in line at Shady Rock's single grocery store.

She went back to the book, but without much hope. She didn't find anything of help, and shut it with a sigh. She leaned back in the chair, wishing now she had never come to Montebello, but knowing she couldn't get away. She knew her face had already been splashed across the pages of the *Montebello Messenger* newspaper, a couple of its less-respected competitors, and more than one magazine. There was no way she could get quietly out of the country, even if she managed to get Luke away from the palace.

She heard a sound from the back of the room, and nearly jumped. And then the absurdity of it hit her, that she, Jessie Chambers, was sitting here thinking about sneaking out of a foreign country and smuggling her baby out with her. How on earth had her life gotten so out of control?

She got up, put the books back, and walked out thinking that her life had careened out of control the day Joe had ridden into it.

Lucas rubbed wearily at his neck, glad to see the last of that bunch. He'd once made the mistake of laughing at his father's lengthy preparations for his annual meetings with the international investors who poured a lot of money into the Montebellan economy. His father had promptly turned them over to him, saying it was time the heir to the throne learned what it took to keep his country among the wealthiest and most successful in the world.

What it took besides hours of reading and looking at spreadsheets and company reports, he'd discovered, was sweet talk, kowtowing, promises of endless stability and a lot of wining and dining. Ordinarily it was merely an annoyance, something he had to get through, hopefully without getting too irritated at the maneuvering and attempts at manipulation for better treatment or trade agreements.

But now, with Jessie and Luke here in the palace, every long, dreary minute was agony. However, it was his responsibility, and he'd learned a lot about responsibility in the last year or so.

"Problem, son?"

He turned to find his father grinning at him. "No more than you ever had with that group," he said. Then, wryly, he added, "But I wouldn't say no to your favorite way to unwind after these things."

King Marcus Sebastiani chuckled. "I'll pour," he said,

and led the way to the small smoking room and bar off the gold drawing room.

A few minutes later, with a small glass of his father's best cognac in his hand, Lucas leaned against the polished cherrywood bar that had been brought here from London back when Montebello had been a British colony.

"I'm sure the meeting went well," his father said.

Lucas opened his mouth to give a full report, but his father didn't give him the chance. To his surprise, Marcus interrupted him, to speak not about the meetings, but about something far more personal.

"Tell me how everything between you and Jessie is progressing."

Startled, Lucas set his glass down on the bar untouched. "What?"

"Don't look so surprised. I do have a vested interest in the mother of my grandson the future king, don't I?" his father said, almost testily.

"Yes, sir," Lucas said very politely, subtly acknowledging his father's tone.

Marcus muttered something under his breath. "Gwen told me to stay out of it."

"My mother is very wise."

"But you're making a hash of it, boy!"

Lucas blinked. "This from the man who was turned down how many times?"

The king of Montebello actually blushed. "That was different."

"Because there wasn't a baby involved?"

"Partly. But also because she was English. It makes a difference, you know, if you've grown up in a monarchy. You're accustomed to it. Americans may understand, but they never quite accept. It's not their way of life."

"I know." Lucas grimaced. "Ironically, it's one of the things I admire about them, this idea that anybody can become anything, and no one has to let anyone or anything else choose for them."

Lucas saw his father's gaze sharpen. "As you had to?"

"I accept things as they are." He remembered Jessie's question, and added, "If I'd had a burning need or desire to become a doctor, an engineer, or something else like that, I might have felt differently. But I didn't. I want to be right where I am."

"Some would say you've been convinced of that by a lifetime of indoctrination," the king said frankly. Lucas knew he'd heard that argument before.

Lucas shrugged. "It hardly matters now. Let's not dwell on it."

"No," his father agreed. "Let's dwell on what you're going to do about your current situation."

"Then I'm going to need that drink," Lucas said grimly, reaching for the glass.

Jessie was surprised when Rudy brought her the small parcel. She thanked the solemn butler, closed the door of her room, and sat on the bench at the foot of the huge four-poster. There was a small vellum card attached to the gaily wrapped package, and she opened it expecting it to be from Lucas, another salvo in his campaign to convince her Montebello was paradise on earth.

It was from Julia.

A little something for the little prince, the card said in a lovely script, and was signed simply "Julia" in a bold yet feminine hand.

Despite the fact that it still rattled her to think of her tiny son as a prince, she was delighted that Julia had thought to send a gift. Her first baby gift, she thought as she carefully removed the thick, expensive-looking wrapping paper, trying not to dwell on what she'd missed.

The small rattle gleamed in the sunlight that shone

through the window. It was obviously not merely silver plate, she could tell that with a look. The handle was solid and curved to perfectly fit a tiny hand. The head was engraved rather ornately, in a pattern that was vaguely familiar, and after a moment she recognized the Sebastiani family crest.

Her delight faded. She stared down at the etched crest, seeing in the lovely lines and the strong, solid ''S'' nothing less than a claim made tangible. The Montebello royal family's determination to have her son was suddenly solid and heavy in her hand.

She felt an odd sense of betrayal. Julia had seemed so nice, so understanding. But it was hard to doubt or deny the significance of this particular gift. And now that she'd seen the gift, that simple, sweet-seeming line written on the card seemed ominous.

A little something for the little prince. The prince who had no choice about being a prince.

She should have realized. No Sebastiani would understand why everyone didn't think Montebello was the best place in the world. Or that being prince, and someday king, might not be everyone's dream job.

And certainly not a job for someone who didn't want it! she thought.

But Julia wouldn't understand that. She was a Montebellan, a princess, and a Sebastiani.

Jessie sighed. She'd dared to hope she might have found a friend here, another new mother who could understand her reservations, her resolve not to take away all her son's choices for his future. She'd looked forward to talking to her again, perhaps even asking her for help.

She sat staring at the gift a while longer before it occurred to her. Maybe she wouldn't have to ask Julia for help. She'd already been invited to Tamir, hadn't she? And it wouldn't surprise anyone if she wanted to take

Luke with her, would it? She'd have to find a time when she could be sure Lucas couldn't accompany her, as she was sure he'd want to do, but surely she could do that?

And maybe, just maybe, she wouldn't be recognized in Tamir. They couldn't be as enamored of the Sebastiani clan as the local press was, could they? Surely her picture wouldn't have appeared on every magazine cover and in every newspaper over there. She could get on a plane and skedaddle for Colorado.

Of course, Lucas could, and no doubt would, come after her with all the force of the Sebastianis behind him. But at least in America she could fight him. She couldn't swear his position wouldn't matter in any court battle, but it would matter less at home than here, that she was sure of.

She could do it. She knew she could. She'd find a way.

As soon as she finished crying her eyes out over being put in the horrible position of having to run from a man she had once loved.

And if she dared admit it, loved still.

Chapter 16

Lucas let out an inward sigh of relief. Something had gotten through to Jessie, because she had relaxed, had once more become the woman he remembered from the ranch. He found it much easier to be with her now, without the strain underlying every word or action. Last night she'd seemed almost giddy at dinner, laughing at his father's awful puns, even the worst, something about good gnus and bad gnus.

His parents had noticed the change, as well, and they'd both given him encouraging nods and smiles. His father had even whispered, on his way out of the room, "Whatever you're doing, keep doing it."

The problem was, he hadn't done anything any differently than he had since they'd arrived here. He'd tried to give her space and time, while at the same time showing her how good life could be here. It hadn't been working at all, at least that he could tell.

So he couldn't explain the sudden change. But that

didn't stop him from feeling good about it. He'd walked her upstairs after dinner last night, and when they'd stopped outside her door, she'd turned to face him. And for a moment he could have sworn she was looking at him with longing, the same longing he felt every day for her.

The same longing he'd seen in her eyes on the ranch when he'd been just a guy called Joe.

It had taken every bit of restraint he had in him to keep from pressing his luck. He'd been aching for her for so long now that it was about to drive him mad. When she unexpectedly kissed him, quick but no less hot and sweet for it, he nearly lost it. But then she was gone, darting into her room and closing the door, leaving him with a disturbing image of that last second before she'd turned away seared into his mind—a woman with utter despair in her eyes.

By morning, he convinced himself he'd imagined that look. He'd wanted to take her to the beach today, now that he'd finished with the last of the financial meetings, but as she'd told him last night, there wasn't much call for a bathing suit on the ranch. So he decided to send her off to his sisters' favorite boutique with instructions to pick out whatever she wanted.

As insurance, he enlisted the help of his sister Julia, who had taken quite a shine to Jessie, to go with her and make sure she didn't run the moment she got inside the exclusive boutique. To his surprise Jessie had agreed easily. She wasn't a shopper, she told him, but then there weren't shops like these in Shady Rock.

Julia had arrived via her husband's helicopter just before noon, proving yet again that Rashid was true to his word; his wife could visit home any time she wished. She hadn't told him that this was a shopping expedition, Julia said with a laugh, or perhaps he wouldn't have been quite so accommodating.

Of course, Lucas knew perfectly well Jessie would gasp at the prices, so he also called ahead to warn the shop's owner, who took great pride in her service to the royal family, to make sure Jessie never saw the cost. Between the eager Ms. Francois and Julia, he was sure the trip would be a success.

When they came back hours later, laden with bags, he was pleased, until he got a look at Jessie. Julia was laughing, but Jessie was looking rather wan, and almost shell-shocked. Julia spotted him and sent Jessie upstairs with instructions to put on the "purple thing" and come back down.

Once Jessie was gone, Julia turned to him. "I tell you, that is the most independent, stubborn woman I've ever met, and given my family that's saying something."

Lucas frowned. "Problem?"

"She was more worried about whether everything could be returned if she changed her mind than anything else."

Lucas smiled. That was his Jessie, all right.

Julia grinned. "I really like her."

"So do I," Lucas said softly.

"Then, big brother, you'd better tell her."

He blinked. "What?"

"She knows 'Joe' loved her. She has no idea about you."

"That's ridiculous. Of course she knows."

Julia sighed. "You know, I thought for a while it was simply Rashid who was so obtuse. Now I know it's men in general."

"You still married him," Lucas pointed out.

"Because he learned," she told him. "And if you don't, you're going to regret it."

"Learned what?"

"To take nothing for granted," Julia retorted, clearly impatient with his ignorance. "Jessie is coming to Tamir for the day tomorrow. With Luke. And you're not invited."

Lucas blinked. "Oh?"

"Yes. It's a girl's day. Rashid is flying to Cyprus for a meeting."

"Oh. Then why is Luke going?"

She gave him a look that, had she not had the same parents, would have called his species into question. He gave up. "All right, all right. Never let it be said I intruded on a sacred female ritual."

"Maybe you're trainable after all," Julia said with exaggerated reluctance.

Lucas grinned at her. When he'd first come home, everyone, including his family, had treated him with such care that it had almost driven him crazy. He'd been delighted the first time his irrepressible sisters began to tease him again, knowing it was the first step back to normalcy.

"Now, when Jessie comes down, be suitably impressed, if you know what's good for you."

"If I'm not, will she skewer me, or you?"

"She'll skewer. I'll hold her purse. Now watch for her, like a proper suitor."

Lucas laughed, but he turned to face the stairway. He did love this sister of his. She'd grown even more confident since she'd married Rashid, proof enough to him that it was a good match. He hoped he would see the same kind of assurance in Jessie, once she was sure of herself and her place in his family. She would come to know that—

His thoughts stopped midstream. All thought stopped, because there was no room for anything but stunned response to the woman at the top of the stairs. She wore some floaty thing that looked for all the world like veils that could part at any moment and reveal the luscious body beneath. The color could be, as Julia had said, purple, although to him it looked like an opal he'd seen once, many colors at once that shifted with the light. Her long, blond hair was down, flowing with the same silken rhythm as the dress, then falling still as she paused above the first step. She had on a pair of strappy sandals that made her feet and ankles look impossibly delicate. He'd never seen her look like this. He'd never seen *any* woman look like this.

Lucas became abruptly aware his mouth was literally hanging open and he shut it with a snap. "Damn," he muttered under his breath.

"Well, now, I'd say that's suitably impressed," Julia said with a barely suppressed giggle. "I guess I'll put away the skewer now."

Slowly, Jessie started down the steps. She kept one hand on the polished mahogany banister, and her eyes downcast almost shyly.

As if any woman who looks like that could possibly be shy. That hair, that body, that dress....

They were a walking declaration, Lucas thought. He just wasn't sure if it was a declaration of intent, of interest or of war.

If it was war, he was already done for. Hit before the first rounds were fired. Casualty number one. And the idea of being a prisoner of war didn't bother him at all, now that he thought about it.

He watched in silent awe until she reached the bottom of the stairs. Julia said softly, "I'll see you tomorrow, Jessie." Jessie flicked a glance at Julia and nodded rather quickly. Julia nodded back and left them there. Alone.

"You look...incredible," Lucas said, barely able to get his voice above a stunned whisper.

"I clean up all right," Jessie said with a shrug, her eyes still lowered, as if she were avoiding his gaze.

"Much, much more than just all right."

Take nothing for granted, Julia had said. He didn't. How could anyone take a woman like this for granted? He reached out and took her hand.

"Let me take you to dinner. Right now, tonight. To the Glass Swan. It's the only place good enough for how you look tonight."

Finally she looked up at him. Maybe it was the unusual color of the dress, but her eyes seemed to shimmer with the same luminescence as the fabric.

"If you promise we won't talk about the future," she said, an odd quiver in her voice.

Right then he would have agreed to anything. "I promise. I'll go change. I won't be long. Don't go anywhere. Please."

She looked so nervous he was half afraid she'd bolt, so he rushed through a quick shower and shave, then dressed with slightly more care in the suit that always made the girls tease him mercilessly, saying he was their brother and not supposed to be so handsome. He chose a dark tie with a small fleur-de-lis pattern in a bluish shade that reminded him of the color of her dress. And realized as his fingers fumbled in knotting it that he was as nervous as she had looked.

This was ridiculous, he lectured the image reflected in the mirror. He was Prince Lucas Sebastiani, not some bashful young swain who'd never taken a beautiful woman out to dinner before.

But he'd never taken Jessie out to dinner before.

He'd never taken Jessie anywhere, he realized with a sudden little shock. As Joe, he hadn't been able to afford it, and there was no real place to go in tiny Shady Rock anyway. And since he'd come back, the only thing he'd done was take her back to the ranch, and then here.

Feeling more than a little remiss—this was the woman he was going to marry, after all, and he'd never even taken her on a date—he paused only to call for his car to be brought around, then rushed back downstairs. His heart sank when he found the foyer empty. He spun around, wondering if she'd just gone somewhere to sit and wait. He'd thought she'd relaxed, but—

He spotted her then, through the open doors that led to the grand ballroom. She was at one of the tall windows, silhouetted by the last rays of the sun. He was seized with a sudden desperation to make certain she stayed here, in his home, and wished he hadn't promised not to speak of their future tonight. He hadn't pressured her at all for a decision, hadn't wanted to press his luck with her, but sooner or later they were going to have to discuss it.

Just not tonight, he thought as he looked at the lovely picture she made standing there in that dress, her hair fired pure gold by the sun. He wouldn't risk ruining this night for anything.

Since this had been an impulse move, he hadn't had time to call ahead to the Glass Swan. But he would call on the way, and knew Louis Montague would rise to the occasion with his usual grace and skill.

Jessie paused at the bottom of the outside steps when she saw the racy blue Italian coupe parked there.

"Yours?" she asked, her voice so neutral he almost wished he had an SUV instead.

"For now," he said, thinking that the best answer he could give. It didn't seem the time to explain to her that he received a new model every year simply so the famous maker could tout that his vehicles were driven by the crown prince of Montebello.

He opened the passenger door for her, and she stepped

past him without further comment. The lustrous fabric of the dress slipped upward as she sat in the low-slung seat, revealing a tantalizing length of leg. He remembered those legs so well; remembered tracing their silken length, marveling at the taut strength there; remembered them in tight jeans as she worked around the ranch, the worn denim hugging her curves as he longed to do with his hands; remembered the feel of them holding him tight and close as she rode him to a completion he'd never known before.

He bit his lip in his effort to tamp down the fire that wanted to roar to life. He sedately shut her door and took his time walking around to the driver's side, since walking wasn't the most comfortable thing to do just now.

Jessie's eyes widened as they walked into the Glass Swan, although Lucas couldn't be sure if it was the rich, luxurious decor or the phalanx of people who greeted them at the door with everything short of a red carpet. As usual, the fuss drew eyes from around the restaurant, but they were quickly through the main dining room and into a smaller, more private area. They walked past a fireplace in one corner, there only for ambience not heat in this Mediterranean climate.

Louis outdid himself. Had he been choreographing the perfect evening, Lucas couldn't have planned it any better. They had a private, candlelit booth overlooking the yacht harbor. And when Louis, stroking his dark goatee, begged Lucas to turn the menu over to him, Lucas did so without a qualm, promising Jessie that the man was unparalleled in providing a meal that was nothing short of heavenly.

This time was no exception. From an appetizer of shrimp in a lemon garlic sauce through the luscious fresh red snapper cooked in paper to the decadent pear and caramel dessert, it was all perfect. And Louis's wife, Mariella, a petite, exotic brunette beauty, waited on them herself, as if they were guests in her home.

The close attention from the proprietors kept him from breaking his promise to Jessie and talking about their future, kept him from trying to make her see how good it could be, how they could make it all work if she just gave it a chance. The fact that he still had no answer for her main concern, that of Luke's future, he tried not to think about.

Somewhere between the appetizer and the main course, Jessie seemed to change. She became more animated, even laughed as the old Jessie used to, as if she'd decided to put their differences aside and enjoy this night. With that example before him, he gave up any thought of forcing the issue, and set himself to the same task, to simply enjoy this evening with her.

And enjoy they did. For now they were just Jessie and Joe, in a fairy-tale setting, savoring this time stolen out of a complicated and painful situation.

When dinner was finally done, and the last drop of wine drunk, they went for a walk along the water, in the light of a three-quarter moon. Jessie's mood held, and when she looked up at him and smiled, his heart seemed to take a little tumble in his chest. He took the chance of slipping his arm around her shoulders, and she didn't pull away.

"It's beautiful," she said softly as they paused at an overlook above the yacht harbor. "I can see why people just want to get on a boat and sail away."

"I've thought of it, more than once," he said wryly. Then, hesitantly. "Do you want to see the family boat?"

"Let me guess," she said. "It's that one?"

She pointed to the largest yacht in sight, anchored out in the turning basin.

"Actually, no. That one belongs to one of the businessmen who came here for our annual meetings." She gave him an odd look that he couldn't interpret, but when she said nothing, he pointed out the lovely but smaller boat at the end of the dock they were looking down on. "That's the *Sophia.* My grandfather had her built, and named her after his queen. Come, I'll show her to you."

He kept his hand on her elbow as they went down the gangway, which was a fairly steep angle at the moment. She managed it easily, however, as he expected she would.

The uniformed watchman aboard the *Sophia* hailed them, then stood aside with great ceremony when he recognized Lucas. He nodded politely to Jessie, and answered Lucas's quiet query with a "Everything is shipshape, Your Highness."

He hadn't been aboard in some time, since seeing his parents off on their anniversary cruise three years ago, in fact. But everything was warmly familiar, and his mother's gracious touch showed in the vessel's furnishings and the rich color scheme. They were of the highest quality, but chosen for practicality and function. It was comfortable and welcoming, indeed a home afloat. He knew that among royal yachts, it was much less ornate— he preferred to think of it as less ostentatious—than most, and he liked it that way.

"It's lovely," Jessie said as he gave her the tour. "Much...simpler than I expected."

"My mother says she has a palace aground, she doesn't need one afloat."

Jessie laughed. "Your mother is a very wise woman."

"Yes, she is."

When they left, the man in uniform stood at attention until they were down the steps and back on the dock. Again Lucas took Jessie's arm as they walked along the boat slip to the main dock. And then she stopped in her tracks. And he knew she'd seen.

She was staring at the sailboat in the next slip. Staring

at the stern, at the name newly painted on the transom above the three oblong portholes.

"*Colorado Dreaming?*" she read aloud. And then she looked at him.

"I renamed her the week I got back."

He didn't mention that the prior name had been a rather racy double entendre he'd chosen when his father had given him the boat when he'd graduated college.

"Why?"

"It fit my...state of mind, I guess." He hesitated, then decided to risk it. "Would you like to go aboard?"

She hesitated in turn. She looked at the stern, read the name again. "Yes," she said at last. "I would."

In a brief moment of panic he wondered what shape he'd last left the boat in. But he decided that with Jessie it didn't matter. She already knew most of his bad habits; as Joe, that was one of the few things he'd brought with him, it seemed.

He led her up the dock steps—several fewer than it took to board the *Sophia*—and once they were on deck pulled out his keys and unlocked the door to the cabin.

"The steps are steep," he said, "so let me go first." The heels on her sandals weren't particularly high, but he guessed she was more used to boots and he didn't want to take any chances.

He watched as Jessie looked around, wondering what she thought. Next to his parents' yacht, this boat was almost utilitarian, devoted much more to function than luxury. The blue and dark green upholstery was rich and inviting, but the teak and stainless steel of the rest, along with the bank of instruments at the navigation station, made it clear this was a boat made for serious sailing.

"My mother picked the colors, since she says I'm hopeless, but the rest is mine," he said.

She didn't speak, merely nodded as she walked slowly

around the main cabin. She looked at the large table with the thickly cushioned horseshoe-shaped banquette. She seemed to admire the compact organization of the galley with the small fridge and microwave, and she smiled when she saw the stove could pivot.

"To stay level at sea?" she guessed, and he nodded.

"Gimbaled, they call it."

She leaned forward to peer out an oblong porthole window. She touched here, ran a finger down a sleek surface there, and as Lucas watched her focus on the tactile, he became aware of a gradual tightening of his body.

Touch me like that, he wanted to say. He didn't.

She paused at the nav-station, looking curiously at all the instruments. "The radio I recognize, but what is all this?"

"Satellite navigation, autopilot, radar, a few other toys."

"And this?" she asked, gesturing toward the velvet-lined box that sat on the first shelf above the chart table.

"A sextant," he said. "The original navigation device. Comes in handy if you have an electronics problem or failure."

"This one looks old," she said.

"It is. It was my...let me see, my great-great-great-grandfather's. The kings of Montebello have always been seagoers, but he was truly a sailor. He thought nothing of sailing to Britain, on a boat much smaller than this one."

Jessie shook her head. "I'd need at least this much boat to brave that," she said frankly. "It's very different than the other, isn't it?"

"It's more a working boat than a home afloat, yes."

Again she shook her head. "I meant it feels different. The shape, and so much is below the deck."

He should have known she hadn't been commenting on the lack of luxury. "Yes, a sailboat is an entirely different feel than a powerboat. Since you have to compensate for the push of the wind above, most of her weight and hull are below.''

"That makes sense." She peeked into the small forward cabin, where there was a crew bunk and lockers for storage. She turned and came back then, to the narrow hallway that led to the stern of the boat. She looked at him questioningly, and he nodded.

"No point in my giving a tour, she's not that big."

The truth was, he was thinking he'd be better off if he kept his itchy hands anchored firmly on the table he was leaning against.

She looked into the first cabin on the left, the one he'd converted into a workshop of sorts, with a workbench, spare parts and tools. And then at the closet that held the small washer and dryer.

"All the comforts and necessities, on a small scale," she murmured, and he smiled. He had a sudden vision of taking off with her, sailing away for an endless string of warm, sunny days and hot nights. His hands gripped the table harder.

She went farther down the hall, glancing in the two staterooms with the small but functional head in between. And then she went to the master cabin, and he nearly held his breath, wondering what she would think.

She stepped through the doorway, paused, he saw her look around. And then she laughed.

"This is wonderful!" she said. "It's like a pirate ship!"

He let out a sigh of relief and walked toward her. The master cabin was his own personal conceit; he'd let his imagination run wild, and his imagination had indeed been in pirate mode. The bed, custom built for his height, ran sideways across the stern. It was atop a bank of shelves and cupboards so you had to climb up to get into it, but it was even with a row of portholes across the stern, enabling you to look out without moving.

With the bunk up against the stern, it left more room in the cabin itself, room enough for a big, rough-hewn desk, over which hung a brass lantern, just like he'd always imagined a pirate captain's cabin would look. Along the sides were hanging closets and more storage.

"The head is modern," he assured her, "even has a small tub. But in here I kind of went...." He shrugged, not sure what word applied.

"Whimsical?" she suggested, still smiling.

"Yeah," he agreed, "that's it."

"It's wonderful," she said. "Makes you want to take off and sail the seven seas."

"Yes, it does. Shall we?"

"What?"

"Sail the seven seas."

"Right now?" She let out a soft sigh. "It sounds lovely."

She turned then, to face him head-on. She studied him for a long silent moment, and he sensed there was something uppermost in her mind she was pondering whether to say or not.

"What, Jessie?"

"Sometimes," she whispered, "I wish we could go back. I miss Joe. His life was so much simpler, I...."

She stopped. And Lucas realized he'd gone so far in trying to convince her that he'd changed, that he wasn't that Playboy Prince who was fodder for the tabloids anymore, that he'd managed to convince her he wasn't the man she'd fallen in love with on her ranch, either.

"But since we can't do that, sailing the seven seas sounds wonderful."

She looked up at him with a world of longing in her eyes, and he lost his battle for self-control. He reached out and touched her hair, brushed her cheek with the backs of his fingers.

"Any self-respecting pirate would be a fool to let you out of this cabin without ravishing you first."

She took a deep, visible breath. She gazed up at him, and he had the crazed thought that she looked as if he were that pirate captain, and about to make her walk the plank.

"I don't think you're a fool," she said softly.

Lucas's heart slammed into overdrive. He stared at her, unable to believe the implication of what she'd said. There had been a sad sort of undertone to her voice, but he couldn't dwell on that, not if she was saying what he thought she was.

"Jessie," he said, and found he couldn't go on.

And then she reached for him. She did nothing more than lay her hand flat on his chest, her palm over his heart, but it was all he needed. All he could bear without pulling her fiercely into his arms.

He still half expected her to pull away when he kissed her, but she didn't. She opened for him, urged him on with teasing flicks of her tongue, and in that moment she was the old Jessie, the woman he'd held and loved in the night on a quiet ranch in Colorado. It was as if the time between had never happened, as if they were as close as they had been before he'd walked out on her.

The Playboy Prince would never have questioned her, would have assumed she had no reservations. But the new Lucas couldn't. He put his hands on her shoulders and broke the kiss, reluctantly, pulling back to look into her face.

"You mean this, Jessie? You want this? I don't want you to regret this tomorrow."

"I want you," she said, and he couldn't deny the truth

of her words, it was glowing hot and intense in her eyes. "And it won't matter tomorrow."

He shuddered under the impact of her words. "I love that dress," he said thickly, "but right now I'd love it more off of you."

She said nothing, simply turned her back to him and lifted her hair. With fingers that were none too steady he found the small tab of the zipper and lowered it. He wanted to go slowly, to savor every inch of lovely skin revealed, but he was still afraid she would change her mind. So instead he let the dress fall, and she stepped out of it.

She turned back, clad now only in a pair of lavender panties and a matching, lacy strapless bra that was somehow no more sexy than her plain cotton underwear had been; sexy, he finally realized, was in the wearer. He picked her up then, lifted her onto the high bunk, before she could change her mind.

He shed his clothes quickly, nearly groaning at the ache of his aroused body. He didn't bother with the steps and was up beside her in a rush.

"Jessie," he breathed, burying his hands in her hair and his face in the soft swell of flesh above the pale bra. "I want to go slow, but—"

"Don't. Don't go slow."

On the last word she reached up and unfastened the front clasp of the bra, and it fell away, freeing her breasts. His hands moved quickly, eagerly to cup them, and lift them to his mouth. He took first one nipple, then the other, and sucked them to pebble hardness, his own body tightening unbearably at her swift, moaning response.

Her eagerness fired him beyond restraint, and he felt as if he'd gone years instead of weeks without touching her like this. Every sign she gave him, every stroke of her hands across his skin, every tiny moan, every arching shift

of her body drove him to a madness he'd never known
with anyone but her.

He moved his hands downward until his fingers
snagged in the silk of her panties. She lifted her hips to
help him slide them off, and the thought of her moving
like that when he was buried inside her made him nearly
lose control right then. When he slid his hands up the
silken length of her legs she parted them for him. He
gently probed through the soft curls, gritting his teeth to
keep from driving himself into the depths of her when he
found her wet and ready. Clamping down on a new surge
of desperate need, he stroked further, until he found the
tiny knot of nerves that made her gasp.

"Don't go slow."

She said it again, breathlessly, and it shattered the last
bit of restraint he had. He levered himself over her, and
she reached up for him in the same moment. In a moment
he was sliding into her, losing himself in her tight, slick
heat. The old magic leapt to life, and he groaned low and
deep in his chest as his entire body cramped with the need
to move.

He drove deep, withdrew, and at her tiny moan of protest, drove forward again. She cried out, and he'd never
heard anything so sweet as her husky voice in that moment. He lowered his head to her breast once more, and
drew one taut nipple into his mouth and flicked it with
his tongue. She cried out again, and her body bowed beneath him, driving him so deep it took the breath out of
him.

And then she convulsed around him, clenching, squeezing, until he could wait no longer and with a final groan
of her name, he let go and flew.

Jessie crept silently back into her room. Eliya was du-
tifully sitting up, stitching as usual on what appeared to

be the same length of silk. She looked up as Jessie came in, and smiled. Jessie went immediately to the crib and looked down at her sleeping son.

"You look lovely," Eliya said.

"Thank you."

Jessie blushed, knowing exactly what she looked like; she'd seen herself in the mirror in the head aboard *Colorado Dreaming,* and known she had little hope of putting herself fully to rights again. Her hair was still in a tangle from Lucas's hands, her body still humming from his touch. She'd gone a little crazy, and Lucas had responded in kind, and it had been exactly what she'd wanted, a night to remember forever. She thought that it must be emblazoned on her face, that she'd spent the evening in a pirate's bed.

Her color deepened at the hot, erotic memories; she could feel the heat flooding her face. At the same time her heart ached inside her, because she knew what was coming. She knew that it was the last time. Because she knew that in the morning she and Luke would leave for Tamir.

And they wouldn't be coming back.

Chapter 17

Jessie hunched over her son as she sat in the back of the taxi, which was an almost luxurious sedan that spoke of Tamir's wealth and strong economy. She touched Luke's cheek, and when he reached up for her finger and clasped it, she smiled through the tears that suddenly welled up in her eyes.

Could she really handle this? She didn't know anything about being a mother. She'd read copiously after she'd discovered her pregnancy, but she had been missing Joe so much, had been feeling so betrayed by his middle-of-the-night desertion, that she wasn't sure how much she had absorbed.

And she had no one close to really turn to. Even if her sister hadn't turned on her, Ursula was hardly the type to give out motherly advice.

She had never realized before how isolated she had become on the ranch. Her nearest neighbors on all sides were elderly or crusty old bachelor men. Since her parents' deaths she'd been so consumed by keeping the ranch going she'd had little time left for maintaining friendships. She, Mrs. Winstead and the ranch hands, plus the wives of the two who were married, had formed a family of sorts, and she'd never really thought about missing the company of women her own age. She'd missed her mother terribly, of course, but that had been a different, separate ache.

It was Julia, she realized with a little shock. It was Julia with her gracious friendliness and easy charm who had reminded her how much she missed the company of women, especially women her own age. She felt a pang of sadness at the fact that the sense of connection with Julia that she'd felt so quickly would be severed before it ever had the chance to develop into something stronger.

Luke squirmed and made a tiny gurgling sound, then his little forehead scrunched up as if in pain. He let out a cry that startled her, then subsided into silence. Trepidation filled her as she looked at him, but he seemed to settle quietly. She checked his diaper, but it didn't need attention. Puzzled, she watched him carefully, but he seemed to have gone right back to sleep.

She sighed, wondering if she would ever learn enough to be comfortable about taking care of him, know when and when not to worry.

Mrs. Winstead could probably help, she thought. She knew a lot, even though she'd never had kids of her own. And Barney had a grandchild barely a year old, so he was even more used to babies. She'd get by, somehow.

She leaned back in the seat of the cab, letting her eyes drift closed. She'd slept little last night; even after she'd packed, she'd been unable to rest. Doubts had assailed her all night long; Lucas had been so sweet, so loving. As she had asked, he hadn't put any pressure at all on her about the future; he didn't bring it up at all. But neither had he spoken of love, so the sweetness of his caresses was lacking the one thing that might have changed her mind.

There were many reasons to accept his proposition, business-like though it was, and only two reasons not to. But those two reasons—her own need to be loved as Joe had loved her, and her son's precious right to choose his own path in life—outweighed all the reasons on the other side by a large margin. And those two reasons made her decision, if not easy, then at least clear-cut.

An image of Lucas from last night formed in her mind, of his eyes bright and fierce as he looked down at her, of the slight tremble in his hands as he touched her, of his husky cry of her name as he climaxed inside her. And suddenly she wasn't at all sure "clear-cut" was the right description.

When the taxi pulled up at the modern, mostly glass airport terminal, it took her several minutes to gather up her purse, the baby and the bag she'd packed for them both. Luke awoke, but made no fuss. Thankful that since the new trade agreement had been signed that Montebellan money was accepted here in Tamir, she got out the last she had for the driver. It constituted an outsize tip, but it was one more way to reinforce the finality of her decision. She knew it was merely symbolic, American dollars spent here just as well, but it was a gesture she needed to make.

Still, she hesitated before handing over the money and dismissing the man. Once she got on that plane, she had as much as declared her independence, and she could well bring down on her head all the might the wealth and power of the Sebastianis could buy.

"Here goes, little one," she whispered to Luke. He cooed back at her, which in her desperation she decided meant he was happy with her, even in the noise of a busy airport terminal. She steeled herself, handed the money to the driver, noted by his expression he was startled by the amount, picked up the bag and slung the strap over her shoulder.

Head up and jaw set, she strode into the terminal.

"She what?" Lucas asked incredulously, staring at the telephone as if it had somehow scrambled the words he was hearing into something impossible to comprehend.

"She was getting on a plane," his stubborn sister insisted. "She had a ticket to Rome, and a list of flights from there to the United States. She was going home, Lucas."

"There has to be a mistake."

"There's no mistake. We started to worry when we found she had slipped away from the palace. When we learned a taxi had been called from nearby for a fare to the airport, we called the company. The driver remembered her because she gave him a very large tip."

"Maybe it was just another blond woman."

"Give it up, Lucas. We have her back with us."

"What?"

"We called airport security, someone Rashid knows. He had already recognized Jessie in the terminal from photos he'd seen on Montebello when he'd been there with Rashid, and remembered which flight she'd checked in for because he thought it curious she would be leaving for America from here."

It was impossible. It made no sense at all. She couldn't have been leaving him, not after last night. They'd had the most passionate night of their lives, there was no way she could simply walk away. Could she?

"What has she told you?" he asked.

"Not much. She's not of a mind to talk at the moment, I'm afraid. She's not happy we stopped her."

"But we were...last night we...she couldn't have been leaving."

"She was," Julia said flatly. "And she was taking Luke with her."

Lucas swore, low and harsh.

"Indeed," his sister said. "So tell me, brother mine, what did you do to drive her away?"

"Me? Nothing! Last night, we worked it all out. I know we did. It was an incredible night, she was so—"

He stopped suddenly, realizing he'd been about to blurt out the details of the night he'd spent with Jessie to the girl who had once spied on his first date with a girl and then blabbed about it to anyone who would listen.

"Let me guess," Julia said dryly, "you had great sex and therefore you decided in a typically male fashion that all was resolved?"

"Well...yes," he said, feeling a bit foolish now that she put it in those terms.

"What is it with men? Rashid thought the same thing, that just because we had the hottest sex on the planet, that there were no obstacles to overcome."

Lucas grimaced. That was more about his sister's private life than he was comfortable knowing. "This is different. Jessie and I, we...she...."

His voice trailed off as he realized they had indeed done no more than have the hottest sex on the planet last night. They'd barely talked at all.

"She what, Lucas? Told you she'd decided to stay?"

"No."

"Then she told you that she no longer cared that her baby's future is cast in stone?"

"No."

Julia sighed. "When you said you loved her, did she say she no longer loved you?"

"Uh...no." His hesitation before he repeated the deadly word a third time betrayed him.

"Lord, Lucas, don't tell me you never told her. Not after I told you she didn't know."

"She didn't want any talk of the future!" he protested. "That was her condition for going out last night."

"And you decided that meant not saying you love her? Good heavens, Lucas, there's no time a woman doesn't want to hear that!"

"Well, how should I know that?" he demanded, feeling more than a little beleaguered. "I've never told a woman I love her before."

"Really? Never?" Julia sounded astonished, then curious. "Not even that little actress you were dating before you ran off to America?"

"No, I didn't, and I did not run off," Lucas said, wondering why it was that nobody could get under his skin like his sisters could. "And could we get back to the point?"

"What is your point?"

"Just let me talk to her."

"I don't think so. If you never told her that you—you Lucas, not the ranch hand she fell for—loved her, and still do, then you deserve what you got. No wonder she thinks you only want her because of Luke."

He blinked. "She what?"

"Lord, you don't even know that much?"

"How should I know that?"

"How can you not? You abandon her and only come back after you have Luke. Instead of proposing, you give her a job description. You never tell her you love her— what do you expect her to think?"

"But I don't understand," he said, knowing he was coming perilously close to whining. "Why would she leave without saying a word? After last night? It was so...extraordinary.''

"Perhaps it was goodbye," Julia suggested.

And suddenly a cascade of images flooded his mind—the look of longing in her eyes last night, the undertone of sadness in her voice.

...it won't matter tomorrow.

God. Could it be? Was that what she'd meant, that it wouldn't matter tomorrow, because she knew even last night that she was going to leave, that it would be their last night together?

It was true. He knew it suddenly, with a gut-knotting certainty. She'd been leaving him.

And she'd been taking his son with her.

What she hadn't counted on, Jessie thought grimly, was how much a blond woman with a baby would stand out in Tamir. Nor had she been aware that the Sebastiani royal family was big news here, as well, in part because of the long-standing enmity that was only recently resolved, and the marriage of Lucas's sister to their own crown prince.

Of course, her own overtipping of the taxi driver hadn't helped. She should have realized that would have made him remember her.

She sat in the back of Julia's limo, cuddling Luke, trying not to fume. Not that she could fault Julia's behavior. Ever since Julia had arrived at the airport to pick Jessie up after she'd been spotted and stopped, she'd been unfailingly sympathetic. In fact, she'd insisted that Jessie listen in on her side of the conversation as she called her "idiot brother," as she had labeled Lucas.

So now, at the cost of having the intimacies of her most private life revealed, she at least knew how she'd been discovered. It seemed the royal family of Tamir had tentacles as long as the Sebastianis did. And her mouth twisted as she realized the unpleasantness of the metaphor she'd unconsciously chosen, and how well it fit her current mood.

Julia replaced the car phone in its cradle in the back seat of the limo. Julia probably never thought twice about it, Jessie mused, whereas she marveled each time she climbed into one of the elaborate vehicles.

After a moment Julia looked at Jessie, shaking her head. "He's just so…male. He assumed because of last night, everything had been fixed between you."

Jessie's cheeks flamed as she recalled Julia's comment to her brother about "great sex." God, would the humiliation never end?

Julia patted her arm. "Don't be embarrassed, Jessie. We're practically related, after all."

The breezy assumption stiffened Jessie's spine. "No, we're not."

Julia studied her for a moment before looking at the baby and saying, "I meant, related through Luke. I am still his aunt, no matter what happens with you and Lucas. At least, I hope I am."

Feeling suddenly chagrined, Jessie apologized. "I'm sorry. Of course you are." Feeling the need for more of an explanation, she went on. "It's just that everyone seems to assume that it's a done deal."

"A…done deal?" Julia asked. "What a descriptive expression. So, what is it, Jessie, Lucas or the expectations of others that has you so determined you won't marry him?"

Jessie grimaced, not liking the sound of it when Julia said it. "My objections are real and valid," she insisted.

"If you mean Luke's future, in a way I can understand that, even if it is very American of you."

"I am American. And so is my son."

"But he is Montebellan, as well."

"And when he's old enough, he can decide for himself which heritage he prefers."

"What if he wants both?"

Jessie looked down at her tiny son, at his innocent, trusting face, and the thought of him ever being disappointed or denied something he badly wanted wrenched at her heart. "Then we'll have to find a way."

"Then why can't you find a way now?"

"Because," Jessie said flatly, "your brother doesn't have an ounce of compromise in him."

"It's not a Sebastiani trait, I'll admit."

"Nor a Chambers one," Jessie confessed.

"But my brother has never been in love before, either." Julia eyed Jessie narrowly. "He does love you, you know."

"So you said."

Julia grinned. "You stick with that, girl. Don't let him off the hook until he tells you himself, and to your satisfaction. He might as well learn now that the words are always necessary. Repeatedly."

Jessie felt herself tear up unexpectedly. "I wish that was all it would take."

"Rashid and I had over a century of feuding to overcome," Julia said. "When the love is true, barriers that seemed insurmountable once are not so difficult."

"How can I jeopardize my son's freedom?"

Julia sighed. "There are many kinds of freedom, Jessie. You and Lucas must find one that you can agree upon."

"And if we can't?"

Julia looked at her then, then shifted her gaze to the window. She sat in silence for a very long time, until Jessie became edgy, wondering if she should speak.

Finally, Julia said quietly, "I was once forced into a marriage I did not want. It was a hell I would not wish on anyone."

"I didn't know," Jessie said, finding it hard to believe the self-confident Julia could be forced into anything.

"I prefer to forget it myself. He thought he was doing what was best, but it was a very long time before I forgave my father."

"I'm sorry," Jessie said, meaning it. And realizing this was the reason behind that pointed exchange of glances between Julia and her father, the king.

Finally, Julia turned her head to look at her once more. "I could not countenance another woman being put in that position. If you will go back and talk to Lucas, if you will truly explore every avenue, and then still feel you must leave, I will help you."

Jessie blinked. "You will?"

"I will. I love my brother, and I love my country, but I know the pain you face, at least some form of it. I will help, if you become convinced there is no other way."

"You are indeed," Jessie said quietly, "your mother's daughter."

As she'd hoped, Julia's smile lit up her face. "Thank you. Now, please, you will stay with us tonight. Give that thickheaded brother of mine a night alone to realize what he's nearly done. Then you can go back and pound some sense into him, I believe you Americans say?"

"That's what we say," Jessie said with a smile. "Thank you, Julia. I can't tell you how much your understanding means to me. And for you, if nothing else, I will try."

Julia's warm smile was thanks enough. "It helps that I once walked in shoes nearly as tight as yours, does it not? If you wish, and if you trust me, you may leave Luke here, so you do not have him to worry about while you are trying to work things out."

"I—" Jessie hesitated, and Julia smiled.

"I understand, and I promise you my feelings will not

be hurt if you say no. There are few I would trust with
my baby, as well.''

That decided her. "No. Please, yes, it will help if I do
not have to worry about him. I'm not," she said frankly,
"quite sure of myself in the role of mother."

"Jessie, my dear, I'm not sure any new mother is. If I
couldn't turn to my own mother for advice, I don't know
what I would do."

"That must be wonderful," Jessie said wistfully.

"You can turn to her, too, you know. There's nothing
that would thrill her more. And of course, we could learn
motherhood together, you and I."

Jessie knew her surprise must show in her face; she'd
never thought of that side of things, that marrying Lucas
would come with a built-in support system of sorts, a
family that she didn't have on her own.

She quashed the familiar pang at the thought of the
sister who had betrayed her, and concentrated on trying
to decide what to do. Finally, she realized that if Julia and
Rashid could set aside the enmity of a century or more,
the least she could do was talk to the father of her son.

Lucas wondered that he hadn't worn a thin spot in the
expensive rug in his retreat, as much pacing as he'd been
doing. Since he'd hung up with Julia, he'd been a wreck.
He'd awakened this morning to find Jessie gone, but
knowing she'd planned to spend the day with Julia, he
hadn't thought much about it. Until his sister had called
with the news he still found so hard to believe.

Last night had been goodbye.

That knowledge colored every memory now. Every remembered touch, every lingering look took on a new significance. Looking back now, he could see them as if
she'd been saving them up, storing them for a time when
she would be gone.

He jammed a hand through his hair and turned to pace back the other way. But if she felt that way, why on earth would she leave?

...you never told her that you—you Lucas, not the ranch hand she fell for—loved her, and still do... No wonder she thinks you only want her because of Luke.

How could she think that? Luke hadn't even existed when they'd fallen in love. For that matter, Lucas Sebastiani hadn't even existed.

You abandon her and only come back after you have Luke. Instead of proposing, you give her a job description. You never tell her you love her—what do you expect her to think?

He didn't want to believe it. Didn't want to think he'd bungled it that badly. And then his own thoughts from last night came back to him, hauntingly. *He'd gone so far in trying to convince her that he'd changed...he'd managed to convince her he wasn't the man she'd fallen in love with on her ranch, either.*

"Damn," he muttered, spinning on his heel to start in the opposite direction. "Now what?"

Irony, he thought, had a very bitter taste. He'd always been more concerned with getting women to leave him alone, be it women with an eye on his future crown for themselves, or their mothers with a drive to matchmake for that crown. He'd been the one dancing to avoid the snare; never had he had to try to get a woman to want him.

Of course, he didn't just want Jessie to want him, he wanted her to love him, like she'd loved Joe.

Like she'd loved Joe....

His pacing came to an abrupt halt. And after a moment, he nodded to himself and reached for the phone.

Chapter 18

Jessie didn't think she'd ever get used to traveling by helicopter. The noise alone gave her a low-grade but persistent headache, and the way it rose and swooped and sometimes seemed to be pointing nose down made her faintly nauseous. She'd give anything for her tired old Ford pickup right about now.

But this was the easiest and quickest way to get from Tamir to Montebello, and it seemed churlish, after all Julia had done, to ask for some other mode of transport this morning. And it wasn't Julia's fault that her night on Tamir had been restless and nearly sleepless, making her less able to deal with flying in the royal family's sleek aircraft.

The helmeted pilot with mirrored sunglasses seemed quite proficient, however, lifting off and landing quite smoothly and neatly in the parking area between the wing of the palace that housed the throne room and the one that housed the picture gallery and map room. As she was clambering out the side door she caught the movement of the pilot from the corner of her eye as he pulled off the shiny sunglasses to give her a grin and a rather snappy salute.

"As they say in your country, I believe, give him hell, Jessie," he said. "And remember, I will come back for you any time, you have only to call."

She stopped in her tracks in shock, realizing that she had been delivered back to Montebello by none other than Rashid Kamal himself.

"You?" she asked.

"I have to take every chance I get to fly," he said. "And besides, last night Julia made me promise you'd get here safely. And back, if that was what you wished." His grin widened. "And last night, after an entire day away from her, I would have promised her anything."

Such pure love and joy glowed in his dark eyes that Jessie felt a strange hollowness inside her. For a moment she envied Julia. What she wouldn't give to have someone look at her like that....

But once, someone had. Joe had.

She yanked her mind out of that futile rut, and with a smile and a quick thank-you to Rashid, she continued carefully down the steps of the chopper. Her hands were free except for her purse; she'd made the decision to leave the bag she'd packed for herself and Luke in Tamir, just in case. She supposed that was hedging her bets, when she'd promised Julia to give this an honest try, but she saw it as a small, subtle reminder of how much was at stake.

To her surprise, there was a welcoming party of sorts waiting for her. Lloyd Gallini and Josie Sabina, standing nearly at attention as she descended.

"Welcome back," Lloyd said, and Jessie wondered if

the barely perceptible hesitation had been on the word "home." "If you will come with us?"

She shivered slightly; the simple words seemed ominous somehow, like something a cop would say to a suspect. She tried to laugh it off, and succeeded to a great extent, but a certain edginess remained.

As she walked toward the palace, the helicopter lifted off, with considerably more speed—and at a more rakish angle—than it had taken on the trip here, and she realized Rashid had actually toned down his flying for her sake. At Julia's suggestion, no doubt, Jessie guessed. The woman thought of everything.

And I'll miss her, Jessie thought, finding it surprising she could feel that way upon such short acquaintance.

She caught herself then, and reminded herself that she had promised Julia to give this an honest try. Just as she had promised Lucas, once. And she had tried, she thought. She had tried, and she didn't see what could possibly change now to make it work.

Once inside the palace, Lloyd closed the doors, turned to her and said formally, "If you would please change into riding attire? Mrs. Sabina will assist you, and then I will escort you to the stables."

Assist? Escort? Jessie wondered, suddenly suspicious that she'd been assigned watchdogs to make certain she didn't leave again.

"And why am I going to the stables?" she asked, trying her best to imitate the imperious tone she'd heard from Queen Gwendolyn on occasion.

"Because Prince Lucas requests it," Lloyd said.

Jessie bit back the sharp response that leapt to her lips, the instant refusal she wanted to give simply because of that annoying assumption that she would dance to Lucas's tune just because he was a prince. A dozen comebacks raced through her mind, but all of them were a bit snappish, and would go against her promise to Julia.

"It's a good thing he requested instead of ordered, or he'd have been disappointed."

That alone startled the staid pair enough to blink at her; an accomplishment that at least made her smile as she went into her room to change her clothes. The sight of baby Luke's empty crib gave her a pang, which was followed by a sudden jolt of fear. What if this was all some elaborate plot? What if Julia had convinced her to leave Luke in Tamir so she could hand him over to her brother?

Shaking, she sank down on the bed. Her heart battled with her gut, and the result was the terrible sort of nausea that she knew from sad experience came when you were afraid you'd been a lethal fool.

You're being ridiculous, she told herself. *You're just overreacting because of what happened before.*

But that didn't help ease the nausea. After all, she'd totally misjudged Ursula. But then, Ursula was—had been—her sister, and who would ever believe such a thing of her own sister?

Jessie pictured Julia in her mind. Julia with her wonderful smile, lovely laugh and impish charm. Pictured her with her own baby son, a look of pure, maternal joy on her face. Tried to imagine that woman taking Luke away from her. She couldn't make the image form. It was impossible, even more impossible than believing the sister she'd always known was self-centered and bitter had done what she'd done.

If Julia is really that kind, Jessie thought, *then I'm too much of a fool to raise a child, and he'd probably be better off here.*

Besides, if that was the plan, they'd have simply gotten rid of her and kept Luke, and probably long ago.

She took several deep breaths to calm herself. When

she was feeling steadier, she got up and went to the closet. She'd had to leave clothing here, in order to keep to the single bag for herself and Luke. Everything she'd acquired since she'd been here hung there; she hadn't felt right taking any of it, and had made sure it could be returned before she'd agreed to take any of it in the first place.

But she'd also, in order to make room for Luke's necessities, had to leave some of her own things. Including, fortunately it seemed now, a pair of jeans and a blue light cotton sweater. She changed quickly; she wanted to find out what was going on, fast.

When she opened her bedroom door after changing, she found Josie waiting outside patiently. "Your leader really must be afraid I'll bolt again," she said. Josie tactfully pretended not to hear her comment, and merely gestured her down the hall to the grand staircase. After descending, they went out the side door where the electric carts were parked. There Lloyd was waiting in the driver's seat of one of them, apparently ready for the escort duty he'd mentioned before.

"I can walk, thank you."

"His Highness was very specific."

"I'm sure he was. I can still walk."

"I'm afraid I could not explain why I allowed that to happen," he said stiffly.

Great. Now I'm responsible for keeping the staff out of trouble.

With a sigh, Jessie climbed into the seat beside him. When he gave her a startled look, she realized he'd expected her to get in the back seat, as if this were a limo and she were royalty.

"I'm just a plain ranch girl from Colorado," she told him rather sharply. "I don't do royal."

He blinked again, and Jessie could have sworn the corners of his mouth twitched. "Very well," was all he said as they started toward the stable.

She'd expected to find Lucas there waiting, perhaps astride his flashy stallion. He wasn't. Instead, when she walked into the barn as Lloyd indicated she should, she found the lovely Ghost saddled and waiting, and beside her Mario, aboard a rather nondescript-looking bay.

It wasn't until she got closer and could see past Mario's horse that she realized with a little shock that the mare was wearing Western tack. A brand-new-looking stock saddle, and a tooled leather bridle with a pair of silver conchos on the headpiece and silver ferrules on the reins.

She looked at the groom in puzzlement, but he merely smiled and shrugged. "I do what His Highness asks, miss. If you will mount and follow me, please?"

She couldn't deny she was touched by the gesture. Closer inspection showed the saddle was from one of Colorado's top custom saddle makers. And when she swung up onto the gray's back, she found—without surprise— that the seat was perfect for her, neither too big nor too small. In fact, it was very similar to her own saddle at home, just newer.

And a lot more expensive, she added to herself as they set out.

They rode out of the stable yard, and the bay turned in a different direction than she'd gone before, up away from the sea instead of toward it. Curiosity kept her silent for the first part of the ride, but as they continued upward, she began to wonder.

"Where are we going?" she asked the groom.

"We are almost there, miss."

"And where is there?" she asked, more patient with this man who so dearly loved horses than she could manage with the rather snootier household staff.

His expression became intense, his brows furrowing, as

if he were concentrating very hard. "Prince Lucas said to tell you it was…his lookout." He gave her a worried look. "This is right? Before he has called it his sanctuary, but this word, this 'lookout,' it means something special to you? He said you would understand."

"Oh, yes," she said softly. "I understand."

His lookout.

Her heart began to hammer in her chest as she tried to analyze what this meant, what his intention was. Did he want to show her a place that was special to him? Or did he want her to be overwhelmed by memories of what had happened at her own lookout, and unable to think of anything but the fire they created together?

She was so fixed on trying to figure out his intent that she almost lost track of where they were going. When Mario pulled the bay to a halt, she came back to herself abruptly and looked around.

The first thing she saw was the incredible view. They'd climbed high enough to have a spectacular, more than one-hundred-eighty-degree panorama of the coastline and the sea, of the city of San Sebastian and the mountains beyond. Yet this spot seemed removed from all of it, as if it were a tiny spot out of time and place.

It was incredibly quiet here. She could smell some sort of exotic, flowery scent, and the air was cool and the sun warm. Now and then a brightly colored bird flitted by, and it all conspired to invite her to dismount and stay a long while just to savor it all.

And then she looked at the place itself, and her breath caught. Behind her, set in a semicircle of trees, was a sort of tent that seemed to be made out of silk scarves of many bright colors, tied open on the side toward the view. It was straight out of exotic tales of the Arabian nights, and Jessie thought it should look silly or overdone, but it didn't. Not here.

Laid out inside it, on a small, low table, was an elegant picnic, with a huge basket and real dishes and sparkling glassware. Drawn irresistibly, she stepped into the unusual tent, surprised at the cool protection the flimsy-looking material actually offered.

Several thick carpets had been laid out on the ground, until it was as soft beneath her feet as any well-padded rug in the palace. The cloth on the table was, she was sure, genuine silk damask, just as the china had to have come directly from the palace dining room, and the heavy crystal she didn't even want to think about. She supposed they wouldn't miss a piece if it were broken, but she'd have nightmares about it, knowing what they must cost.

She turned to make a comment to Mario, only to find that both he and his horse had vanished. Startled, she looked around, but there was no sign of the groom or his horse anywhere, not even on the trail. Ghost was tied carefully to a low branch, and placidly dozing in the warm sun, as if the other horse and rider had never been here at all.

For several long, quiet minutes she simply stood there, not particularly concerned about being up here alone—she could find her way back, after all—and soaking in the beauty of this spot. She did wonder where Lucas was, why he'd arranged it this way rather than being here when she arrived, but supposed he had a reason.

She wasn't sure how long she'd been simply standing there, feeling the peace, when something tickling the edges of her vision became too clear to ignore. She turned then, and looked down the hill she'd just ascended. Although they were still a distance away, there was no mistaking the sleek black horse. Even from here the graceful stride and flowing mane and tail were obvious.

She gathered now that this had been Lucas's plan, to arrive himself after she was already up here. Still, she couldn't help but wonder why he hadn't just ridden up here with her in the first place, instead of having Mario bring her here and leave her waiting.

Nervous about this first face-to-face meeting with him since she'd attempted to leave, Jessie returned to the table, thinking she could at least open the basket to see if there were any preparations she could make.

She dug in and found napkins that matched the rich tablecloth, a bottle of wine, some rich Brie cheese, grapes, two servings of what appeared to be a luscious chicken with rice dish, and silverware trimmed in gold that she had no doubt was real.

She placed a napkin with each plate, arranged the utensils and glasses with great care, and then turned to the food, hoping to dispel her nervousness in action. But as the sound of the horse's steady gait came closer, her nervousness increased instead.

Finally, when she could tell by the sound that he had topped the rise and was only a few yards away, she took a deep breath, braced herself, and turned to face Lucas Sebastiani, crown prince of Montebello.

But it wasn't Lucas she saw.

It was Joe.

Chapter 19

Jessie stared, the picnic forgotten.

It was Joe.

Not Lucas, the royal prince, but Joe. Wearing the same battered hat, Western-style shirt, worn jeans and battered boots he'd worn on her ranch. He'd kept them, she thought, stunned. He even rode a Western saddle that looked odd yet endearingly familiar on the hot-blooded black horse.

Her heart hammered in her chest at the flood of sweet memories that nearly swamped her. Joe. Her Joe, who had been so lost, who had worked so hard to chase away the demon of his lost past; Joe who had so reluctantly but so completely fallen in love with her.

Joe, who had fathered her child.

Her common sense was telling her that this was still Lucas, but her heart was crying out to Joe.

The black came to a sharp halt with a snort and a toss of his dark head. His rider dismounted with the fluid grace that had first drawn her to an itinerant cowboy who had rather wearily explained that he couldn't give her any references or any identification, simply because he had no idea who he was or where he was from.

She simply stood there, because she didn't know what else to do. She knew she was breathing too quickly, knew her pulse was racing, but could do nothing to calm herself. Not when she was face-to-face with a dream, with the man she'd never thought she'd see again in this life.

He walked toward her, not with Lucas's innate confidence that bordered on arrogance, but with Joe's quiet demeanor that had seemed almost shy to her at the time. Even his expression was the same; hesitant, uncertain.

He came to a halt in front of her. And then he reached up to drag off that work-stained black Stetson and jam a hand through his tangled hair, exactly as Joe had the day he'd come to her door looking for work. And when he spoke, her breath stopped, for he used the same words Joe had spoken then.

"I heard you needed someone. I can't give you any references, because I'm new at this. But I'll work hard and well, that much I can promise."

"That's all I ask of anyone." She whispered the words she'd said that day.

Joe smiled. She couldn't deny that it was him, that it was the man she'd fallen for who stood there smiling that shy smile at her. And in that moment she felt again the sweet joy of falling in love, and it was so strong she thought she would do just about anything to feel that way again.

Anything except sacrifice a child's future.

"I never quite understood why you hired me," he said.

"To be honest, neither do I," she said, her mouth twisting into a rueful smile. "It was very foolish. I know the guys thought I'd fallen right off for a pretty face."

He grimaced. "Believe me, I know. They made that pretty clear from the very first day. They're all very protective of you, you know."

She smiled. "They've been with me for ages. Some of them saw me grow up on the ranch, so yes, they feel protective."

"Not nearly as protective as I felt," he said. "I knew from that first day that you were...different from any woman I'd ever known."

Her brow creased. "How could you know that, without your memory?"

His mouth quirked wryly. "The same way I knew that I was good with horses, I guess. It wasn't in the brain, it was gut-deep."

He stepped into the tent then, and looked around, as if assessing how it looked.

"Was this your idea?" she asked.

His gaze went to her face. "Yes. I told them I wanted a romantic picnic set up." Then he shrugged, almost sheepishly. "It's a bit over the top, I guess."

"No. It's lovely." She hesitated, then plunged ahead. "And dressing like Joe?"

His expression became very solemn. "I wanted to show you I'm still that man, Jessie. He's here inside me, that man who fell in love with you."

Jessie felt her cheeks heat, and took a deep breath. She wasn't ready for this, after all, she decided, and quickly suggested they eat the lovely meal, needing the distraction to deal with this new turn.

The meal was, as all meals were at the palace, excellent. The chicken was moist, the rice fluffy, the cheese rich and creamy, and the wine a light, perfect complement. They didn't say much, and they both ate slowly. It was as if they both knew that afterward would come the conversation that would set the course for the rest of their lives, and neither was in a hurry to get there.

But finally the meal was undeniably done, the dishes, glasses and utensils put back in the basket, the cloth and napkins folded with more care than was necessary, considering Jessie knew they'd go immediately to the palace laundry when they were returned.

And finally there was nothing left to do, nothing left to busy herself with. She opened her mouth, ready to say something inane about the view, or even the weather, but shut it again when she realized how obvious it would be that she was avoiding the real issue.

Lucas seemed to hesitate, as well, but she knew him, even in this guise, well enough to know he would plunge in eventually. And he did. But not in the way she expected.

"There was something else I knew in my gut when I came to your ranch," he said. "Even though I didn't know much of anything about myself."

"What?"

"That I'd been lonely for a long time."

Jessie stared at him. "Lonely?"

"Now, looking back, I know how right that feeling was. I've been surrounded by people, sometimes hundreds or even thousands of them, yet I was lonely."

"They say you can sometimes be the loneliest in a crowd," she said, and he nodded.

"When fate dropped me on your doorstep, that was one of the few things I was sure about. I knew it the minute I looked in your eyes. I thought, 'Well, here she is, at last.'"

Jessie blinked. "That soon?"

He nodded. "That soon. Maybe because I didn't have any of this—" he gestured widely, as if to encompass not just the palace but the entire country and his life in it

"—to cloud my thinking. I knew all I had to know, that you were the woman to end that loneliness."

Jessie felt a tremendous pressure ease, a pressure she hadn't known the strength of until now, when it released.

"I used to think about it a lot," she admitted. "How amazing it was that we'd been thrown together by chance and yet...."

"We fell in love?" When she nodded, he added quietly, "Maybe it wasn't chance at all. I don't know. But what I do know is how much luckier we are than the rest of my family, including my parents."

She blinked. "Luckier?"

"Yes. Because unlike all of them, we fell in love without who I am ever being a factor, in any way."

She'd never thought of it that way, and now she turned it over and over in her mind as he went on.

"You didn't set your sights on the prince of Montebello, or a crown of your own, and I wasn't looking for the perfect woman to wear that crown, for the sake of my country. Joe had his own problems, true, but generally we were just two people who met and fell in love, simply, like real people do."

"We had the complications after, not before," she said slowly.

"Exactly. But we have the knowledge that it truly didn't have any part in how we feel about each other. And that's something to treasure, believe me."

...how we feel about each other.

The quiet assumption that that love still existed between them was balm to her battered heart. And as if Lucas realized it, he suddenly slipped off the bench where they'd been sitting, down on his knees before her.

"I've been a fool, just as my sister said. I thought you knew I still felt about you the way I had then. I thought it was a given. I was trying so hard to be fair about what it would mean for you to marry me, that I didn't think about telling you again what I thought you already knew.''

"I knew Joe loved me," she began.

"And I should have realized that to you, Lucas is a very different person. I'm sorry, Jessie. But let me tell you now, that I love you even more now as Lucas than I did as Joe back then.''

"More?" It was greedy, perhaps, but she wanted—no, she *needed*—to hear this.

"Yes, more. And not just because you're the mother of my son, although that added a whole new dimension to my feelings. I love the way you're willing to fight for him, the way you're willing to stand up to anyone who gets in your way when you think you're right, the way you aren't intimidated by anyone's rank or position.''

"That's what you think," she muttered.

He grinned at her then. "Honey, there's a big difference between being amazed and being intimidated. An intimidated woman wouldn't have used the princess of two countries to help her escape.''

She felt a pang of guilt at the characterization of what she'd done, but she was too surprised by his grin—and the endearment—to dwell on that. Instead she gave him a wary, sideways look.

"You're not angry about that? That I...just left. Or tried to?"

"How can I be mad at what you did, when I did the same thing to you?''

She hadn't thought of that, either. "Yes, I guess you did.''

"And I have to think you did it for the same reason I did, because you honestly thought it was the best thing to do at the time.''

"I did. It was." She corrected herself. "At least, I thought it was."

And then it hit her. She knew now that he, Lucas, loved her, but now what? What had she gained, except a more painful parting? Because the most pressing reason of all hadn't changed at all, hadn't been magically altered by his declaration. Love didn't remove all obstacles, she thought. Some it made harder and higher.

"Jessie?" An odd note had come into his voice. He was still kneeling in front of her, with a rather desperate expression on his face. "Did I wait too long? Or have I killed the love you had for Joe by turning out to be Lucas instead?"

"No," she said softly. "I love you. That's what was so hard, why I was so afraid. I didn't *want* to love a prince, but I couldn't seem to help it."

Relief softened his expression. "Thank God," he murmured. "I was afraid we were going to lose this. Lose what we have, what we found that night on my boat...."

Heat flooded her at the memories his simple words summoned up. It blazed into an inferno when his voice went thick and husky.

"I'd love to make love to you here, in my special place. Just like we did in yours, on the ranch."

In that moment she wanted nothing more than to say yes, to have him over her, under her, in her, naked in the sun in this impossibly romantic place. She wanted him so badly she nearly ached with it.

But an image of a sleeping child who had no one else to fight for him crowded out even those hot images, and she knew she couldn't put this off any longer.

"I want it, too. If that were all it took to build a marriage, a family, a life together, then we would have it made," she said.

Lucas sat back on his heels, looking at her steadily. "But that's not all it takes, is it?"

"No. I'm sorry, Lucas, but that I love you still doesn't change the fact that I can't do this to Luke, to his future. And I won't."

Lucas sighed. "It's not a bad life."

"No, I can see that. Many would say I'm a fool not to want this kind of life for my child. I know he would have more material advantages here, being raised royal. But it's not a free life, and that's worth more to me."

At that, Lucas sat on the thick carpet, and reached up to tug her down beside him. Cross-legged, they sat facing each other. They had often taken up just these positions in front of the fireplace in her ranch house, and she wondered if he remembered that, if that was why he'd done it.

"I've been thinking a lot about this," he said. His mouth quirked as he added, "I had a lot of time alone to do it, all night last night."

So did I, she thought, remembering the long hours spent shoring up her determination, telling herself over and over what she had to do, trying to convince herself that there was no reason good enough to sacrifice her son's freedom to choose his own path.

"There's got to be a way, Jessie. We can do this, I know we can."

Remembering her promise to Julia, Jessie said, "I'm willing to listen to anything."

He gave her a grateful look. "I was thinking...what if we—all of us, you, me, and Luke—spend all our vacations on the ranch? We could go at least four or five times a year, and the summer visit could be a couple of months. And you can't tell me," he said with a crooked grin, "that it wouldn't be nice to spend the worst of the winter here in the sun."

"No, I can't, but it's not fair to expect the hands to do all the hard winter work while I loll in the sun."

"So, we rotate 'em out of there. Bring one of them with you for a vacation in Montebello each year."

At the image of Barney lounging on a sandy beach, Jessie couldn't help but smile. "Now, that's a plan."

"And come to think of it, we could send a few of my family to the ranch. Give them a taste of real life some of them badly need."

He said it with such a wry undertone that she couldn't help but laugh. And when she did, he smiled widely at her.

"See? There's always a way. And you'll have the resources to do whatever is needed on the ranch, even give the hands a raise. I'm not," he said quickly, guessing accurately at the cause of her suddenly mutinous look, "suggesting that you should or would marry me for the money, I'm just saying that it's there, it's a fact, and you should take it into account."

The spark of irritation subsided at his simple, honest declaration.

"And when the time comes," Lucas went on, "Luke can do as I did, and go to college in the States."

That still didn't resolve the basic issue of Luke's choice of a future for himself, but Jessie didn't have the heart to say anything just now, not when Lucas was trying so hard.

"And I promise you, you'll have all the help you need to learn whatever you need to learn to be at ease here, to find whatever role you want to fill in Montebello, as high or as low profile as you wish."

"Is there such a thing as a low profile when you're involved?" she asked wryly, remembering how quickly she'd been recognized at the Tamir airport.

"We'll find one," he said, sounding determined. "No

one will force you to do anything you're not comfortable with. And if they try, they'll be dealing with me.''

Jessie sat quietly for a long time. She knew he was trying; in fact, was trying harder to compromise than she'd ever expected him to. But finally she had to make her point.

"If it was just me," she said softly, "then maybe. But none of this changes the biggest problem. You still expect me to accept that Luke has no choice about what he will become. That his future is already decided for him. And I can't do that. I'm sorry, Lucas, but I just can't.''

"Jessie—"

"I know you could fight me in court on this, and I know with your wealth and power you could probably win. I hope you won't make me, or your son, go through that.''

He stared at her for a moment. "You think I'd do that? Sue you for custody?''

She shrugged. "What else can I think? You've made it clear that there's no negotiation on this, that Luke must be what you say he must be. But I can't—and won't— back down, either. My son will be whatever he *wants* to be.''

She thought she saw a flicker of something like admiration in his face. Then he let out a long, compressed breath.

"I've been thinking about that, too," he said finally. "But first, tell me something. Would you want more children?''

Jessie blinked, startled. "More children?''

He nodded, and for an instant she saw Joe's shyness in his eyes. "More, besides Luke. With me, I mean. You know, if…."

His voice trailed off awkwardly, and she couldn't believe Prince Lucas of Montebello felt awkward very often.

''I always wanted three or four,'' she admitted. ''But after Luke…it was so hard I'm not sure now.''

''I'm sure that was a lot worse than it would be with proper care and attention,'' Lucas pointed out.

''I suppose.'' Then she frowned at him. ''But what was your point?''

He sucked in an audible breath before saying, ''I was thinking that, if you were willing to have more children…well, surely one of them will want the job, if Luke really, truly doesn't. Although it's rarely been used, our law allows me the right to designate any heir I choose.''

Jessie was stunned into silence at the size of the compromise he was offering. She'd read enough, in her searching for precedents in Montebellan law, to know that what he was saying would be a historical first. That he would bend this far amazed her. And told her volumes about his feelings for her, because she knew he could easily have opted to fight her for custody. And there was only one reason she could think of that he would do this instead—he'd meant it when he said he still loved her, even more than Joe had.

''Meet me in the middle, Jessie,'' he said softly. ''What we have is worth at least that.''

He'd come so far, she thought, how could she not take at least a step or two in turn? But there was one last thing to consider, one last precedent she had to see set.

''What if we have a daughter?'' she asked. ''What if she's the one who wants to give her life to Montebello? Will you promise she will get that chance? Will you name her your heir?''

A slow, rueful smile curved Lucas's mouth. ''I should have known that was coming,'' he said. He appeared to think for a minute, then took a deep breath and said, ''All right, Jessie. Yes, I'll promise you that. If it's a daughter who wants the job, I'll give it to her. I can't promise the country will accept it, but I'll make it clear she's my choice.''

And Jessie could guess what kind of heat he might take over a decision like that. That he was willing to, for her, told her everything she needed to know.

''In that case, Your Highness,'' she said, ''you have a deal.''

And with those words, the simple Colorado rancher agreed to someday become a queen.

Chapter 20

The media was having a field day. It had been a very long time since so much royalty had been gathered in one place. Every Sebastiani and every Kamal, both by blood and by marriage, and everyone close to them, representing several royal families, was in San Sebastian for the long awaited, much anticipated wedding of Montebello's Crown Prince Lucas Sebastiani to his American bride- and princess-to-be.

The entire country—indeed, the entire world—knew most of the story by now; the Noble Men, the Brothers of Darkness, the undercover work of Rashid Kamal, his brother, Hassan, and Lucas Sebastiani, the plotted murder and kidnapping and extortion using Lucas's baby son. It was the stuff of tabloids to some; to others the stuff of legend. The only certainty was that none of it would soon be forgotten.

Those who oohed and ahhed over such dramatics, and found it almost unbearably exciting, would likely have

been surprised if they knew how much all the people involved in the dangerous, chaotic and admittedly exciting
doings of the past couple of years wished simply for
peace.

Some, Lucas in particular, went even further and
wished for a long period of uninterrupted routine.

"Boredom," he told Jessie the weekend before their
wedding when she had dropped into the chair in his retreat, clearly exhausted from all the turmoil surrounding
the preparations for the biggest royal wedding in years.

"What?" she asked.

"Boredom. A long, yawn-inducing stretch of pure, un-
mitigated boredom. That's what you need. And I wouldn't
mind it myself, for that matter."

She sighed. "I'll vote for that."

"Maybe we should have eloped after all."

She gave him a sideways and rather dangerous look.
"As I recall, I suggested that in the first place."

He grimaced. "I know. But it really wouldn't have
been fair to my mother. She's been looking forward to
this since I was born."

Jessie relented then. Lucas knew she'd come to adore
his mother, and that the feeling was mutual. His head-
strong fiancée had agreed to many things he knew she
would rather not have done just to please her future
mother-in-law. Not to curry favor, not out of fear—his
Jessie wasn't afraid of much of anything—but because she
wanted Gwendolyn to be happy.

Lucas had seen the transformation early, after Jessie
had balked at the part of the budget—rather extraordinary
even for a royal wedding—set aside simply for her dress.
She had mutinously told Lucas she would buy a dress off
the rack, thank you, and give the leftover thousands to
charity.

They had compromised by giving the huge commission

for the attendants's dresses to Ms. Sally Tucker of Shady Rock, Colorado, who was nothing less than gleeful about the unexpected plum. The lovely dresses she'd designed and had made had been delivered two days ago, and Jessie had been delighted to send back to the woman the official papers designating her "Designer to the Royal Family of Montebello" for her to use in her shop.

"I'm glad you chose Julia to be your chief attendant," he said.

Jessie smiled. "That still sounds odd. I'm used to matron of honor. But I'm just glad she said yes. There's really no one else I feel so close to just now."

Had she not assured him she had reached a certain calm about her sister, Lucas would have thought she was thinking of Ursula. As it was, he was just glad she and his sister were becoming so close.

He was also glad she had chosen Elena Kamal as her other attendant. The wife of Hassan Kamal, the young woman had risked her life, putting herself between Lucas and a bullet to save him during his captivity by the Brothers of Darkness. That alone, Jessie had said, was reason enough, but she also liked the courageous young woman who had had to fight for her place in a world peopled by men who liked to think they knew just what a woman's place should be.

He himself, at his father's request, had chosen Rashid as his supporter, or "best man" as Jessie would have called it. He'd wanted his friend Nick Chiara, but the newlywed doctor had graciously but firmly opted out; he wasn't up to playing a star part in this drama, he'd said.

Besides, he'd told Lucas with a grin, who was he to deprive the world of the chance to see the two highest profile royal couples extant in one ceremony, Rashid and Julia and now Lucas and Jessie? Lucas had laughed, but hastened to warn Nick not to say that in front of Jessie.

"A little skittish, is she?" Nick had asked.

"Ready to bolt like one of her wild horses at home," Lucas had answered ruefully.

"Can't blame her." Nick's answer was cheerful, but clearly heartfelt. "I'm just on the perimeter, and it sometimes drives me nuts."

With that in mind now Lucas got to his feet, went to the chair Jessie was curled up in and sat on the arm. He put his hand gently around her shoulders. She leaned back, looked up at him and smiled, but it was a very weary smile, and he could see the effort behind it.

Now, he thought. He'd been waiting for just the right moment.

"I've been thinking," he said softly.

"About?"

"Our honeymoon."

"Oh."

The smile was a bit better this time. He didn't think it was for the destination, which had been announced as a private island near Tahiti. He'd come to know her rather well, so he guessed the smile was probably for the length of time. When he'd told her they would be expected to take at least a month, she'd brightened considerably.

"What about it?" she asked.

"I think we should go someplace else."

She blinked. "We should? But I thought all the plans were made?"

"Plans are made to be canceled."

"For some, anyway," she muttered with a slight grimace that told him that, as usual, she was thinking about those who would be inconvenienced by an unexpected cancellation. But he thought she would forgive him in a minute.

"Well, I can change the flight plan back, I suppose,"

he said thoughtfully. "I'm sure Barney and the others will understand."

She went very still. "What?"

He gave her a crooked grin. "I thought we'd go to the ranch instead."

He didn't get a chance to see if this smile was the best one of all, although he knew without seeing that it was, because she had leapt up and thrown her arms around him before he even caught a glimpse of her face.

She supposed giggling wasn't the best approach to her wedding day, but Jessie couldn't help it.

Here she was, in a ridiculously expensive dress—albeit a beautiful one, lush satin with a capelike, pearl-beaded train that trailed at least fifteen feet behind her—riding in, of all things, a gilded carriage through the streets of Montebello. It seemed absurd to her, given that she'd been in the palace already, and the ceremony was to take place in the royal garden, but it was part of the ritual, the bride put on display for the people. Little did they know she'd much rather be up top driving this four-up of beautiful horses.

She shifted nervously on the richly upholstered carriage seat. She felt the slight touch of something at her ankle, and managed an inward smile. Lucas had given her the tiny golden horseshoe, explaining the old British tradition that Montebello had adopted in its days as a crown colony.

"Thank Dunstan of Canterbury, later Saint Dunstan. Legend has it," he'd said, "that one day the devil approached Dunstan to make horseshoes for him. Of course the cloven feet were a clue, and Dunstan chained him to the wall, supposedly to attach the shoes. He only let him go after he promised never to bother a house with a horseshoe. So today, the bride carries a replica of a horseshoe for good luck."

I'll need that luck just to get through this, Jessie thought now, as they passed another cheering crowd and another phalanx of television cameras. The thought of her wedding being of interest to the world still seemed so incredible. Just as it still gave her a chill to think of someday being queen to the thousands who lined the streets every foot of the way.

If she let down her guard, terror would fill her and she'd be like some fugitive bride in a movie, running for her life—or her sanity, she thought, barely remembering to wave and smile as best she could.

"It will be all right, dear," Gwendolyn said from the seat across from her. "You have it in you, I know you do."

Jessie looked at the woman who would be her mother-in-law by day's end. She was looking at her with great empathy.

"You do understand, don't you?"

"Oh, yes. I was quite simply terrified on the way to my wedding to Marcus. I was a simple teacher, I was certain there was no way I could ever be a proper queen to these people."

"But you are," Jessie said softly.

"If I am, it's because Marcus has taught me. As Lucas will teach you. That, and because I've come to love them as my own."

"And they adore you."

"As they will you, my dear. I promise you. They're a good, kind people, and they need only see how happy you make my son, and they will love you for that alone. Until, of course," she added with that warm, gracious smile Jessie had come to love, "they get to know you. Then they will love you for yourself."

She couldn't have said anything better to reassure Jessie. Searching for a way to thank the woman, she said softly, "I wish my mother could be here. But since she can't be, I'm very, very glad you are."

A pleased smile curved Gwendolyn's mouth. "Thank you for that, Jessie. That means a great deal to me. And I hope you know that I am very, very glad to be here with you."

That sense of female camaraderie got Jessie through the rest of the ride. Julia was waiting on the steps to the palace, where the entire Sebastiani and Kamal families—a huge number, all of whose names she hadn't learned yet—lined the way through the front doors and out to the royal garden where the other invited guests were seated.

"Wait until you see Lucas," she whispered. "Even if he is my brother, I have to say he looks magnificent in all his royal regalia."

Jessie had seen the traditional Sebastiani wedding attire in the portraits in the gallery and in photographs in the archives. It hadn't taken much to picture the tall, broad-shouldered Lucas being able to carry off the elaborate getup. A lesser man would look silly, she thought, but not Lucas.

She was barely aware of the gathering around her, although she heard good wishes called out to her in many voices, some she recognized, some she did not. Eliya was there with baby Luke for a last-minute kiss and pat.

And then, at the end of the line of people, Julia leaned over and whispered in her ear.

"Here's your first wedding present from Lucas, Jessie."

Puzzled, since Lucas had already given her back her grandmother's ring—another thing Ursula had stolen from Jess, which had made its way into Lucas's hands—Jessie looked where Julia pointed. And gasped in delight when

Mrs. Winstead and Barney stepped forward, both of them dressed to the nines in a way she'd never seen before.

"Oh, Jessie, you look so beautiful. My little girl," Mrs. Winstead said, nearly weeping as she hugged Jessie tightly. And Barney gave them both a bear hug that nearly stopped Jessie from breathing.

"That man of yours, he insisted," Barney said. "Sent a private plane for us, and put us up in the fanciest hotel I've ever seen so it would be a surprise for you."

Jessie was so warmed by Lucas's thoughtfulness, her apprehension faded a little. But as Julia guided her through the foyer, then through the grand ballroom where the reception was already being set up by what seemed like a battalion of caterers, Jessie's heart began to pound anew as she thought one last time of what she was about to commit herself to.

Lucas, she chanted to herself. She was committing herself to the man she loved, the man she'd loved as simply Joe, and the man who came with all these trappings. Because she had finally realized that no matter the trappings, the core of the man was the same. That the Playboy Prince had just been Lucas without direction. As Joe he'd found that, and now he was a steady point on the compass, never wavering.

And then, as she stepped out into the glorious Montebellan sunshine, she saw him. Standing tall and straight and looking more than worthy of the elaborate attire. And waiting for her. Waiting for her with as much love in his eyes as she could ever have prayed to see.

She was only vaguely aware of the hush that fell over the guests as they saw her. The music began, a grand royal march composed by some eighteenth-century Montebellan, as she walked slowly toward him. At last she was there and he reached for her hand. The moment she felt his fingers clasp hers, her nerves vanished.

"Did you like your present?" he whispered, and she poured all the love she was feeling into her expression as she nodded. "Good. We'll bring the second part back with us from the ranch. I can't wait to see you and Brat take on some of our bigger blowhards in the quarter mile."

And right there, with a crowd in person and half the world watching on television, the bride burst into joyous, unabashed laughter. Her groom grinned widely, and winked at her.

And out in the gathered throng, all those who had also found their forever loves turned and smiled at them, Sebastianis and Kamals and all the others. And not one of them doubted that the entwined futures of Montebello and Tamir were as solidly bright as the future of the bride and groom they watched pledge themselves to each other.

* * * * *

If you enjoyed what you just read,
then we've got an offer you can't resist!

Take 2 bestselling love stories FREE!

Plus get a FREE surprise gift!

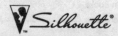

$ Saving Money Has Never Been This Easy! $

Just fill out and send in this form from any October, November and December 2002 books and we will send you a coupon booklet worth a total savings of $20.00 off future purchases of Harlequin and Silhouette books in 2003.

Yes! It's that easy!

I accept your incredible offer!
Please send me a coupon booklet:

Name (PLEASE PRINT)

Address _____ Apt. #

City _____ State/Prov. _____ Zip/Postal Code

In a typical month, how many
Harlequin and Silhouette novels do you read?

❏ **0-2**　　　　　❏ **3+**

097KJKDNC7　　　　　　　　　097KJKDNDP

Please send this form to:
  In the U.S.: Harlequin Books, P.O. Box 9071, Buffalo, NY 14269-9071
  In Canada: Harlequin Books, P.O. Box 609, Fort Erie, Ontario L2A 5X3

Allow 4-6 weeks for delivery. Limit one coupon booklet per household. Must be postmarked no later than January 15, 2003.

HARLEQUIN®
Makes any time special®

Silhouette®
Where love comes alive™

PHQ402

COMING NEXT MONTH

#1195 WHAT A MAN'S GOTTA DO—Karen Templeton
Single mom Mala Koleski wasn't looking for a husband—especially one like Eddie King, the sexy bad-boy-next-door she'd grown up with. When he blew back into town, alluring as ever, she swore nothing would come of their fun-filled flirtation. But was this no-strings-attached former rebel about to sign up as a family man?

#1196 ALIAS SMITH AND JONES—Kylie Brant
The Tremaine Tradition
To find her missing brother, Analiese Tremaine became Ann Smith and traveled to the South Pacific, where he'd last been seen. Her only assistance came from a mysterious man who went by the name Jones. As they searched the jungle, their passion grew hotter than the island nights. And though they had to keep their identities secret, their attraction was impossible to hide!

#1197 ALL A MAN CAN ASK—Virginia Kantra
Trouble in Eden
Hotshot Chicago detective Aleksy Denko tracked his suspect to Eden, Illinois, where a convenient cabin made the perfect base—except for stubborn, fragile Faye Harper, who refused to leave. To preserve his cover, Aleksy found himself playing house with the shy art teacher—and liking it. Until his suspect cornered Faye. Then Aleksy realized he could handle danger, but how could he handle life without Faye?

#1198 UNDER SIEGE—Catherine Mann
Wingmen Warriors
He only meant to pay a courtesy call to military widow Julia Sinclair after her son's birth, but Lt. Col. Zach Dawson ended up making an unconventional proposal. A single father wary of women, Zach asked Julia to be his wife for one year. Soon their false marriage led to real emotions and had Zach wondering what it would take to win Julia's love for life.

#1199 A KISS IN THE DARK—Jenna Mills
Falsely accused of murder, Bethany St. Croix had one chance to save herself and her unborn child: Dylan St. Croix, her ex-husband's cousin. They had shared a powerful love but now were divided by painful differences. Drawn together again, could they put their past aside in time to save their future?

#1200 NORTHERN EXPOSURE—Debra Lee Brown
Searching for a new life, fashion photographer Wendy Walters fled the city streets for the Alaskan wilderness. There she met Joe Peterson, a rugged game warden set on keeping her off his land and out of his heart. But when Wendy was targeted by an assassin, Joe rushed to her rescue, and suddenly the heat burning between them was hot enough to melt any ice.

INTIMATE MOMENTS